PLEASUREHOUSE
13

C000150347

PLEASUREHOUSE 13

Agnetha Anders

First published in 1991 by
Nexus
338 Ladbroke Grove
London W10 5AH

Typeset by Phoenix Photosetting, Chatham, Kent
Printed and bound in Great Britain by
Cox & Wyman Ltd, Reading, Berks

ISBN 0 352 32805 3

In an office sits a man who works. In this year of 2030, those few people who work have Class One status.

In another office sits a man who provides pleasure. Pleasure providers have Class Two status.

In walled cities sit the rest. They are the don't knows and the don't matters. They have Class Three status.

And on a wild hill far, far away, nobody sits, until a woman called Ann begins to change everything.

[1]

EVERYONE ELSE MIGHT be fucking themselves silly as per normal on a Tuesday, but there was a nasty flashing spot of trouble on Twozec Salkeld's screen.

For normal instance – there was normal pigging, poking and contentment among the Threes in City MK (as Milton Keynes was now called). The MK Threes were, as normal, so bombed out and shagged out that they couldn't be bothered to make the kind of waves which caused trouble on Salkeld's screen.

City HH was also calm. The last spot of bother in what used to be Hemel Hempstead had been a year or two ago, when the Regional Centre computer sent in double food but no alcohol. Everything went unstable for a day and a half, until the computer system was fixed and the Threes of HH, whatever their turn-on, could wallow continuously in it once again.

Tuesday's reports to Salkeld from the Pleasurehouses continued to indicate the required percentage of full satisfaction with all the ad-lib sex, sport, entertainment etc., etc., which it was Salkeld's business to provide.

Except, of course, this morning, 26 September 2030, there was that irritating problem for Class Two Executive Salkeld.

A possible answer to his problem, even if he didn't yet know it, was currently sitting naked in her kitchen about fifteen kilometres from Salkeld's office. She was very beautiful, not tall but with the sort of body which

1

often illustrated downmarket reading matter. She was in a state of eager anticipation. Today was her own private treat day. Her eyes glittered as she speculated gleefully on how she would spend the next hour or two, and positively gleamed as she compared that in her mind with the pallid, mechanical, missionary instant her husband provided as a weekly passion allowance.

Up in the Berkshire Downs she sat, in the large, picturesque, period farmhouse so typically favoured as a residence by Class One.

There she was, Ann, Salkeld's potential answer, splendid and solo, sitting on an old oak chair worn glassy smooth by centuries, wearing it still more glassy smooth with eager little squirms of her bottom. Her eyes were fixed on the kitchen window, chin cupped in hands, elbows and glorious tits resting on the kitchen table top at White Horse Farm. She was Ann Richmond, 36, not to mention 40, 29, 38. She wanted her heart's desire and got something like it when Lancelot Brough, 17, arrived at the window and very nearly broke the glass with his eyeballs.

Ann swung up and moved to the door with that certain special walk that female dancers have, a sort of flat-footed duck walk yet a light and bouncy movement with the lower leg thrown out from the knee joint.

Ann, the lovely Ann, got to the door and opened it standing behind, hidden from view although there would be no-one to see. Having non-marital sex outside the Pleasurehouse, even having a regular relationship with a student under full privilege age, was not a desta-bilising offence. But probably it was against the wishes of the Social Committee, so there would still be trouble if it came out. Oh well. So bloody fucking shitting bloody what. The bored Ann took the risk. Being a wife in these days meant being strictly non-working. You

2

were supposed to be a mother and homemaker only, when all the homemaking was done for you anyway by the robot and the computer. It was not exciting.

In walked the boy with a fragile bearing of self-assuredness. Back at college he was like a king, among other boys envious of the number of his conquests and the size of his weapon, and among those girls who were keen to surrender their sovereignty. But here he was a mere apprentice to a great sorceress and he always felt a peculiar mix of sensations when he saw Ann – powerful desire, wonderment at his good luck, and anxiety about what she might do.

'Don't speak, boy,' whispered Ann. 'Just pick me up and carry me.'

This superb woman had grey-green eyes, deep red hair just short of shoulder length, and a mature, slightly aquiline, subtle and remote beauty that reminded the boy somehow of days long gone by, of those actresses they used to call 'film stars', or the legendary symbols of animal femininity like the Roman Empress Messalina who outperformed the city's top prostitute. He carried her upstairs to the attic bedroom she reserved for adventures.

He lifted her with her legs over his left arm and his right arm round her back. Her left arm was round his neck while her right swung free, her fingertips brushing ever so lightly against his thighs as he mounted the stairs.

He breathed more heavily than normal with the effort of carrying Ann, and he inhaled her perfume deeply. Its reverberations filled his head. She wore something quite unlike the sort of stuff the girls at college had. Their perfumes' messages were unmistakable, as matter-of-fact and open as their attitudes. With them the scent was either 'Miss Permafrost

3

Discusses Thermodynamics in the Refectory', or 'Fuck Me Sideways and Bring All Your Friends'.

Ann's perfume, however, was from another world. It had all sorts of complicated messages in the background, all kinds of depths and dark corners – and he could smell her through it. Her smell was of hair, and skin, and excitement, and it all mingled deliciously with those few drops of distilled essence which, if he only knew it, came out of a little bottle, which came out of a fancy box, which came out of a pack of six given to Ann in return for certain favours in Paris, as long ago as 2012.

By the time he turned along the landing her palm was on his vital part. She idly wondered if she could, from her current position, undo his zip, get his cock, fit it between her cheeks and let it find its own way home.

She had the zip down anyway by the time he placed her on the blue duvet, so she ordered him to stand still while she sat on the bed edge and lovingly extracted the warm, soft as silk, hard as iron glory which, with the vigour of its youth, could give her hours of delight. There was another side to youth, however, and that was the initial overexcitement of, as it used to be called, the bull at the gate.

Ann felt that surge of emotion within her as she held the boy up to her lips. She wanted the first bed-shivering, sense-quivering moment, the first of maybe four or five that she knew that thing in her hand could give her. She wanted him pushing and shoving on top of her, in her, all over her, but she couldn't have it yet.

Sure enough, the closeness of her face to his cock, the soft sensation of brushing breath on it, the thought that any moment her tongue would run its roughness along it . . . all this proved too much for the lad. As she stroked the sturdy scimitar she felt it begin to pulse

4

inside her fist. Like lightning she loosed the waistband fastenings of his trousers and whipped them and the tiny briefs he always wore, down to below his knees. Her lips opened just enough as she fed the boy's personal vibrator into her mouth.

Back and forth she went, pursing and sucking as he let go with the first of the day. Fellatio was routine for her. She got no great pleasure from it, but she knew it was a supreme feeling for him and so, like the artist she was, she made certain she gave her best performance. She knew (from great experience) just how to suck in rhythm with his spurts, just how to squeeze the most ecstatic feelings for him so that he was soon looking down on her with an even more devoted, ever-grateful and adoring expression on his young face.

He had quite a nice face, actually, thought Ann as she looked up, swallowing. Sort of craggy, with scrubby blond hair, just a few freckles and a little snubby nose. Little and snubby was soon a description equally apt for the item she held in her hand.

'Come on boy,' she said. 'Shoes and socks . . . off!'

This was their private cue, dating from the first time he'd had her, which had been after a dinner at the college where Ann's husband Arthur Richmond was on the Technical Committee and the senior boy Brough had been seated on her left.

She'd had her stockings round her ankles and her shoes on as she leant over the back of the Founder's Chair on the stage of the school hall, and she had wondered what on earth would be the reaction if the curtains opened onto the port and cheese below. Now, whenever she said shoes-and-socks . . . off, each had to strip as fast as they could, and the last one to be naked was underling and the winner was overlord.

The boy had got shoes, socks and trousers off before

he twigged. The luxurious wife Richmond lay, already without a vestige of clothing, as she had been since before he arrived, a half-smile on her reflective red lips as she watched the boy's frantic Pavlovian reaction.

'Caught you,' she said, as he completed his strip at a more leisurely pace. 'Now, I'm the big boss for the day.'

The boy Lancelot was hesitant, wondering where this all-knowing, never-fazed woman would take him if he let her put him in too weak a position. So, he hoped she would keep it to a little light trick or two, a token, just enough to add a hint of spice.

Just a hint, thought Ann, as she rummaged through a drawer for the roll of sticking plaster. Binding thumbs with plaster is hardly the real thing, but still, can't have everything.

'Hands behind head, boy,' she commanded, 'and sit up.'

She quickly taped his thumbs together behind his neck, making sure to include plenty of blond hair just in case he should think of bringing his hands forward over the top.

'Lie back.' My, she loved this. Power gave her good sensations. It always had, and issuing orders was fun, whether it was to a troupe of chorus girls when she'd been captain and choreographer all those years ago, or to a muscular, hard, youthful man who delighted her eyes and her most secret wishes right now.

In both cases, the chorus girls and the boy, she was in command because she knew the most. Knowledge is power, she thought, and power is an aphrodisiac.

He lay back as ordered and, swinging her leg over him like mounting a bicycle, she presented her divine red muff to his lips. At full stretch she could rub her considerable saddlebags against his stomach, give his crossbar a little lick and, while he was busy exploring her seat with his tongue, tape his big toes together.

He tried to protest at this double securing, but he was really in no position. The protest went unheeded and was largely unintelligible. Muffled, as it were, thought Ann.

She gave herself two or three minutes of pivoting on his tongue but was careful not to let herself slip too far. She had plans for young Brough.

Suddenly, lifting away and kneeling beside him, she kissed him on the lips. She pushed her tongue into his mouth, tasting her own fluids and snorting her own pheromones like a line of coke. Then –

'Back to that college next week, is it, Lancelot?' she whispered. 'Back to that dreadful concentration camp of sadists and woofters?'

Colleges for future members of Class One were high-powered educational establishments which naturally concentrated their academic efforts on computer systems, programming languages, robotics and the like, but they retained much of the philosophy and lifestyle of the old public schools.

'But,' continued Ann, 'you'll be a senior prefect now, won't you, Lancelot? You'll be able to beat those naughty little boys and girls with your cane, won't you, Lancelot?'

Since she was saying all this while fondling his assembly into a more riotous state, Lancelot was a bit slow catching on, and was too relaxed to stop her as she moved sharply, flipped him over like a nurse giving a bed-bath, and sat on his calves. The small riding crop was behind her, hidden under the bottom of the duvet, and the grin of complete amusement was on her mouth, and the glint of purified lust was in her eyes.

Lancelot tried to lift her off with a kind of swimming butterfly kick as she tickled his darkest little corner with the leather tab on the whip end, but a quick and hard flicker of the whip across both buttocks stopped him dead.

'Now, Lancelot. What is it we're going to do to those little boys and girls? What do you call them? Faggots?'

'Fags, Ann, fags. For goodness' sake, look, you know I'm not terribly keen on . . .'

He stopped dead again, as she flicked that evil little tab across his white buttocks, one-two, then thrust it into the crack at the top of his legs and pressed it up hard against his balls. Go on, you big bastard, she thought as he raised his hips from the bed and she raised herself slightly to allow his legs to slide. You great big fucking machine, you with the strength and the biceps, you do what I tell you – she almost spoke aloud as she pressed the whip up harder to lift him further and further until he was kneeling, hands behind head, forehead on the pillow, arse in the air, feet tied by toes, and Ann dismounting as she slipped the whip from its position of ultimate power.

'Don't move.' She spoke matter of factly, as if the instruction were unnecessary, to be taken as read, assumed. 'Now Lancelot, remember when you were a fag thingy, and how you used to get a hard-on when the big boys beat you?'

Oh why did I ever let that out, thought the increasingly worried Lancelot.

'Well Lancelot, I'm now going to take you back in time, and I want you to pretend that I'm just another big, big boy.' By all the gods above and stuff me gently but I love this bit, she continued – to herself.

'Ow! Fucking hell!' cried Lancelot, as she thwacked him smartly right across both cheeks.

8

'Language, Brough, language. I won't have such language in my class.'

Lancelot confined himself to sharp intakes of breath for the next three strokes, while Ann paused after each to see if she was having the desired effect on his member. She wagged it this way and that with the end of the whip, like an old farmer she remembered seeing as a girl, moving a lamb's tail with his walking stick to see if it had been castrated properly. No farmers now, she thought, just Food Production Facilities and robots. But this little lambikins certainly is no gelding . . .

'Dear oh dear, Lancie baby. Dear dear dear. We shall have to beat you harder. I can see that being nice to you isn't appreciated.'

And she gave him two real crackers, two full strength ones that had him arching and yelping.

'Fucking bitch! Aargg!' he shouted as he brought hands, arms and a large tuft of hair over his head then turned and grabbed the whip. 'I'll show you being nice!'

The two thumbs went together for her throat, and the fingers spread round and forced her back on the bed. His knees moved up between her legs in short jumps and he spread her apart as far as he could. His cock was bouncing hard now, nodding its eagerness and swaying in its search for the spot. He collapsed onto her, they met like an armour-piercing shell going up the spout, he flipped his hands behind her head and kissed her fiercely.

Ann Richmond moaned and sighed. Lancelot Brough bounded and rebounded, hard and regular, plain and deep. Ann Richmond, (36), ex-professional dancer, mature and plentiful, let herself go. Lancelot Brough, (17), boy stallion, vigorous and dedicated, went for the big fences.

They came together in a huge, panting, floorboard-squeaking, window-rattling climax and when their breathing became regular and their heartbeats had slowed to near normal, the pink plaster was snipped, their eyes closed and they slept.

Ten minutes or so later, Ann was awake. The boy slept on, his head in the crook of her arm, resting on the universe's most comfortable pillow.

As she often did in quiet moments, Ann contemplated her life and in particular her status as a Onewife. She'd had the choice, she knew, and if she'd chosen correctly she'd have been a Two, probably not an Executive, probably just a Local Unit Supervisor, but being a Twoloc was a hell of a lot better than being a Onewife had turned out.

For the umpteenth time she let her mind tick back to the time of the Change. When was it, 2018, or 19, she never could be sure. She'd been abroad with her dancers, dashing between European capitals, rehearsing, performing, resting, having a fantastic time. She never read the English papers, and there was very little on the TV news in Europe about Britain since it'd been kicked out of the Community.

Technology in Britain had become increasingly dominant. While the rest of Europe was backtracking, deliberately making life more old-fashioned so as to preserve a need for people to work, Britain had embraced one technical revolution after another. By the middle of the second decade of the 21st century, the only people who worked in Britain were the systems analysts and robotics engineers who developed and maintained the technology which did absolutely everything.

Everybody in the country had all the consumable goods they wanted, so the concepts of wealth and status began to change. Soon, the only people that mattered were the technologists – and the entertainers.

This new superclass got itself organised. Elections were computerised, so that the next election was fixed. Laws were swiftly passed and a new society was created, entirely based on us and them.

'Us' were in two sections: Class Two consisted of pleasure-givers and pleasure-providers for Class One, which consisted of those who worked to sustain the plentifulness of everything. 'Us' wanted a spacious, elegant, aristocratic lifestyle which necessitated the removal from the countryside of all those scurrying crowds, hateful modern buildings and everything else vulgar.

'Them' were Class Three. They originated from every social stratum, from the erstwhile rich and high born to the downtrodden and hopeless lowlife. But they had something in common. None of them qualified as a technologist or an entertainer.

Class One and their robots built a series of walled cities, rounded up the Threes and told them they could do what they liked except leave the city they were put in. So, they just consumed. They had everything they could possibly want, except freedom.

The government then passed its last law, abolishing itself and placing all power in the hands of a few committees of volunteers, and left the country to run itself like clockwork – or more properly, electronic microcircuitry.

This was the Britain Ann came home to at the end of her tour. Obviously she and her girls were entertainers. Some kept on dancing, but Ann started a promising career in pleasure management. One of her clients was Arthur Richmond, a quiet, reliable sort, the year's top college graduate.

Arthur hardly used the facilities of the Pleasurehouse where Ann was an assistant department head. He just wanted to talk, and he told her how he wanted a live-in, permanent spouse and a family.

Marriage and children were forbidden for Twos and discouraged for Ones. The whole point of the Change had been to preserve the best things in life for the elite few. Also, the population of Ones, and therefore of Twos, needed to decline as technology became even more hypercapable. The few children that were required came from gene-controlled, artificially ferti-lised implants.

But you could, in certain cases, get married and have kids just like the old days. The discouragement was that there was no divorce, and either but not both of the spouses could continue working as a One. The other would be a permanent house-spouse.

Arthur Richmond wanted a proper wife, and kids. He was a top man, a brilliant mind. He could swing it. Ann had a blind urge to have children. She married Arthur.

Then they found out she couldn't have any. Which explains why now she was in her bed with a boychild who was not at all in the original gameplan.

Young Lancelot Brough had been quietly awake for a minute or two. While Ann was contemplating her fate, he contemplated at the closest of quarters the pillow on which he had slept.

It was a large, firm, generously curved breast with a nipple which, he now saw, must be all of a centimetre high. Around the base of it was a pinky brown circle, also raised but only slightly and with a higher rim around it as the border with the white china surface of the lovely globe. The rimmed disc had numerous min-uscule hairs and tiny little hills and pits in it. Under a microscope that must look like a wild terrain where only giant reeds can survive. He sniffed in its odour. Like her neck, the same smells, perfume, skin, body fluids, were there but in different proportions. More body, less perfume. He blew gently on it to get the reeds waving in the wind.

It was a beautiful breast, he thought. His heart went out to that breast. It induced in him a wish to write a poem while simultaneously licking it.

The young girls he knew might have boobies which were more pert, more nearly perfect like those you see on sculptures. But this lady, this bountiful garden of delights, had so much more to interest a chap. And even though her tits were big, they did hold their shape and they were firm and bouncy. What sumptuousness, yes, that was the word, sumptuous.

His hand went to this glorious object of desire and his rod began to stiffen. Ann rolled over to see the time on the bedside clock. Lancelot thus had a hand trapped under her on her right breast. The other went to her left. Her left hand reached behind, found his fast-rising cock and swiftly drew it to its full height.

She thrust out her bottom a little, raised her left thigh slightly, diddled her little pleasure peg with the big round end of his knob, then guided him right in. The sheer satisfaction of it almost send her straight back to sleep. It was like a really good massage, a sunlamp and a jacuzzi all at once. It was just wonderful, totally, utterly, wonderful.

He pumped her gently at first, giving most of his attention to those luscious breasts and those centimetre-long nipples which he could feel hardening and growing as he tickled their tips with the centres of his palms. Round and round the garden, like a teddy bear . . . she gave the groan he knew, the groan which was the signal for all systems go.

She rolled flat on her stomach and he began the big pushes from behind. Almost immediately she groaned again, louder this time and meaning her first climax of the bout. He felt the extra lubrication make his journeys in and out that much more slippery.

With the energy of youth he speeded up and thrust even harder. She came again, really copiously this time, and the boy felt as if her juices had given him a second skin over his tool which was also now operating in what seemed to be a much bigger space. Sensation diminished as the steel-hard member went back and forth no less effectively for Ann but automatically for Lancelot.

He felt himself becoming detached. I could do this all day, he thought. This is what they call 'giving her one'. I'm nothing more than a reciprocating pump, an engine for engendering, in, out, in, out, there she goes again, that's three.

He raised himself up on his hands and looked down at her back, her beautiful back, those curves, the big, ample, lovely, *sumptuous* bottom, with the shaft of his prick slurping in and out, in and out. And a wicked idea occurred to him.

On the count of seventeen, he thought, since that's my age. One! Two! Three! Four! In went his most powerful thrusts, with every millimetre of length and circumference and every kilojoule of energy he had, slap, slap he went, eleven, twelve, thirteen. She came yet again, a fourth flow which gave him even more love-oil for what he wanted, fourteen, fifteen, sixteen, SEVENTEEN!

In a quick movement he pulled out, grabbed himself for extra firm direction, presented the head of his cock to her little back gathering and drove it in with one stroke.

'WaagoooooOOWFF!' she cried in a combined gasp

14

of outrage and trill of ecstasy. Lancelot had never felt anything like it, a magic mixture of close-fitting tightness but with all that extract of delight acquired from the other entrance giving him easy sliding.

He didn't carry on counting. If he had he wouldn't have got through another seventeen. Just two or three pushes in this new haven and he was into the final phase, jerking and bucking as he came with a gush into (for him) unknown territory.

Ann had been making curious half-whispered wails, a high sound that meant wonderful moments, but which also expressed total surrender, the complete absence of the last vestige of self control. Then, they lay exhausted and splayed out, silent except for their breathing which took a long, long time to grow quieter. His prick stayed up, not allowed by the grasp of her muscles to slacken and drop out as it would have done had he been at a more orthodox destination. Eventually, Ann spoke.

'What made you do that, boy wonder?'

'I don't know. It just came to me to do it. I hope I . . .'

'Don't you worry none, honey chile, You ain't de first to go in by de trademan's entrance. Why, when we poor dancin' folks was lookin' fo' a job, we got front line chorus if de Great White Chief could stuff our ass, yeah boy.'

'It was the first time for me, anyway,' said Lancelot, all prim and proper, not liking her frankness about her past, not understanding her theatrical argot, and feeling threads of jealousy for those older men, the men with the power, who had enjoyed the younger Ann when, he knew from her photographs, she had been a quite spectacular beauty.

'Don't be such a pompous little fart, Lancelot.

15

Everybody has to use what resources they've got in this world. And don't think this arse-banditry is something you'll be having every day, young Lochinvar. Conditions have to be right. I'm not having you dry-drilling whenever you fancy it. Conservation is very important in these matters. There's such a thing as over-exploitation, you know, and leaving the landscape exhausted. Think buggery, think green.'

She pulled herself away from him and turned to kiss his mouth. He looked into her eyes, her green eyes, such a powerful combination with the deep red hair.

'Green?' he said. 'I used to be green. But I'm learning.'

[2]

CLASS TWO EXECUTIVE Salkeld was responsible for entertainment and pleasure provision in an area roughly the same as the previous administrative boundaries of Bedfordshire, Leicestershire, Northants and Warwickshire. There were some lovely old towns, like Warwick and Kenilworth, which had had their nasty twentieth century buildings cleared away leaving a nostalgic, romantic kind of urban dwelling place with plenty of space and comfort.

The great ugly sprawls like Birmingham had of course been demolished and their populations removed to new walled cities based on more compact, easily controlled areas like Coventry. But these were not Twozec Salkeld's concerns today. He had trouble on his screen, and it came from Pleasurehouse 13.

Like most of the Pleasurehouses, 13 was based in a fine old mansion, a great house of the past which, before the Change, had become an anachronism in a vulgar age. Once again it fulfilled its original purpose as centre of high life, taste and culture for the privileged minority.

13 was designated for the use of female Ones. It was at a village called Althorp, near Northampton, and so most of its clients were those who spent their working hours cerebrating at Regional Computer Centre NN, one of the three power centres of the entire country and a most sensitive and important place. Any discontent from the Ones at NN would immediately come to the

notice of the Amenities Committee, and failure to rectify the situation could well mean destabilisation for the Twozec responsible.

The last time Salkeld had visited Pleasurehouse 13 all had been well. Every department had been smoothly run by the manager, a Local Unit Supervisor called Spencer, and the Northampton female Ones clearly got all the top-quality rest and recreation they needed. Salkeld had been especially impressed with the Racquetsport, Swimming and Gymnasium departments, and the Theatre, and said so in his report, but his memory of the place was dominated by something he'd watched through the two-way mirrors in the Luxury department.

A fairly mousey looking One, an absolute genius in memory-circuit conceptualising according to Spencer, had come in to a studio, pressed the communications channel and ordered four boys and a girl. They arrived in their normal indoor working clothes – sweatshirts, slacks and trainers. The One told the four boys to take off everything except the shirts and stand in a line by the wall. She stood in front of them and beckoned the girl who then carefully and slowly stripped the One naked. She had a good body, quite hard and muscular, with small firm breasts whose nipples pointed upwards, and with her hair down she looked much less the bluestocking and much more the athlete.

She turned to the girl, kissed her on the lips, and stripped her too. She was a contrast, much more the classic feminine female type, big titted, big arsed, narrow waisted and obviously built for fun. The One knelt and ran her tongue up the inside of the girl's thighs. The girl spread herself slightly, bent her knees a little, and grasped the back of the One's head. Soon she was bumping and grinding in a slow, gentle way, but the

18

One got up, stepped over to the large circular bed, lay on her back and put her hands under own buttocks to provide a better angle for the girl to get to work.

While the girl employed some of the advanced tongue techniques she had learned during training, the One stole an occasional glance at the line of four boys, standing in just their shirts with their varied array of jewellery stirring. When the One thought a boy was sufficiently excited, she beckoned him over and took his semi-hard cock, first in her hand, and then in her mouth. Soon it was fully erect. She waved the girl away, got up, lay the boy on his back on the bed, straddled him facing his feet, and sat on his pillar of strength with a slow but decisive movement.

When she leaned back on her elbows, Salkeld could see that the cock was up her rectum. The girl knelt again and went on with her licking, the One giving her a sharp cuff when she thought the girl's tongue was straying to her boy colleague's benefit.

A second boy was beckoned. He was already fairly hard, and a brief suck was all he needed to become fully attentive. The girl retired again, the boy got into the press-up position over the reclining One and went into her from the front.

After a minute or two, she rattled out some swift commands. The press-up boy turned himself clockwise as far as he could, leaving room for the girl to place a pillow on the One's muscular stomach and put a knee on it. The other she placed behind the One's head, so she was straddled sideways with her fuzzbox over the One's face.

The remaining boys also knelt, behind the girl and in front. Together, they entered her arse and quim there right above the One's eyes, who squirmed with delight as, at her signal, the boys who were into her began moving in regular rhythm.

Somehow the girl managed to lower herself enough so that the One's tongue could reach up to hanging balls and thrusting poles. The One's feet were now kicking in a frenzy, her hands were rasping up and down the girl's body, her torso was jerking as both hard cocks fucked it at once, and her mouth roamed and groaned over the other cocks which were fucking above her.

As the kicking reached a tremendous climax, the One grabbed the cocks in front of her face, shouted something at the girl – who leapt off – and jammed the ends of both red and glistening members into her mouth. She could only get a little of each between her lips, and as they came the cream gel spilled out between her teeth and down her chin, her neck and between her breasts. At the same time she bucked and heaved with her hips as the other boys made their final surges inside her.

Salkeld had turned from the mirror, his own prick standing up despite his telling himself that he was a professional who'd seen it all. But thinking about it now, back in the present, Salkeld realised he'd missed something. What he'd watched through that mirror had been more like a carefully staged theatrical event than an act of wild abandon. How long ago had it been – a year? Nine months? Some of the Ones – what had she been, a memory-circuit conceptualiser? – were clearly applying the intellectual disciplines and principles of systems analysis they used during the day to their after-dinner stints. There's a line from Francis Bacon, he mused, about mathematics making men subtle. Bloody right. More theatre, that's what they want in Pleasurehouse 13.

The flashing blip on his screen speeded up, which meant he had to make some response to any top priority message. The only such message he had had was about Pleasurehouse 13. He couldn't avoid the issue any longer. Something must be done. He acknowledged the flashing blip with 'Thank you, I am dealing' – that would keep them quiet for a short time, anyway – and spoke to the screen. 'Get me Twozec Rafferty,' he said.

'I am so sorry, sir,' replied the screen after a second or two. 'Twozec Rafferty is not available at this time.'

'Why the fuck not?' shouted Salkeld.

'I am so sorry, sir, Twozec Rafferty is in the Forest making special arrangements, and cannot be reached at this time.'

'The Forest' was in fact Sherwood Forest, replanted across half of several counties to provide leisure pursuits for the Ones. 'Special arrangements' probably had something to do with the new craze for witchcraft, since the last time he'd heard from North Midlands Region Twozec Rafferty, he was setting up tutorials for his people on rituals and spells.

'As soon as you hear from Twozec Rafferty, present him with my compliments and tell him I'd be most grateful for a call.'

'Thank you sir. Have a nice day.'

'Fuck off, you electronic bastard,' Salkeld muttered to his screen, and sat back on his chair. Rafferty and he were a good partnership in times of difficulty. His was a great scheming brain, Rafferty's was a practical. If Salkeld could imagine some brilliant stroke to achieve their end, Rafferty could engineer the necessary action. The screen buzzed.

'Excuse me sir, but Onestudent Lancelot Brough is here to see you. His presence here today has been requested by the Amenities Committee. Thank you, sir.'

'Just give me a moment,' replied Salkeld. He read through the file on Brough which the computer had

21

brought up on the screen for him. Nothing unusual for an average Onestudent, good study records, full participation in early-day privileges . . . hang on, what's this? 'While ensuring the ongoing stability of society, the Committee has had it brought to its notice that Onestudent Brough is having a fully integrated relationship with Onewife Richmond, of White Horse Farm blah blah etc etc.

'In view of Onezec Richmond's special value as a leading Intelligence Engineer, stability in his chosen lifestyle is important and this potentially unstable relationship should be terminated. It is suggested that Onestudent Brough is suitable for transfer as a Trainee Two.'

'Send the bugger in,' said Salkeld to his screen, in no mood to mess around with wayward students who couldn't keep their cocks in the hot little pockets provided for them every weekend at Onestudent R & R.

Brough came in, trying to look unconcerned but only succeeding in looking bemused. Whatever his prowess with women – young and old – Brough was still a boy. He could not but feel awed in the presence of an exalted individual like Salkeld, who gestured to a seat having summed up exactly where Brough was at in half a second.

'Lancelot, isn't it? Lancelot, or just Lance?'

'My friends call me Lance.'

'I see. And among those friends, would you happen to number a lady called Ann Richmond?'

Lancelot Brough blushed and said 'Oh.'

'Yes, Lance. Oh. Oh, oh, and double fucking oh. You see, your problem, Lance, is this. You have allowed yourself to be distracted. The investment of care and attention lavished on you by your tutors is being jeopardised – so they complain to me. "How

22

come," they say in that reasonably outraged and surprised way of theirs, "how come that the pleasure and entertainment you provide for Onestudent Brough is insufficient? How come," they say, "that he finds it necessary to leave his studies of the Laws of the Universe, to go and wave his willy in front of a respectable Onewife?"

'Now, the thing is, Lance, every other Onestudent in your year is perfectly satisfied. Every weekend we Twos have provided you junior Ones with boys and girls of your own age, as well as more senior and practised personnel to help you advance your pleasure knowledge. So, either you have truly extraordinary appetites, the need to satisfy which transcends your natural concern for your own stability, or Onewife Richmond is so enormously attractive that all else diminishes. Hm?'

'Well, actually,' replied Brough, 'I suppose it's a bit of both.'

Salkeld had to admire the boy's coolness. Maybe they were right and he was wasted in the Ones. Maybe he could make a good Two, perhaps even a Twozec eventually.

'In which case, Onestudent Brough, I shall have to persuade your superiors at college that their recommendation is unsuitable. They have suggested an alternative, you see, in view of your behaviour, to the future previously mapped out for you in agricultural robotics. But I think you might be better off this morning, or lunchtime as it now nearly is, Lance, by giving a quite different choice your full consideration.'

'But sir, firstly I wasn't doing anything destabilising. Secondly, I don't know what the college wanted me to do . . .'

'BaseNat, Lance, a posting to BaseNat.'

Salkeld was bluffing, just to test Lance a little. The Institute for Basic Research into the Nature of Technology, built on the site of a ruined monastery on the Skerrig Islands off the Kerry coast, could never have been a real option for Brough. You needed an IQ of over 180 and the personality of a sea urchin to work there. But Lancelot didn't think about that. He just knew it was the only One establishment in the entire country where the nearest pleasurehouse was a wet and windy boat ride away, the boat only went monthly, and even then hardly any of the super-intellectual troglodytes left their holes to go.

'Therefore,' continued Salkeld, 'you might like to consider changing your career direction towards the Twos.'

'I've always thought I would make a good Two, sir, and I'm ready to start immediately. I never did like agricultural robotics anyway. But if I had, and I regarded this move as a bitter blow to the career prospects provided for me by their Excellencies of the Amenities Committee, I should have to say it was worth it, sir. Onewife Richmond is a truly remarkable woman, and her experience of the entertainments world has broadened the outlook of a grateful young technical specialist.'

'I'll put you down as a possibility for specialisation in communications and media,' said Salkeld, impressed. 'I think it may be possible to transfer you to the next intake of Trainees. In fact, we might be able to do something sooner, since I just happen to know that a particularly promising young man has had to be destabilised and so there is a place on the course now running. You've only missed a week, so you'll soon catch up.'

'Er, what was he destabilised for?'

'Repeatedly refusing to take Examination B, which involves fellating any pair of your classmates in front of the whole college, and then giving a technical talk on the experience.'

'But I thought heteros and homos were kept separate.'

'They are. But in case of emergency, all must be prepared to do their duty. Now, are you prepared to do your duty, or would you rather go to BaseNat?'

'Examination B, here we come.'

'Good. Let's see, where are the Trainees at the moment . . . right, the boys are out on a half-day seminar at the Zoo, learning how to assist in acts of bestiality. The girls are in aerobics.'

Salkeld pressed a key and a picture came up on his screen of the aerobics class. Thirty beautiful girls bounced, kicked, bopped and swung to the music as the instructress called out the moves. Most of them were the familiar hourglass types, all tits and bum, but some were different. There was a little dark piece with a turned-up nose that Salkeld thought looked like a famous actress from the old movie theatre called Audrey Hepburn. She seemed slightly distanced from the rest – maybe not feeling a hundred per cent today.

All of them, except the instructress, were perfectly nude. Lancelot Brough stared in fascination. 'Excuse me, Twozec Salkeld, but are we Trainees allowed to, er, mix with our female colleagues?'

'During term time, certainly, that is a matter for individual choice, providing that you are not out on a practical, in which case you must conserve all your energies and attentions. Also, of course, during the vacations you will be posted to a holiday job in a pleasurehouse – light duties, but again no off-duty mixing between Trainees.'

'But it's term time now? And when is my first practical?'

'Let's see . . . in fourteen days. You'll have an intensive forty-eight-hour course in City work, and then you'll go on active service for three days to a City house of some kind. Meanwhile you have a fortnight of unrestricted access to your female classmates, always assuming that they are as interested in you. Now, if you'll excuse me, I have some pressing matters to attend to. My assistant will help you settle in.'

As soon as Brough was out of the room, Salkeld keyed in his demand for his own unrestricted access – to the file on Onewife Richmond. Somehow he was beginning to feel that there was a connection between her and his salvation on the now urgent matter of the trouble at Pleasurehouse 13.

Up came the file. The pictures were quite something. There were groups of girls in feathered headdresses, girls in little Scottish outfits with mini-kilts, girls in grass skirts and floral garlands. There were some of a girl, draped over a bar stool, wearing a bath towel.

This same girl could be discerned at the front of the crowd in all the other pictures. She was very beautiful. She had red hair, green eyes and a magnificent pair of knockers. And she looked straight at the camera with eyes that said 'Notice me, and don't ever forget me.' On the bottoms of the pictures it said things like 'Scarborough Summer Show' and 'Dick Whittington, Nottingham'.

Salkeld was an entertainment professional and he easily recognised the picture collection for what it was – mementoes of a chorus girl from the old theatre, probably around its very last days before the Change.

The facts in the file bore this out. Onewife Ann

26

Richmond, née Cuillin, left school at 16 and joined a dance troupe. With spells of modelling and waitressing she kept herself going until regular dance work took over. She was captain of the chorus at 19, worked in France and Germany, organised her own dance troupe and took them all round Europe, then . . . how very interesting . . . was a Trainee on the first ever intake of Twos after the Change. Suddenly married Onezec Richmond, no children. Extra material available.

The last phrase referred to information beyond the normal scope of a personnel file, available to those with high access rankings – such as a Regional Twozec like Salkeld. He keyed in his access code. The screen flickered and a pattern of dots ran across it, which usually meant the system was processing images from the old technology – film, videotape – into the new standard known popularly as CLIT – Conductive Light/Image Technology.

The first extracts were from old television shows – dance numbers, with the young Onewife Richmond there at the front. Then there was something else, much poorer quality despite all the image enhancement the system automatically gave it. The sound was crackly and the vision narrow angled, as if from a small, fixed camera.

The scene was some sort of office – Salkeld could see part of a desk, a window, a few potted plants and a chair. The film had started partway through what appeared to be a job interview. The motive for the interviewer to record such an event in this way soon became apparent.

A man's voice was saying '. . . my dear, I *know* you're good enough, but so are others. In every agent's office in London there's a beautiful girl, ready to work hard. So tell me, why should I hire you rather than any of them for the French trip?'

'Right,' said a young female voice. 'I think perhaps you haven't had a chance to appreciate everything I've got to offer.'

There were a few indeterminate rustling sounds. Salkeld had heard such sounds so many times that he recognised them easily. He could hear a button being undone at 100 paces, and could tell what was the article of clothing being removed. The unmistakable swish of cloth being pulled past skin and more cloth told him that here was a shirt being pulled out of a waistband. He heard a zip being pulled, and the sound of something soft hitting something hard. He concluded she must have taken off a short, wraparound skirt and thrown it on a chair.

All this was happening off screen. He'd seen nothing yet, but the files were on Ann Richmond and this made his prick twitch and rise. He reached down to adjust himself in case it should rise some more and get trapped.

Salkeld was a pro. He noted his own reaction. After all he'd seen and done, a small sound and its associations seemed to be enough to stir his excitement. This Ann Richmond is some woman, obviously. Back on film, the dialogue continued.

'Very nice, darling,' said the man. 'Why don't you walk over here, a little closer?'

Into the camera's view walked the now familiar hourglass figure and red hair of theyoung woman who would become Onewife Ann Richmond. The hair was down, quite long, about nipple length, observed Salkeld. The hourglass figure was partly concealed by a black lace brassiere and a black G-string. She shook her head a little, allowing the hair to swing back and forth

28

over a truly superb cleavage, then she turned her back and appeared to have difficulty unfastening the bra. She looked over her shoulder – and a man came into vision. He was about sixty, bald, short, ugly and handsome at the same time. He unclipped her bra and stepped back.

She turned round and the black lace fell down her arms. She let it slip onto one hand, then onto the floor. She shook her hair behind her back. She stood there, slightly taller than the very short man, with the proudest bosom Salkeld had ever seen. They really were a wonderful pair of tits. Not so huge as to be grossly out of proportion, but big, and quite able to support themselves.

The man took a gorgeous fruit in each hand. He weighed them, he gently fondled them, he kissed them.

'Excellent qualifications for French work, wouldn't you say?' asked the girl.

'Certainly enough to earn you serious consideration, my dear,' said the man. His index fingers each stroked to the end of a breast, then down her sides to her hips and the tiny strand of black cord which was all she now had on. With a sudden movement he tugged and broke it, and thrust some fingers from his right hand into her dark red crevice. Equally quick and sudden, she tore his trousers and pants down and grasped a very large and eager sword.

Funny how short, muscular men often have the biggest cocks, mused Salkeld, as he watched the man lean back against the desk. Putting her hands round his neck, the dancer got her legs on the desk on either side of him with a double high kick. With one hand the man felt for his destination, and with the other he guided the monster home. She seemed to accommodate it quite well, and with her feet flat on the desktop was doing a series of swinging squats.

29

After a while, his hands went to her armpits. He lifted her off and turned. She stood on the desk, so her pussy was level with his face. He parted the lips with his fingers, ran his tongue around inside, then lifted her up again, turned her round, and placed her on her knees, bum away from him, on the desk.

All these moves happened swiftly in succession and with considerable ease and grace. Salkeld realised he was watching the young danseuse in partnership with another professional – an ex-hoofer, maybe, or acrobat.

The man's hand went to his desk drawer. There, among the pens and pencils, was a dildo. He operated a switch, there was a buzzing noise, and he reached over and behind the submissive, kneeling form of the woman and inserted the vibrator – Salkeld could not tell exactly where. For her part, she grabbed the great, bounding, swaying, flesh and blood thing in front of her and rammed as much of it as she could in her mouth.

He moved back and forth as if he were fucking for his life. Where she put it all Salkeld could only wonder. As his speed built up, she reached behind her to nudge the vibrator further in, and then on an instant it was all over. He was wiping his cock on his handkerchief and putting his clothes back on. She was coughing and spitting into the wastepaper basket, saying she didn't mind a snack at lunchtime but never could manage a big meal.

The vibrator was placed somewhere out of camera. The now immaculate man also went out of shot, presumably back behind his desk. The last sequence showed a still-naked young Ann Richmond, née Cuillin, leaning over the desk to sign something.

While his erection went down, Salkeld searched the cross-reference files for more information on this ever-surprising woman. Meanwhile Lancelot Brough, new status Trainee Two, was being looked after by Salkeld's assistant, a Two of Administrator status. She was about 28, dark hair strained back into a tight bun, heavy spectacles, sensible tailored dark blue suit, white blouse, and with a fine gold chain on her neck the only ornament.

'My name's Lancelot Brough,' he said, feeling the need to be confident over the top of his butterflies. After Salkeld this woman was much less titanic but still had a no-messing air which stopped Brough short of his usual approach to women, which supposed they found him sexually irresistible.

'I'm to join the intake, er, Miss . . .'

'TwoAd Wilson to you, young man. Has Twozec Salkeld entered your statistics?'

'Statistics? I don't really know if . . .'

'Typical. Always forgets the nitty-gritty. You see, Brough, despite whatever marvellous talents and god-like capabilities you may possess, you cannot become a Two unless you meet a simple physical criterion. Were you the most highly qualified and brilliantly recommended Trainee in the history of the cosmos, there would be no point in starting you on the course unless you measured up.'

'Measured up?' said Brough, quivering slightly, inferring from her tone that if he didn't, not only would he be rejected but whatever it was that didn't measure up would be removed without anaesthetic and placed on view in the foyer.

'It's not so much the length, as the total volume – when erect, of course.'

'Erect? Volume? I see, well, I don't know, I mean, I've never had cause to . . .'

'Don't worry, Brough. I'll show you what to do.'

With this, TwoAd Wilson, known throughout the

national Administrative Twoservice as a remorseless and successful practical joker, led the innocent Lancelot Brough off to Training Room F. Here there were tables and chairs, a large pad of paper on an easel, various cameras and screens, and all the usual paraphernalia of any training department.

'Right, Brough, strip off, will you? Come on, hurry up boy. Oh dear, won't it stand up on its own? Very well, come here.'

TwoAd Wilson secretly pressed a few buttons. A hidden camera turned towards them, a recorder began whirring softly, but Brough remained unaware.

'Place it in my hand, please. Thank you. Now, let's see if we can't . . . there, that's beginning to look a little better.'

Wilson had scratched her fingernail down Brough's cock, and then taken a blob of spittle from her mouth and run it round the glans. A few gentle strokes and it reared. A few more pulls with her hand right round it and Brough's mighty member, quite famous in its own way back at Onecollege, was in its pomp.

Wilson led him by it over to the easel. She motioned him to stand sideways to the pad, and she drew carefully around his erect profile. Then she took him to the sideboard, filled a dish right to the brim with white wine and placed that in another, larger dish.

Taking great pains not to get her fingers in she pushed his prick into the wine, which overflowed into the larger dish.

'Just have to measure the volume of fluid displaced, and we've got the total volume of your penis, haven't we?'

'But surely there must be more accurate ways of doing it?' said Brough, suddenly nervous. This crazy woman and her archaic measuring methods could ruin his career before it had started. He'd already left the Ones, now he'd be refused admission by the Twos, and that meant destabilisation and a ghastly life in the City.

'Look, TwoAd Wilson, I say, why not use a proper electronic instrument? If you've spilt any of this stuff, my measurement will be less. I mean, it might not be enough.'

'No, no, this is quite accurate enough.' She ran her finger and thumb in a ring down the length of his cock, squeegeeing off the drops of wine that were wetting it. Instead of shaking the drops into the measuring bowl, to Brough's dismay she flicked them away across the room. Then she decanted the displaced wine from the bowl into a small measuring jug, the sort used for mixing cocktails. While she fussed about the measurements, and put a ruler up against the silhouette she'd drawn on the pad, then punched a calculator and made a few notes, Brough stood there, his cock in his hand, gently wanking himself almost subconsciously.

Wilson looked at him over the top of her glasses. 'Average circumference', she said, 'multiplied by length, gives us total surface area. Very important.'

By the time she'd finished taking those dimensions with a small cloth tape measure, Brough's obelisk was quivering wildly with frustration. With the highest level of skill, Wilson touched and brushed and stroked as she measured, featherlight, somehow managing to increase excitement in every tiny nerve end as she went about the job of describing his manhood in geometric terms.

With difficulty he stopped himself from giving himself a few quick jerks. It wouldn't be quite the thing, he thought, to come all over the carpet in front of this disinterested administrator.

She looked at him with dead-pan face. 'I hear you're

quite a performer, Lancelot. I've seen the reports on your weekend R & R from our people. Some of our girls gave you special mention. It's a professional activity for them of course, giving the Onestudents much needed relief, but they can get involved sometimes if their customers are really something extra.'

All the time she was speaking she was having a fidget, first with her blouse, which somehow came slightly unbuttoned, then with her skirt, which managed to ride up a bit.

Brough was strained beyond belief. If something didn't happen soon he expected the heat his prick was generating to set off the fire alarm.

'I think I'd quite like to try some myself,' continued Wilson. 'You just stay there while I change into something more comfortable.'

She left the door into the next room ajar. Brough could see her lift her skirt to undo her suspenders and begin rolling down a stocking. Then the door swung a little more shut and he could see no more.

'Won't be long,' she called. 'What sort of thing do you like? Diaphanous negligée, or perhaps basque and fishnets, or maybe nothing but a neat little velvet collar . . . ? I think nothing, don't you? Oh, I can't wait. Such a lovely long one. I want it straight in, bang bang, no fooling about with foreplay. There. Nearly ready. Just the bra to come off . . . and the panties to come down . . . there. My nippled are all hard. Ah, I can feel my pussy getting wetter, my oh my, I'm nearly coming already. I've got to have that big steamer right in, as far as it will go . . .'

She opened the door just as Brough, unable to contain himself any longer, spilled involuntarily.

'What a pity,' she said as, fully dressed, she snapped away with her camera on fast motor wind. Brough's

34

indignity was preserved on a sequence of a dozen still pictures, which were transmitted on the closed-circuit CLIT that evening, and on a CLIT recording which, weeks later, suddenly appeared in the middle of a TV tutorial on diet and health.

[3]

The following day, Lance Brough was supposedly due to present himself for more athletic bliss at the hands of the experienced Ann Richmond, but he was busy trying to catch up with the others on his training course. He hadn't got in touch with her and – O, the thoughtlessness of youth – the selfish bugger probably never would.

And so a somewhat older and wiser man was taking Brough's place on the date, a certain senior executive in the entertainment business. He parked the little hover-bubble he used for local travel about a mile from the house. He would take his time, walking, slowly, looking at the fine views in the golden light of a brisk, sunny, early autumn morning. And he would keep himself out of sight.

Today the lovely Ann wasn't looking wistfully out of the window, anyway. She was filling in time before she expected Brough to arrive by finishing off her story and reading it into the network. There weren't many releases for a bored Onewife, but writing stories and putting them on the network, under a pseudonym of course, was at least a bit of fun. Ann had built up quite a readership, or listenership really, since most people preferred to have the network read the story out to them than read it themselves off the screen. And each time somebody accessed a story, the network logged the incident. So Ann could ask the database for her latest figures and take a small amount of satisfaction to compensate for her screamingly boring life otherwise. Apart from Brough that is. And the boy before him. And the boy before him.

Today's story, which had taken her all week to write, was another example of the old formula. Girl meets boy. Girl loses boy. Girl gets boy back again. It always worked. Even the most intelligent, technological of the female Ones would fall for it. Pillocks.

She began reading to the screen. 'Story library. New material. File under Historical Romance, by Sylvie Du Lac. Begins. Blurb. *True Love Will Find a Way* is the latest from favourite authoress Sylvie du Lac. Set in London in the 1960s, it is a sensitive analysis of the passionate relationship between beauty and the beast, a girl who has everything and a man whose charm rests in his personality, not his face. And, as with all Miss du Lac's work, her light touch of humour is very much in evidence. Ends blurb. Story begins. *True love will find a way*.

'There I was, sitting in the departure lounge at Heathrow Airport sobbing my heart out and surrounded by suitcases. Well, who cares about excess baggage when you'd rather be dead?

'Outside the majestic jetliners took off, winging their way to faraway places, rushing silently through the cold night air. Inside, the passengers were safe and warm – business people, holiday-makers, lovers – while the stars twinkled down as they had since the world began.

'I must look awful! I thought. Whatever would Cyril say . . . ? Blast it. There I was again, what would Cyril say, what would Cyril think. I had to start thinking for myself!

'This was why I was starting a new life. This was why I was flying to Spain to a family I knew almost nothing

38

about, to be nanny to a rich, aristocratic little boy I had never met.

'Spain! What was it like? Warm, starlit nights, the sound of guitars? Would the Contessa really trust me with her son and heir? She looked superb in the photograph – beautiful dark eyes, jet black hair, long, elegant neck.

'What charm, what natural authority she showed. How it shone, even out of a photograph of her bringing off those two men, one with each hand. I wondered who they were. They looked more like workmen than members of the Spanish nobility. Still, you can't always tell, can you?

'Somehow my musings led me back to the day I first met Cyril. We both worked in an ad agency at the time. Cyril Lofthouse was a new art director, just joined us from up north somewhere. He was not really outstanding as far as looks went – short, fat, midriff shirt button always undone, lank hair down to dandruffed shoulders, horn-rimmed glasses and a wart on the end of his nose. However, a girl in the accounts department said he had the biggest willy she'd ever seen, and she'd seen some.

'Anyway, I was typing some letters in my office one evening, about six o'clock. Cyril just about knocked my office door down as he stormed in.

'"Where's that prat? Mick O'Reilly, account director! He couldn't direct a cycling proficiency test. What's the idea of putting this job into the studio at this hour? Storyboards for a campaign of six commercials, for a 10.30 meeting tomorrow? Bloody Irish wanker."

'Well, I wasn't having that from an uncouth northern yob.

'"*Mister* O'Reilly is in a meeting, actually. If you wouldn't mind waiting . . . ?"

39

Cyril threw open Mick's door. Disappearing at the same moment through the other door we both glimpsed a girl from the accounts department trying to do up her bra. Mick had tidied his hair but forgotten to zip his flies.

'"Hello, Cyril," he said. "What can I do for you this fine day?"

'"How long has this job been kicking around on your desk?" Cyril stormed.

'I quickly scanned Mick's antique partner's desk for scuff marks from my high heels, but could see none.

'"Oh, that," said Mick. "Sorry. Doris lost it in her pending tray. Look, I know there's not much time, but . . ."

'"Don't blame it on the stupid little cow!" said Cyril. "You hired her."

'He meant me, of course. My blood boiled.

'"As it happens, me and my writer have nothing to do between now and 5am, so you'll get your storyboards. Next time, you're more likely to get a shillelagh up your colon!"

'The door banged, and I just had time to look up how to spell "Shillelagh" before Mick was putting my hand inside his trousers. I didn't really see why I should have to complete work started by the accounts department, and told him so several times.

'Next morning, Cyril brought the ideas for the TV campaign and threw them on my desk. He struck a pose and declared:

'"There once was an adman called Mick,

Who used to make pretty girls sick.

T'was not what he said

As he took them to bed,

But the . . . please complete in not more than seven syllables. Answers on an office memo pad before 12.30

40

today. Winner to be given lunch by an art director of her choice."

'He looked me up and down. I could almost see him taking inventory. Long reddish blonde hair, mysterious smoky grey-green eyes, pert little turned-up nose with three freckles, generously curved red lips, and a very nice pair of 38Cs even if I say so myself.

'Our eyes met. I saw, deep behind the grease-smeared and dusty lenses of his glasses, an infinite spark of light, like a star, twinkling. Then, he just turned and went. Nothing more was said. But I knew even then that something wonderful was going to happen.

'Mick went off to his 10.30 meeting, so I had two hours to finish the limerick. I'd nearly done it when, like a thunderbolt from the blue, the phone rang.

'"Come on, Doris. It's after half twelve!" said those hard, northern accents. "Meet you in the foyer."

'We jumped in a taxi and in less than three quarters of an hour we had crossed over two miles of London's busy streets to La Grenouille Bienvenue. Well, what a laugh. Cyril gave me nine different endings to the limerick before we'd even finished the starter. I had mange tout in aspic, by the way, and he had something I'd never seen before, called "*boudin noir avec des pois masses*".

'Life seemed so wonderful. We got through two bottles of cold, white wine and three of something rich and red which Cyril said was called Coats de Throats. I could only just manage the After Eights, and by the time the taxi came at 5.30 I was at sixes and sevens.

'We went back to his place, a partitioned-off quarter of a warehouse floor near the Blackwall Tunnel. We kissed. So this was what it was all about. The walking

41

on air, the tears of pure joy at being head over heels and young and crazy. We kissed again.

'No long weeks of wooing. No conventional courtship. We both knew what had to happen, so why delay for the sake of propriety? He just turned me round, pulled my knickers down, stood me against the wall and gave me one.

'I could see the stars reflected in the river outside Cyril's window. It was midnight now. We'd had forty winks, been down the pub for a few jars, and come back for more sex. Cyril snored gently beside me, his lank, greasy hair flopping on the dark stained pillow. He farted.

'Men! I don't know. They're just like little boys, some of them. But still, that was a very happy time.

'After a few weeks he took me up to Lancashire to stay with his parents. His father was a retired Hotpot Scavenger, whatever that is – I was obviously supposed to know! – and his mother did the doorsteps for the next four streets.

'Cyril told me he was proud of his heritage, but I could see he preferred drink and sex.

'We went over into the Yorkshire Dales and walked for miles in the pouring rain. I know the countryside was wild and beautiful, but I couldn't see it. All we saw were wet sheep, and this wonderful little black and white dog which could make them go where he wanted.

'Next day we went over into another Yorkshire Dale, where it was raining as well. We stayed in a pub all afternoon watching a game called Rugby League on the television, then went for a walk.

'A gnarled, grizzled old shepherd gave us both a good laugh as he wrestled for half an hour with a sheep, so vigorously that his trousers came down. Then that same little black and white dog we'd seen yesterday (what a marvel – it gets everywhere!) came and barked so that the old man got up and went.

'Back in London, things took a turn for the worse. Cyril started finding reasons not to invite me back to his place. After the third weekend in a row that he'd gone to parties that I wouldn't like, I guessed that the end wasn't very far away.

'Sure enough, it came. I'd been trying to cure Cyril's wart and it was the day when he had to dig the steak up and feed it to the pigeons. We were sitting in the park, and I was telling Cyril about the jumble sale my mother was organising, when he suddenly got up, gave me ten pounds, and marched off.

'"Taxi home!" he explained over his shoulder.

'I cried. My, how I cried. It was quite some time before I could find the strength to walk from the park and find a cab. The endless stream of car lights went by outside the misted window, like red and white stars.

'I must have left the tenner on the bench, because the only way I could pay my fare was by helping the driver to eat his chocolate beans. He balanced them on the end of his wotsit and I had to pick them up with my lips. I was quite good at it, actually, and he thought so too and said I had to try and pick them up with my tonsils.

'The end of an era, I thought. "There aren't any red ones, you've had them all." Life would return to dull old normal. "Yes, I like the orange ones the best, too." I mustn't cry. Cyril hated weepy girls.

'"Yes, I bet you would," I replied to the driver's saying that he wished he had a pound for every chocolate bean that girls had swallowed in his cab over the years . . .

'So long ago, so long ago. And now I was flying away,

43

away so that I couldn't be tormented by the second wart which had grown, much to Cyril's disgust, beside the first one.

'I'd been in Spain six months when it happened. The stars that night seemed brighter than usual, as if some mysterious force was filling them with extra energy. I suddenly knew in some mysterious way that something wonderful was going to happen soon.

'Gunther, the German boy I'd been dating, was being especially obnoxious. I pretended to be all warm and excited, told him to lie down on the grass, and then kicked him ever so hard in the crutch.

'I related this story – only in outline of course – in my next letter to my parents, more as something funny than anything else. I was a bit surprised, therefore, when a week or two later the parlour maid came in while I was photographing the Contessa with two of the gardeners.

'The maid was insistent that an "Eeengleesh" was here to see me. Things had got to a critical stage with the gardeners, so I showed the maid how to work the camera and went to the library.

'There, waiting, was Cyril.

'"You're not safe out here with these foreigners," he said. "You're coming home with me."

'Suddenly I was kissing him. How it happened I'll never know, but I was in his arms. Without consciously moving we found ourselves outside on the immaculate lawns, beneath an orange tree. The moon shone blue silver, edging the night with soft music. The stars twinkled down as they had ever since the world began.

'We seemed to float on the greensward. I lay gazing at the stars, pinpoints of eternity, infinitesimal sparks of excitement in the purple void of mystery.

'We made love. Idly I toyed with a lank, greasy lock

of his hair. As he began to move faster and faster, his head came up and in the light of the far, far stars I noticed that there were now three warts on his nose.

'OK, screen. Story ends.' Now, she muttered to herself for a bit of something more physical than literary. Although, of course, it could be construed as research for my next passionate analysis of the heart-searing relationship between etc etc.

Ann had decided not to be naked for the boy's arrival this time. Instead she would wear a tee shirt, an old, worn, thin, used to be sort of greeny coloured tee shirt – and nothing but the shirt, apart from a headscarf that is, because she also decided to fill in the waiting time by flicking cobwebs from the ceiling with a feather duster. The old oak beams and joists of the farmhouse were ideal spider country, and since Ann didn't want the spiders destroyed along with their means of making a living, she wouldn't let the house robot apply its vacuum atomiser.

With spiders' webs occupying Ann, there was an opportunity for Salkeld to sneak a look through the living room window and see a handsome, well rounded bottom on top of tiptoeing, finely muscled legs, on top of a footstool. His eyes travelled back up from the stool, paused for some time again on the admirable buttocks and considered why the little waist-length shirt should make the entire spectacle so utterly decadent and so much more entrancing than would a completely naked body. He watched the movements through the shirt, and below it, as she reached up with her duster to knock down the spiders' hard work.

Ann had resolved not to hear the boy when he came in, so she didn't look round when someone entered the room. She didn't start when the hand touched the inside of her left knee. Salkeld stood behind her and ran

45

his fingers up the inside of her thigh. Ann raised a mental eyebrow at a slight departure from what she was expecting when Salkeld's fingers waited at the heavenly door, teasing, will-he-won't-he, not like the normal boy Brough who usually wants his pudding on the same plate as his main course. Still, I decided to ignore him, so ignore him I shall, thought Ann. Just keep dusting, baby.

She found dusting increasingly difficult as Salkeld worked her most sensitive nerve ends for all they were worth. Quite soon, she was sure, had it not been for the force of gravity she would have been floating gently upwards, balanced on a couple of fingertips and the force field they were generating. As it was, the feather duster had stopped, Ann had her eyes closed and was desperately trying to stop herself falling backwards. It's no good, she thought, I've just got to turn round.

With the smoothest of movements she high-kicked with her left leg and spun to her left on the ball of her right foot. The kick would have gone over Brough's head. Salkeld was a good six inches taller than Brough, and so he got a powerful sideswipe from a fast-moving ankle bone smack on the temple.

Salkeld went down as he would after receiving a full-blooded right cross from a bare-knuckle fighter. On the subject of the pain in her ankle, Ann made a few remarks to herself which themselves would not have been out of place at the ringside, and then looked at the prone man on her living room floor.

She knew what he was, rather than who. If he'd been a One he would have had on the superbly comfortable two-piece they all wore during working hours, a costume not unlike the old track suits Ann remembered, except these were made of some natural fibre

46

mixture with silk and wool which managed to be cool in the heat and warm in the cold.

This man, on the other hand, was wearing a business suit in the style that hadn't changed for almost a hundred years. She could see it was made of the finest material, but then all suits were. It was dark blue with a lighter stripe. He had a cream coloured silk shirt, and a tie with yellow and red diagonal stripes which obviously meant he was a member of something or other. Clearly he was a senior Two.

Ann took all this in, then remembered what she herself was wearing. Not a lot. She looked down at the swells and peaks and valleys of her breasts covered in old, no, very old thin green cotton. She looked at the edge of the shirt, at the gentle swell of her belly, at the deep, dark red triangle – the 'hairy diadem' she remembered from a poem – and stepped down from the stool.

So, Mister Smartypants Class Two, you'd come creeping into a girl's house, would you? Come sneaking and creeping, and diddling her while she was doing the housework?

And what have you done with my fancy boy, she continued, silently, to herself. What have you done with the only beam of light in my tunnel? You know about him, don't you. You must have known it was his hand I was expecting. You took advantage. You wanted to catch me out, and look where it's got you. Still, you're not half bad, and I did kick you rather hard.

Salkeld was conscious by now but playing not. Through the narrowest of eyes he saw her beautifully sculptured ankles, the ankles that can kill, he thought. They turned and went into the next room. They returned, and she knelt beside him with some water and a cloth. She dabbed at his temple and brow, saying nothing. Salkeld was calculating hard. His initial position of superiority was lost, and instead of having some fun bringing a woman out of embarrassment into wherever he wanted, he was lying on the carpet with a bad head.

Play for time, play for time, he told himself. Enjoy the moment. It's not every day you have your fevered brow mopped by the finest pair of tits in England. In fact, Salkeld couldn't see those. As he squinted he could only see a pair of knees, skin tight across them, and the insides of a pair of thighs going away in narrowing perspective to a dark target. So, she still hasn't put any more clothes on, thought Salkeld. She can't know why I'm here, although she must connect it with Brough, and she's going to tough it out. Either that or she's absent-minded, which I doubt, or she's just plain raving for a screw, which I also doubt.

He decided it was time to wake up. With a convincing series of sighs, small movements and blinks, he managed to get himself up on one forearm, with his head resting between those Rubens thighs. She patted his cheek and coughed. He did a little cuddle up, trying to get a touch nearer the top.

Suddenly she stood. Salkeld's head banged down on the floor. The crafty bitch! That's two-nothing to her and I don't even look as if I'm in the game.

Trying to preserve his air of total ignorance of the immediate surroundings and the immediate past, Salkeld hauled himself into an armchair. Ann sat down briskly, opposite him. She crossed her legs, lit a cigarette, exhaled in a narrow stream and said, 'OK. What the fuck do you want?'

Quite a lot, my lady, quite a lot, he thought. But aloud he replied, 'They never told me you learned the martial arts while you were working abroad.'

'Very good, Mister. Now. Numero uno, if you want

48

me to get in a twitch and ask you how you know I've worked abroad, and who "They" are, I'm going to disappoint you because I don't give a stuff. Numero due, if you want another kick, Marshall Fart, I can do it from here and you'll get it in the balls this time.'

'Please, please,' he said, spreading his hands out in a placatory gesture. 'Let's not assume we're on different sides. You are on edge because the unexpected has happened. I am here because, as you so delicately put it, I want something.'

'And even though you so delicately put your index and middle fingers in my quim, a bit of diddling isn't all, I suppose.'

'Er, no, quite.'

Salkeld was beginning to have an idea. His first aim had been to recruit Ann Richmond into the Twos as a lecturer/demonstrator at the Training College. With her experience and proclivities she would be ideal. Now he saw there was more quality to her than ordinarily required in a training officer.

'My name is Salkeld. I'm the Class Two Executive in charge of entertainment provision for this region.'

'A real live Twozec! No wonder you felt free to stick your hand in my crutch.'

'Please. It was a foolish game, an attempt to score points. I apologise – not for touching your remarkable person, but for attempting to mislead you. Now, if you will accept my status as apologiser and favour-beggar – ' Ann nodded, 'I will explain why I am here.

'It was necessary to redirect the career of Lance Brough away from a future as a rather average One in agricultural robotics. This necessity arose owing to his extramural activities. He was potentially a disruptive influence. He could have been the cause of instability. In the new bargain, with Brough as a trainee Two,' Ann

49

allowed herself a small grin, 'and your husband remaining undisturbed in his calm, useful and peaceful furrow, and all husbands everywhere likewise saved from aggravation from Brough, the only sufferer is you.

'With Brough out of your life, you have no one left to bring a little variety into your – as you see it – most unsatisfactory routine. I think I may be able to help you there.'

Ann burst out laughing. 'Look, sweetheart, you may be a handsome devil and frightfully suave, but you ain't no young buck stud. I wouldn't mind you coming into my life occasionally, and that would be a particular sort of treat. I mean, you could say nice things, seduce me slowly, and I could lie back and think of opera, champagne and fur coats. But you are no replacement for four times an hour with a seventeen year old. That's a quite different sort of treat. That's quantity rather than quality, and I'm in charge.'

'I was thinking more of offering you a job,' said Salkeld.

'A job? Me? A humble Onewife? Not allowed, old boy. No going back. Once you are committed to the rare and rarified state of matrimony, you can't get out of it. It's against the law, or something.'

For the first time in this interview, Ann showed a weakness. The bitter memory of her bad fortune flicked across her eyes and made her look, just for a moment, unhappily vulnerable.

'It would be difficult, I agree, but I think I could arrange a short secondment, a sort of consultancy. You know – special skills unavailable elsewhere, dancer-manager brought out of retirement just for this once. It's been done before. Of course, it wouldn't be repeatable, that is, unless circumstances were to change.'

50

Ann was interested now. The thought of doing something different, even if was for only a few weeks, was thrilling in the extreme.

'You mean I'd be a choreographer? In a pleasurehouse theatre? It would be wonderful, but . . . I don't think you'd be going to all this trouble just to get a show on the road. Or just because I've lost my young cockerel's morning cocking. Come on, Salkeld, let's see the whites of your eyes.'

Ann was on a big-dipper ride at the moment. First she was trying to stay cool and in command, then she almost collapsed under the dead weight of her own future, then she thought a brilliant interlude was round the corner, and now she realised there was more to it. More to it, good, or more to it, bad?

Salkeld didn't answer straight away. His eye had been taken by a photograph on a shelf, of two heads looking happy. On the left was a serious young man with a proud, slightly pompous smile. On the right was a stunningly beautiful young woman. Salkeld was an entertainment historian as well as a capable executive, and in his mind he blended a mid-20th century French film actress with an Italian one. Jeanne Moreau plus Gina Lollobrigida equals Ann Richmond.

'You were extraordinarily lovely when you were married,' said Salkeld.

'And now I'm just an old bat with big tits. But you can call me Ann.'

'I'm having a spot of bother at Pleasurehouse 13, Ann. On the face of it, nothing can be the matter. The management is excellent, the Local Unit Supervisor running the team is among the best we've got, and the staff are as good as any. But there is trouble. There is discontent. The Ones of Northampton are complaining, and that means a formidable group of females,

51

among the most important in the entire country.'

'And if you don't crack it, my lord Salkeld, the Amenities Committee'll bust you down to Punch and Judy man.'

'At least, Ann, at least. So I'm going to request an extra big show for the winter season at Theatre 13, with you as choreographer. But really you'll be there to find out what's going on. You'll be my spy. I can stall the Committee for a while. I can assure them that matters are in hand. But I must find out what this problem is, and I won't do it by descending on them and asking.'

'What do I tell my husband?'

'Whatever you like. I'm quite sure he will be totally convinced by whatever you say.'

'OK, it's a deal. Let's celebrate. I've got a very nice bottle of Pouilly-Fuissé in the cooler. Wasted on that boy, of course. Might as well give him vodka and donkey piss, he wouldn't notice.'

'That sounds very pleasant – the Pouilly-Fuissé I mean.'

'OK, blue eyes. A glass of the dry and flinty will await you in five minutes. Upstairs. Top floor.'

With that Ann, already feeling slightly drunk on excitement, uncurled her naked legs, stood, did a little wiggle and a dip to show she knew he knew that she knew that he knew, and did her dancer's duck walk out of the room.

Salkeld waited until the clinking of glass had stopped going up the stairs, then slowly climbed after it. The large bulge in his trousers was hidden, he thought, by fastening his jacket.

Giggling to herself with him still downstairs, she had whipped off her shirt, opened the wine and poured the glasses. She placed these on the left and right of the window sill, so wide it was almost a window seat. She leant forward on her elbows, chin cupped in hands, looking out of the window at the countryside just beginning to turn from summer to autumn. She giggled again.

Salkeld walked into the room and stopped. His perspective showed the fabulous arse he'd already admired, assertively aiming at him, the feet below quite well apart. There was a glass of wine to each side. Ann looked up to see his reflection in the window.

'You've forgotten your umbrella and briefcase, Class Two Executive Salkeld.' Ann had wanted to have some fun with this guy, and he was turning out very well. She gave her arse a wriggle and resumed her contemplation of the rural splendour below.

Salkeld took his tie off first. Funny how habits never die, he thought. He folded his clothes neatly and placed them on a chaise, then turned towards that delicious bum.

He steered his column up against the crack in her cheeks and rubbed a little.

'Oh, sorry,' he said. 'First things first.'

He reached forward for the wine, placed one next to her elbow and took the other for himself. 'Good luck,' he said, as he took a drink and, rightly judging that this woman was now so eager for him that her pussy would be running, at the same time pushed his cock unguided into it.

Ann gave a little gurgle, reached for her wine and sipped.

'So, that's how you get to be a Twozec,' she sighed in mock adoration. 'Being able to do two things at once.'

'My dear,' said Salkeld 'this is a fine wine. You have the finest of bodies. Were it not so, and thus totally occupying, I can assure you I could add to the show by simultaneously tap-dancing while playing "Putting on the Ritz" on the pipes of Pan.'

Ann was, despite his wisecracks and her self-possession, at the foothills of orgasm. The peak was not far away. She put her wine down, braced her feet more firmly and wider apart, put her left hand down on the window sill and reached behind her with the other. She found the bouncing balls she wanted. Her fingernail traced the point where they joined the root of the fearsome stem, now powering in and out with a heavy regularity.

As she squeezed gently and let go with a small murmuring groan, Salkeld put aside his careless air too. His glass also placed firmly down, he reached forward and grabbed a tit in each hand. He felt their marvellous weight, their skin and shape so inexplicably exciting. He felt them moving as he moved.

Salkeld pressed the insides of his arms into Ann's body as he increased his speed. His hands held the great, hardly credible breasts. His elbows gripped the smoothly curved waist. His groin thumped and smacked against the glorious roundness of her cheeks. She was coming, he could feel it. He went into a mad dash, a final flourish, a spasm of ins and outs as his own moment approached and then surged up into her.

Ann felt her inner glove contracting and gripping as she came with him, the sudden hot jet of him forcing its way past her self-willed muscles. There was another involuntary clenching, and another, then a declining, dimming but completely satisfying series of fireworks until the last push was made and the last candle exploded.

Ann raised her forehead from the window sill, reached for her glass and drained it.

'Well, my highly trained entertainment executive friend. Do you do encores?'

'Right at this moment an interval followed by a few

curtain calls might be more in order. More wine, my dear?'

They took the bottle to bed. Ann, glowing and replete, was not now in the mood to discuss her future employment. To learn about the other of today's surprises, the man Salkeld himself, did not require so much effort from her.

Answering her questions he was not terribly forthcoming about his life before the Change, but with her personal knowledge of a type of pre-Change young man who had had lots of money and liked spending it on photographic models, actresses and dancers, Ann put five beans together. She guessed he had lived on his wits, gambling, fixing and high-class pimping for the rich and reclusive.

Some day she would find out how right she was, but today Salkeld was comparing himself as a trainee Two with that most recent entrant to the college, Lancelot Brough.

'Of course in those days we were far more worried about the Threes. Most of them had been long-term unemployed before the Change. Labourers and skilled workers had been replaced by robots; clerks, middle managers and members of the professions by artificial-intelligence computers. Those people, plus the idle rich, the politicians, the forces of law and order and various other rumps of the old ways, made up quite a wodge of people. Far, far more than the rest of us.

'So, calling them Threes and shoving them all together into the new walled cities seemed like putting a lid on a mixture of chemicals which was about to start fizzing. We hoped that an unlimited and continuous supply of absolutely everything would keep them quiet, but we didn't know. If you were a young Two posted to city duty, you were nervous.'

Ann drained her glass again, nestled up to him with her hand cradling his balls and her head on his chest. She was beginning to feel that a new life was on its way, but for the moment it was story time.

'Well, I never found life as a Two so trying,' she said. 'There was always the occasional young One who hadn't quite grasped the system yet, and thought he could come on stage and screw you there and then in the middle of a routine. But that soon settled down. And when I transferred from theatre to pleasurehouse, junior management couldn't have been nicer. Then I met Arthur.'

'If you hadn't, you could have been the Twozec around here.'

'I've always had the imagination and the sense of theatre, and I know how and why people enjoy themselves, but I think I would need a really good politico-admin person to fill in my gaps.' Ann gave Salkeld's balls a gentle reminder as she whispered that last remark. Salkeld said:

'Yes, I hope that soon there will be an opportunity to, er, fill a gap, but a chap of my age needs more than five minutes and a glass of Pouilly-Fuissé to recover from a bout with a woman like you, Ann.'

Ann sighed and groaned in mock despair.

'When will I ever find Mr Right? You're either terrific at it but can only do it once, or you've got the energy reserves of a Herdwick tup but the technique of a tidal wave.'

'What very picturesque language you do use, Ann. Might I enquire as to the approximate nature and whereabouts of an Arkwright tup?'

'Herdwick, bubble brain. My grandfather was a farmer up on the fells in the north. He always reckoned that when it came to tupping, meaning the ram giving a length to the ewe, there was no gentleman of the ovine classes so eager to please, nor so able to deliver, as the Herdwick ram. This beast was every woman's dream. But I'm so sorry. I interrupted your life history. Now, where were we? You were an unfortunate rookie in the Two squad deputed to keep the trogs happy.'

'Not just the lower orders, Ann, I keep reminding you. It was everybody who could neither design a robot nor star in, or produce, some form of pleasurable pastime. There were belted earls as well as the great mass of unemployed hooligans, navvies, ex-factory girls and screaming tarts. Anyway, I was posted to City HX, built in a bowl with a new wall around the rim, and previously known as Halifax. The wall was up and electrified and a couple of the new supercentres had been built.'

'What on earth is a supercentre?'

'A disaster, basically. The planners of the Change had got it wrong. They thought that the Threes would be like the Ones, wanting their pleasures highly organised. But they didn't. They thought the idea of free beer and free sex was marvellous, but they wanted to keep it local. Also, the yobs and the scum didn't want to mix with the erstwhile nobs, and vice versa. So they didn't want one-stop joy shopping at a supercentre.

'So what went on was a sort of self-selection process. Ostensibly similar nightclubs would automatically go different ways. Club A would become your high society type full of hooray Henrys and squeaking frightfully-frightfullies, and another would have the common herd doing their mindless thing to the music.

'And you still had lowlife pubs where people would bet on the horseracing telesatted from China, but they couldn't bet money, because there wasn't any, and they couldn't bet goods, because everybody had all they wanted, so they bet forfeits. They'd bet fingers, or ears. They'd bet they could drink half a pint of their own blood. Doesn't happen now, of course. Well, not so much.

'You had girls still walking the streets, and men picking them up and screwing them in shop doorways for free, even though there was a fully signposted and completely kitted out Supercentre with Sex District not a hundred metres away.'

'And what were you doing in among all this? Doesn't sound quite the thing for a future Twozec Salkeld.'

'Oh yes it was. You might think we have it pretty good, but we come up the hard way. What I was doing initially was the sex theatres. We called them the off-fucks, because there were strippers constantly taking their own and the audience's clothes off, and you could go upstairs any time for a quick one. They'd been set up in a fairly hurried and haphazard way, and my job was to organise them into a co-operative, see that there was a constant supply of girls, install a good manageress and so on.'

'Manageress? Always?'

'There wasn't a particular policy. It was just that no men wanted to do anything like that. Class Three had regressed almost instantly to a male-dominated society. The men were mostly stronger physically, there were no civilising pressures, and so they were happy to drink, smoke and be tossed off all day. Some women wanted to do something more positive, and whatever psychological motives they may have had, if that meant providing sex and drugs and rock and roll, great.'

'Rock and roll. Whatever happened to rock and roll?'

'It's still going strong in the cities. They have theatres where they project pictures of the old concerts.

Chick Berry, Jerry Lee Lewis, Status Quo. All been dead for years.'

'I think it was Chuck Berry, not Chick.'

'Was it? Anyway, these concerts are the only time you can guarantee that in a city theatre audience there will be no one knobbing the person in the next seat. Any normal kind of show and the cleaning robots have the most appalling time trying to get dried semen off the upholstery. But not after rock and roll. But what was I saying? Ah yes, the off-fucks. Well, at first the problem was quantity. There was an endless stream of men wanting to take advantage of the new free sex, but we hadn't got enough girls. Then I had this brainwave of offering girls a chance to escape the life of a Three by becoming a pleasure-source outside the city for the new technical aristocrats, but first they had to do a spell inside with their fellow drones.

'Obviously I had to get them young. They had to work for, say, nine extremely hard months in an off-fuck, then do six months training at Twocollege, and still graduate luscious and lovely for the systems analysts.

'I began by going to the discos. Lots of pretty girls all with empty heads suitable only for nodding to their synthetic dance music. No good. So I tried the streets and the pubs. I got beaten up three times, once by the women.'

'Tell me,' said Ann, thinking that a bit of rough stuff might get Salkeld going again.

'I went in a pub. It was a big place, several rooms but no carpet on the floor in any of them. The lights were bright around the bars, reflecting faces and bottles in the spotty mirrors, but everywhere else seemed in shadows. You had an impression of solidity, as if the pub was built to withstand an aeon of mistreatment, of

59

violent blows to its fabric and the more subtle decay of thick air and things spilt.

'There was loud music. The overwhelming sensation was the smell of yesterday's cigarette smoke, and the day's before that, and back to the first smoke when the pub opened – maybe a century before, 1920s sort of time. If you got near the toilets you could smell them. If you got near the people you could smell them too, the result of putting the same clothes on again and again without washing. Interesting point, you see. New clothes were freely available, robot laundries and dry cleaners likewise, but they didn't perceive the need.

'Ugly old people sat in couples staring into space. Young, overweight men leered at the barmaids and belched and farted and laughed with wide open, half-toothless mouths at obscene jokes.

'A few girls sat on bar stools, alone, each gazing into a glass and chain-smoking cigarettes. A group of nocturnal animals – pasty, middle-aged, hungover-looking men – watched the sport on the telesat.

'I got a beer from the robot and just sat around, looking. There was a girl playing darts, totally unsuitable for training as a Two but she did look as if she could exhaust ten men an hour. She was about your height, a bit shorter, with the most enormous bosom you have ever seen. It was contained, just, inside a studded leather jacket. The rest of her, equally bulbous, was doing its best to get out of a pair of skintight jeans. She had a cigarette always in her mouth, and if she caught any man trying to look down the front of her jacket, she'd put her darts and her pint of lager down, grasp her own lapels, pull them apart and say "Ere. Wanna fuckin eyeful, do yer?"

'After a while she came over to me and sat down. She said something like "ello, darlin, you look like you

60

might av bin a customer in the old days. Looking for a bit of business, are yer?" I said that in a manner of speaking I was, and could we go somewhere. To much nudging and whispering from the rest of the clientele, we went out and so to her place. She turned the telesat on to the game show channel, got us a couple of tins of beer out of the cooler, lit a cigarette and took her clothes off.

'It was utterly amazing. I've never seen so much flesh hanging off such a small basic structure. Her breasts hung to her waist, huge sacks of lard, and she stank. Layers of perfume on top of not very much washing. "Wotcherwant, then?" she said. "Suck or a fuck?" I said something like "um", or it might have been "er". She knelt before me, her lard sacks resting on my knees. "Like em?" she said. "Biggest fuckin tits in Halifax, they are." Then she threw her cigarette across the room and dug for my private member.

'I can tell you, Ann, there was not much to find just at that moment. But she did manage to drag out a little winkle. "What the fuck's this?" she said. "I'm used to big fuckers." Then another amazing thing happened. She took some teeth out. She had a plate with the top four teeth on, and she removed this and balanced it carefully on top of a small pile of metal foil dishes which obviously had come last week from the autotandoori.

'"Lost my fuckin teeth in a fuckin punch-up," she informed me. Well, she went to work on my poor willy, and sure enough, with the gap between her teeth, there was an unusual sensation. I began to swell. She grunted and sweated, sucked and licked. After what seemed like an age, I came.

'"Thank you," I said. "A highly professional job. Now, I've got an offer for you. How would you like to be a star in a sex theatre?"'

'She didn't like the idea. I could tell that, because she said "Wodyer think I am, cunt face, a fuckin slave? A fuckin machine with obligations? I don't want none of that. What I want right now is to get some fuckin thing out of tonight."

'So she lit another cigarette, got her can of beer in her hand, pushed me back on the couch and sat on my face. I have to tell you, Ann, I thought my moment had come. I was drowning, suffocating, being eaten alive by a gigantic pussy with a manic urge to push my chin up into my nose. This is not funny, Ann. I might never have survived. From somewhere out there I heard the command "Lick, you bastard, lick" and so I licked. I had this wild image of my face coming out of the experience looking like a Pizza Quattro Stagioni.

"The stench was dreadful. Then I heard her voice again. "Ere. You heard this one? What did fish smell like, before women went swimmin? Good, eh?" Then she began to speed up. "You fuckin dirty bastard. Go on, go on, go on, go on . . ." And she came. I can't describe it. Just say I was thankful it was over. But it wasn't.

'She called out, "Irene. Come on in 'ere." And a black girl came in, tall, muscular like a body-builder, very short hair, hard as nails, with a chrysanthemum tattooed on her forehead. She didn't smile. "Irene," says my friend. "This cunt 'ere likes sex. He wants me to go and work in a brothel, suckin fuckin cocks all day long. What do you think, Irene?" I sat up as Irene walked towards me. All I could see was the blue ink of the chrysanthemum on her forehead. I stared and stared. As she got near enough, without any warning, she smashed me across the face with the back of her hand. I felt the blood run from the rings she was wearing, and fell back.

'The fat white darts player sat across my legs. Irene grabbed my hand and made as if to break the fingers. Remember, Ann, that I was young, fit, strong, tall and a decent weight for my height. These women reduced me to nothing. Fat Whitey then carefully tipped her beer over me. There was a tiny little pool of it in my navel. With equal care she stubbed her cigarette out in it. This didn't hurt too much, because the beer quenched the fire. But the next bit did.

'Irene whipped my hands behind my back. Whitey punched me in the mouth. From somewhere they produced some cord, like picture cord, and tied my ankles together. They pulled them up my back and tied feet to wrists, then lifted me. I got a mad, swirling picture of this luxurious room, newly appointed to Standard Three which was like the old five-star hotels used to be, and it was filthy, this room. Dirty glasses and plates everywhere, cigarette packets, full ashtrays. And now I could see a hole in the ceiling. They'd knocked a hole through to the steel girder and hung a hook from it. They hung me from the hook. I dangled head down – but this wouldn't do, so they put another cord through my armpits and adjusted me until I hung level, looking down at the carpet, about a metre below my eyes.

'Irene lay down below me. She flipped off her shoes, each with the other foot. She wriggled her black trousers down. Fat Whitey pulled her black sweat shirt off for her, lovingly fingering the nipples of a near-breastless chest as she did so.

'Irene, slowly, ever so slowly, hooked her thumbs in her pants, pulled them down and rolled them off. Then, she raised her hips up with her hands, swung her body back so her weight was on her neck and shoulders and she opened her legs wide, still with her hips supported in the air. She had a chrysanthemum tattooed on the inside of each thigh. Her friend (and mine!) knelt and gave tongue.

'Irene stared at me in defiant dislike. This is sex, her eyes told me, and you can't give it to me. Her foot shot out in a karate kick and just about took my cheekbone off. "Don't look, you fucking pervert," she said. So I closed my eyes. Another kick split both lips open. "Open your fuckin' eyes, you shitbag, or I'll kick them out from here. Just you look straight at me, not at what I'm doin." So I stared into her eyes, and the chrysanthemum, and saw her coming in the backs of those eyes, those deep, deep brown and black crystal globes with an ancient hatred in them.

'All the time I could smell her, and the fat white one, and I could hear all the noises, all the eating noises, and in my peripheral vision I could sense the movements, but I kept staring into those eyes because the next kick would have put a big hole where my nose used to be.'

'They got up and went out of my line of vision. It sounded like they were getting dressed, and soon I saw two pairs of shoes. They didn't hurtle up into my face this time. Instead I heard the sound of matches striking, smoke being inhaled, and then felt a wasp sting on the top of each of my feet. Smoke again, and more burns, this time on my shins. They were just touching me with the red hot cigarette ends, enough to burn but not enough to go right through the skin.

'I was yelping, of course, and they were laughing. A burn on each of my knees was followed by a gradual progression up my thighs. They were sitting on the floor below me now, the smoke was going in my eyes, and they were sticking their cigarette ends in the air towards my most vulnerable area.

'First, they scorched the hair off my testicles. They did this with a cigarette lighter – and I was crying now.

Then they lit more cigarettes. They got a couple of tins of beer, and just sat, and drank, and smoked.

'Then Irene reached up, pulled back my foreskin and burnt me right on the end. Whitey reached up, pulled my knees apart, and thrust her cigarette up my bum-hole. The next thing I remember I was in some sort of cart or barrow, on a rough pathway. The women were talking to me. "You're the first from outside," they were saying. "Usually we just bump off the more disgusting specimens of our own lot. Well, nobody cares any more, do they? Reduces the numbers a bit, doesn't it? And they're such fucking scabs and shitarses they deserve it. But you, you're more of a laugh. You're one of them, aren't you? From out there. Our first. But we'll get more of you, and we'll do the same." There were more punches, and then I was falling, and I hit cold water.

'I woke on land, and a man was cutting my bonds. He was talking. Something about hearing the splash. "Saw Pam the Pram and her mate Irene, evil bastards they are, so I went in for you, not that I like swimming in the canal even now it's clean and got fish in, well, I remember it when you could have dissolved a dog in it, but anyway, I don't usually bother when Pam throws 'em in 'cos they're usually DOA if you know what I mean. But we had a chat about Pam and her sort at the last meetin' and decided that we should include an anti-killing statement in the new constitution. And that presupposes rescuin' people from bein killed, so 'ere you are." By now I was free and rubbing my body, trying to get the circulation going again.

'"Constitution?" I said. "What constitution?" He said, "Aven't you heard? It's because there's no laws now, no coppers or owt, and everythin's provided, and anythin goes kind of, some of us thought it was a good chance to start all over again. So we meet, and talk, and maybe someday something will come of it."'

"'But what's the point? I said to him. You've got everything you . . ." "*You*?" he said. "You? So you're an outsider, are you, and I've been shootin' my mouth off. I've a good fuckin' mind to chuck you back in. The casualty centre is four blocks that way. Good fuckin' night."

'A few days later, transferred to a Class Two sanitorium, I wondered what to do. I didn't care about Pam and her pram, but what my rescuer had said sounded like the birth of a revolutionary movement. Clearly, the Threes were not getting enough aces.'

'Aces?' said Ann, idly scratching the root of his dick with her little finger nail.

'Activities, Consumables and Enervators. Aces. Like bread and circuses. Sex and football is A, food and fancy clothes is C, and booze, drugs and rock and roll is E. Fill your life with those and you have no time for revolution. Anyway, I got some help in and we set up a big recruitment drive, put on loads of stunts, and within a few months there were no more slags on the streets, hardly any murders, Pam the Pram had disappeared, and everyone was having a jolly good time. And I got my first promotion. To mmmmmmmmm.'

He felt hair brushing his thighs and stomach. He felt lips closing around his still rather limp member. He felt a tongue working its way up and down, round and round, the tip of it finding that most sensitive spot. Ann had her eyes closed in concentration – tongue tip on the glans, suck and lift. She lifted her head to look at the wet and glistening, half raised cock. She bent down, and took both his balls in her mouth as she worked his cock with her hand. Now it was really stiffening. Her lips hovered, her mouth open, brushing his helmet rim.

She breathed hotly on it, then took it right in, not in deep-throat style but to the side of her mouth, in her cheek.

Salkeld was hard now, and ready. Ann wanted no preliminaries. She just wanted IT. She swung her leg over and began to bump and grind, like she'd been taught all those years ago. She felt his prick grow even more, and she got hotter. She got faster. Ann was wild now, thinking of nothing but the gallop, concentrating totally on that thing going in and out, and on the most exciting ways of making every little bit of it rub her up the right way.

Salkeld let it all happen. He would want something more in a moment, but now he was simply providing a pole for her to prance on. He watched her magnificent breasts, bouncing and shaking with frenzied effort. What a superb woman, he thought. What a combination of mind and animal.

She exploded with a series of wails and ohs, juddered and shuddered and wet him from knee to ribcage, and collapsed on top of him. She was half senseless. Salkeld drew out, held his cock between finger and thumb, and thrust it up and into the next available aperture. She hardly noticed. She had been to the Elysian Fields and was still out.

Salkeld lay still, waiting. Gradually she came to realise what she had had inserted and where. Slowly she moved, a more restrained version of the bumps and grinds this time, while Salkeld began to feel his own spring welling up. He thrust upwards with his hips. She moved faster. He shot, five, six, seven times, and without speaking they fell back and slept.

Salkeld woke with his half shrunken rod still in the tight little hole. Ann woke as he pulled out.

'Tomorrow,' he said, 'I want to talk business. In the office. I'll pick you up. Same time.'

By the time he'd showered and dressed, she was asleep again, the red hair cascading over the pillow, the sheet covering one perfect and excellent breast while the other was revealed. Glory be to the highest, thought Salkeld, and he strolled back to his hoverbubble a lighter-hearted man.

Ann dreamt. She was back in her youth, a time when babysitting was still a fairly usual thing for teenage girls to do because not every family yet had a domestic robot or indeed trusted it if they did have one. She was being taken home by a friend of her father's, after looking after his small children for the evening. Her own parents were away. She would be alone in the house.

As they pulled up outside the door, Ann asked the man if he'd like a coffee. She made sure her skirt rode well up her thigh as she got out, and again when she sat opposite him with the coffees served. In her dream, as in reality, Ann knew all about the effects she could have on men. She had a fantastically desirable body, a beautiful face, and a light in those green, green eyes that flashed not 'Go' but 'Come on!'

They chatted. Ann did some eye and thigh flashing and watched the man stir uncomfortably. She had selected him from a number of unwitting candidates to be her first sexual experience, but hadn't worked out very much more than that. So far she had him excited but he was on the sofa and she was on the armchair opposite. 'I'll show you my holiday photographs,' she said, and sat beside him with a selection of sizzling beach pictures featuring a topless Ann Cuillin aged fifteen and looking ready for anything. In the photographs she seemed always to be licking an ice-cream or sucking a straw, looking directly into the camera lens and gathering her bosom between her arms to make her cleavage even more spectacular.

The man was now at bursting point. 'My suntan's nearly faded now – look,' she said as she lifted up her jumper so that he could see her midriff and just the very slightest beginnings of her magnificent breasts which were unrestrained beneath the thin wool. The man couldn't stop himself now. He grabbed the sweater and lifted it over her head. After a brief moment of wonderment and admiration at the sight of such miracles, he buried his head between them.

She felt him undo his trousers and push them down. He pulled up her skirt, quite roughly, and almost tore her pants off. This was not what she'd imagined. The man was a charming, smooth, sophisticated type and she had expected more romance. She felt panic. She tried to get him off. 'No you don't, little prickteaser,' he said to her through a mouth closed with determination.

'Please, I might have a baby,' she cried, her eyes tight shut. 'If that's your problem . . .' he said, and lifted her heels onto his shoulders. He knelt upright. His right hand went to her crutch. His thumb went in her pussy, and his middle finger went up her arse. She bucked and wrestled but couldn't escape. She opened her eyes and it wasn't her daddy's friend after all. It was a huge black man, with a chrysanthemum tattooed on his forehead. He began to wank himself, slowly, while pushing his hand as hard as he could up both her orifices.

'You've got to learn how to keep the seven dwarfs happy if you want to be Snow White,' said the man. She reached up and held his burning meat in both hands. She pumped it once, twice, three times, and he came in enormous spurts, great long streams that covered her tits, her tummy, her neck, and shot into her open mouth. There seemed no end to the flow. More and more of it came, and she said, 'How do I stop it?'

'Put it in your mouth and it'll stop,' said a voice. Ann looked round and saw her mother, watching. She was with Salkeld, and Ann's husband Arthur. They nodded approvingly as Ann, with her eyes on her mother, pushed her young novice's mouth over the drinking fountain and eventually got the end of the black man's giant of a cock between her lips. Still the river wouldn't stop. Her mother was lying! Worse, her mother was laughing, sharing the joke with Salkeld and Arthur . . .

Ann Richmond awoke with a thumb in her mouth and the fingers of her other hand frantically rubbing the little joystick hidden just inside her golden gate. She was sweating, more as in a hot flush than through exercise. Still partly in her dream she kept rubbing, harder and faster. She came with a shiver and said to herself, I've tried to be Snow White. This time, my lord Salkeld of the Dance, I'll audition for the Wicked Queen.

[4]

A fortnight later, Class Two Executives Salkeld and
Rafferty sat in vast leather armchairs beside the fire in
the private management room of Pleasurehouse 13. It
was an inglenook fireplace with a great oak bressumer
beam carved with coats of arms, and seasoned
hardwood logs were burning in the dog grate. Behind
him a George III dining table was set with Victorian
glass and china for lunch, which would be served
shortly. Meanwhile, this pair of matching pleasure professionals discussed the problem which surrounded
them.

'As far as I can work out it's all about attitude,' said
Salkeld. 'Not a single One who has complained has
been able to say anything specific. Just a lot of didn't
like it, it wasn't as good as it used to be, nothing really
factual to go on.'

'If it's attitude, it's motivation, and if it's
motivation, it's management,' replied Rafferty. 'Get
rid of Spencer.'

'I can't do that, not without more evidence. He's
extremely popular with the customers, and several of
them, including the most senior lady Onezec in Regional Computer Centre NN, expect him to leave his
general management duties frequently to do something
more personally active. There'd be a revolt if I destabilised him. Even so, I take your point. It must be to do
with him.'

'Then I suggest you get your spy in tomorrow. Don't

71

leave it 'til next month or whatever. I also suggest you run a check on all the Twos working here, particularly the younger and more recently recruited, to see if they have anything in common – city of provenance, for example.'

'Why should that have anything to do with it?' said Salkeld in surprise. 'You can't tell me there's any difference between where they bloody come from.'

'Not officially, no, nor even unofficially. I'm only telling you that my own observations, instincts, sixth, seventh and eighth senses and the eye in the back of my head, all tell me that some of the new Twos we're getting are fifth columnists.'

'A fifth column? For whom, for Christ's sake?'

'That I don't know,' Rafferty responded, draining his G&T and ringing for lunch. 'I can't work out whether they're sent by the Amenities Committee to check us managers out, or whether they're representing something a whole lot more sinister.'

'Come on, Raffery. The Amenities Committee doesn't mess about with spies. If that lot want you they'll have you, served with parsley butter on Wedgwood.'

'Used to be like that, I'll admit,' Rafferty said as they sat at the table, beneath chandeliers and below massive portraits of red-coated and bewigged generals. The waiter brought them a dish of gigantic prawns which had been split and marinated in lime juice and rice wine, then fiercely fried in a secret amalgam of oil, soy sauce, garlic, lemon grass and various hot, dark and flavourful powders.

The diners had a happy few moments with these, and said a silent thank you to the wise and wonderful but unknown Kim Doo Ik who had smuggled his son and daughter out of the everlasting wars in Korea and

Vietnam to Japan and thence to Britain. Miss Kim now offered her services as a lithe young Two, and her brother cooked the most delicious food as the Pleasurehouse second chef.

'What do you mean, used to be?' said Salkeld when the prawns were finished and fingers were being dipped in lemon-scented water.

'I just think there's a bit of unrest going around, and the Amenities Committee is keen to find out what it is without disturbing the status quo. Or, maybe they've got themselves organised in the cities, and there's a puritan backlash or something. Anyway, I have spotted a thread joining up four young Twos I've had to destabilise recently. They were all from the same city. HX. Used to be . . .'

'Halifax, I know,' interrupted Salkeld. 'I did a spell there, and there was some minor trouble, but I was sure I'd got it pacified and stable. Well, bugger me.'

'Would that be instead of a sorbet, after this?' inquired the waiter as he served Salkeld with an utterly delicious concoction of poultry and vegetables called Six Jewels at a Wedding with a Duck.

'You fucking behave yourself, Anthony, or I'll have you transferred to be a lavatory attendant in LN,' snapped Salkeld, not in the mood for camping. 'Now fuck off out of it.'

The rest of the meal was consumed in silence, both men deep in thought about the first serious hint of instability since the new Order had settled down.

'I think I'll have my brandy upstairs,' said Salkeld, eventually, and gruffly.

'Not a bad thought, my man,' said Rafferty. 'Miss Kim, I assume? I fancy a bit of Ghita myself. That is the thing about oriental food. You always want something else Oriental soon afterwards.'

The Korean girl, so polite, formal and deferential that it was impossible to call her by any name more familiar than Miss Kim, received Salkeld with her usual charm. She showed him to a rocking chair, bowed, and left for a moment to get him a large brandy. When she returned with that, she did as she always did for her Mr Salkeld. She sat on the arm of the chair and spoke to the telesat screen. As the picture started, she put her arm round his neck and leant her cheek against his.

From time to time he took a sip of his brandy, but otherwise they were motionless as they watched the screen together, two pairs of eyes, both worldly, but from different worlds. Miss Kim had not been brought up to expect the service of others. Salkeld hadn't either, to start with, but by heaven he expected it now. He looked the part, too, more distinguished now after years of the very best of everything had given a few lived-in creases to his face and a few grey hairs to his immaculately groomed temples, trimmed that morning as they were every morning at 08.30. This was immediately after the cut-throat shave performed by a Mr Harold Gilbert, late many years of Jas. Gilbert & Sons of Market Harborough. Harold was far too old to be a Two, even a sub-Two as the personal servant class were called, but Salkeld regarded Harold as his personal perk.

It was surprising, Miss Kim was musing to herself, how someone so thoroughly familiar with every aspect of professional sex could still not feel contempt for the dramatised product of his own industry. But, no question, Salkeld always liked to watch before doing.

On the screen, six well dressed people sat around a table as if at a fancy dress dinner party. One man had on a historic army uniform jacket, the sort of thing they wore at the Charge of the Light Brigade. Another had a

74

laboratory coat, open to show a mauve shirt and a large purple bow-tie. He wore a pair of gold-wire framed half-glasses, over the top of which he kept peering in what was obviously supposed to be an absent-minded way, but under the make-up he looked too young to be that kind of absent minded. The third man was in clerical collar and plain black shirtfront. He sat tall, a powerfully built African or West Indian.

The three women were all glamorous. One had on a shimmering red dress which was cut as low as a dress could be and still keep its contents within. The second girl was in a white tailored suit, and the third had a vivid blue silk pyjama outfit with mandarin collar. They were playing some kind of board game.

The man in glasses threw a die and moved a little counter around the board. The camera zoomed in to reveal that the counter was a miniature erect penis on a plinth. As a result of his move he drew a card from a pack, then threw again. His next card made him smile.

'In the dining room,' he said. 'With Mrs White.'

The girl in the white suit got to her feet.

'Why, Professor,' she said, 'we are already in the dining room. Do you mean now, in front of all these people?'

In fact, Mrs White didn't seem to mind too much. She stood, walked around the table and took off her suit jacket to reveal that it was her only upper garment and that she had a very large pair of knockers.

Her skirt came off too, and she had nothing underneath that either. She stood in front of the fireplace, naked except for a pair of high-heeled shoes, and waited. The Professor rose from the table and went to meet her. The camera zoomed in on his trouser front as she unzipped him and took out a very healthy looking prick which would have been more appropriate on Tarzan than a Professor.

She skinned it slowly back and forth, then knelt and kissed it. She rolled back onto the hearthrug.

'I don't think you'll be needing the lead piping,' she giggled, as the Professor kicked off his shoes, dropped his pants, whipped off his bow tie, pulled his shirt hurriedly over his head, and lay down beside her. He parted his legs, she got on top, and the camera viewed the action from between his feet. Up and down went a gorgeously rounded bum, alternately hiding and exposing the complete length of a rod which, if not professorial, was certainly of academic interest. Anyone with a cock like that would make his living with it.

Occasionally the picture cut to a front view, to show the glorious jiggings and joggings of Mrs White's equally interesting breasts, and there was just the odd cut to the audience, still at table, whose attention could hardly be said to be riveted. The army officer had his hand down the front of the red dress, and the girl in the pyjamas was clearly looking for loose change in the reverend's trouser pocket.

Mrs White began to move faster, and the Professor became more urgent. Suddenly she slipped off him and turned her body round the other way. Now the camera looked from between the man's feet at a lovely face, a tumbling cloud of blonde hair, a great dangling pair of heavyweights and a brightly lipsticked mouth closing over the end of an enormously erect penis.

She could only get a little of it between her lips, so she gave it more stimulation with her hand. At exactly the right moment she drew away, pushed her chest forward, and took eight or nine long, shining spurts all over her miraculous tits.

The camera went back to the table. The army officer

threw the die twice and announced that his partner was to be Mrs Peacock, the lady in blue silk.

'In the kitchen.' He added. 'With the dagger.'

The scene moved to a small room with a table in the middle and a few pans hanging on a rack.

The girl came in first, and turned to her man as he entered.

'Well, Colonel,' she said. 'Not quite the ideal place?'

'Rules are rules, and must be obeyed,' said the army chap in what might have been a real Scots accent. You could now see that he was dressed as from an old Highland regiment, for he had on a kilt. He bent to his stocking and pulled out a dagger, then stepped towards the girl.

In one movement he slit her silk top and tossed it away. Another swift movement with the dagger and she had on no trousers – which meant she had on nothing but a pair of light sandals. She stepped out of those and, keeping a mocking eye firmly on the man's face, ran her hands up inside his kilt.

'As if I didn't know!' she said, as her hands came out from under and went to his waist. Kilt and sporran were soon on the floor and she led him across the room by his prick.

'Kitchens do have their advantages,' she murmured as she reached inside a cupboard to find a sugar bowl. She knelt, gave his cock a wet suck, then dipped it in the sugar. The next five minutes were spent licking the grains of sugar from his twitching red member, one at a time. The camera got right in on this scene, and you could count the grains as she got near the end of her task.

With her sweet tooth satisfied and his prick at breaking point, she stood, turned, leant forward with her arms and chin flat on the table, and he took her there, standing up. Half a dozen thrusts and he was done, as you saw clearly when he pulled out to spend, and the camera again got in really close to watch the creamy rivulets of life run down the channel between her cheeks.

Back in the dining room, the reverend gentleman was already busy. He had a rope, and with it he was tying the red-dress girl's hands behind her back.

'It said, in the billiard room,' he shouted, and dragged her off by the rope. The picture cut to the billiard room, and there he pushed her to the floor where she knelt, abject, like someone awaiting the axe. Instead of an axe she got an eye-level view of a massive black chopper as he quickly undressed. He pulled her to her feet.

'Miss Scarlett, this is no time for prayers.' He delved into her neckline and pulled out another pair of breasts just like Mrs White's, full and round and very ample. He ripped the dress downwards. It came apart and fell off. He took a gold bangle from her wrist and hung it on his prick, right at the base where it swung a little and tapped the bottom of its ornate circumference against his balls.

'Now, Miss Scarlett. Taste gold!'

He threw her down on her knees again and she took the whole of his prick into her mouth. Admittedly it was not as big as Professor Plum's but it was still of highly creditable dimensions. In it went, up to the hilt, right up inside her cheek rather than into the back of her throat.

He didn't move much, but just enjoyed the sensation. Then, he pulled out and, with her hands still tied, he lifted her onto the billiard table. She sat on the D, her own sweet pocket pretty well on the brown spot. He put a red on the pink spot, a white on the black spot, and took the easiest of shots. The red rolled gently up and bumped against her fur. He chalked the end of his cue and walked towards her.

She looked scared. This was a cue which was not in the script, obviously. But instead he put the cue back in its rack, pulled her down full length on the table by her ankles, took his own private cue and screwed her long and rigorously on the table. As he approached his climax he knelt and pointed his big black banana at the camera and with a short sequence of abrupt movements from the hips he spattered the lens. The picture faded to black. The end.

Miss Kim meanwhile hadn't moved. She knew if she tried stimulating Salkeld while he was watching a film he would go off like a rocket, and he preferred to take his pleasures more slowly. He drained his brandy, stood, and walked towards the massage table. He stripped, handing his clothes one by one to the Korean girl who placed them carefully on hangers. Then he put a large white towel around his waist and walked to the bathroom. There was the sound of a shower, just for a minute or two, then he returned and lay, face down, on the padded table.

In the corner of the room was a small, polished wood cupboard with riotously coloured Oriental patterns on it – writhing dragons, finely dressed women, parasols, trees, mountains, birds. Inside was an array of bottles and jars, mostly with labels in Chinese and Korean, mostly – if literal translations could be made – with names like 'Heavenly Averter of Love Calamities' and 'Strength of the Tiger Inside the Hunger of the Fire'. Miss Kim had no idea what ingredients were in them but she knew how they worked.

She selected two bottles – a largish blue one, something resembling a quarter of Scotch in shape, flat and slightly curved like a hip flask; and a dark green one, much smaller, with a tiny cork in the top. She checked the labels.

The larger one was handwritten although the person using the brush had taken trouble to ornament it with coloured drawings of flowers and, for some reason, a frog. This preparation was called 'Peerless whimsicality engendered in the richly mellowed', whose effect was to relax the main muscles of the body, even quite a tense, knotty body, especially when massaged in by the small and skilful hands and knees of a naked Korean girl.

Miss Kim was indeed naked by now, having slipped off her single garment, a black silk wrap-over, as she came back to the table from the cupboard.

Salkeld liked fine things and the beautiful body of Miss Kim was exactly suited to his eye. She was shortish, slim, built entirely in fine lines and showing purity of design from every angle. Her breasts were small, her hips were not much bigger than a boy's, but she was the very epitome of woman as art.

She was also a very clever girl. She placed the little green bottle nearby on the mantelpiece in readiness, and shook an amount of transparent, oily liquor from the blue bottle into her palm. The air was suddenly laden with a smell so strong you could almost feel it. Incense was in there, and something strongly alcoholic, and something floral, and another elusive, reluctant aroma which reminded Salkeld of a kind of sweet there had been when he was a boy. You sucked this brown, flat lozenge when you had a sore throat, what was it called, began with V . . .

The effect of the atmosphere was almost literally knock-out. The ether in the ointment was soporific enough, and added to the rhythms of Miss Kim's breathing there seemed no reason for, nor possibility of, staying awake. Sleep for eternity presented itself as such a good idea, as she rubbed her hands briefly together and began to work the fluid into the man's back. Up to the shoulders she went, down to his buttocks, down to his heels and the soles of his feet, up to his neck, until his entire back surface was covered in a thin, glossy film.

She then got onto the table and 'walked' him up and down, on her knees. She knelt on his shoulders and pummelled his arse cheeks with her fists. She knelt on his waist and dug deep into his spine.

At a signal from Salkeld, which was no more than a half-raising of the little finger of his left hand, she dismounted and rolled him over onto his back. The towel fell aside, revealing a lengthy but floppy organ. This was obviously expected – not a function of lack of desire or ability but rather a side effect of inhaling the aromatics produced by energetic application of Chinese muscle relaxant.

Miss Kim rang a bell-push at the mantelpiece and took up the small green bottle. The translation of the label was particularly difficult, and the nearest she could get in English was something like 'One Strong Volunteer will Breach the Rampart while Six Conscripted Soldiers Spit on their Hands'.

Miss Kim removed the cork, which had a glass rod coming from it. With enormous care she placed one drop from the rod onto the end of her tongue, and replaced the cork with her tongue still out. She was thinking to herself whatever the Korean is for 'Hurry up for fuck's sake' because the taste of this highly concentrated liquid was bitter in the extreme.

The door opened and another girl came in. She came across and stood on one side of Salkeld's naked, prone

81

body and Miss Kim stood on the other. The two girls leant forward. The new arrival put out her tongue and touched the end of Miss Kim's, so that she collected half the drop. Now it tasted of almonds. With tongues touching they lowered their heads as far as they could, then, with hands behind backs, they gently licked the length of his tool, just once, so that all of it, top and sides, was touched but none of it more than once.

They then went back to its root and placed their tongues underneath the beast – which was now beginning to stir – so that the tips met again. Slowly they moved their tongues down the shaft. Now there was a taste of fruit, a kind of wild berry taste, sour-sweet with a complex background.

The knob began to lift. They kept in touch. By the time they simultaneously reached the end, it was standing proud.

The other, younger girl retired silently, with an envious look at the career she herself was training for, as Miss Kim straddled the Salkeld flagpole, facing his feet. With him well in she stretched out, her spare, slim body directly on top of his, her toes near his ears and her hands on his ankles. There she lay, apparently still, while he enjoyed the most interesting fuck to be had in any Pleasurehouse.

With no movement visible from the outside, she contracted and agitated her avenue of cherry blossom so that he felt he was, in effect, being fellated by a vagina. Her muscular control was utterly amazing, and as he felt his charge rising she somehow felt it too and increased the suction. He came in absolute purity of successful pleasure, with a gush of sensation impossible in ordinary sex. He came, and he came, and he came, with a little boy's cry of ecstatic delirium.

He only ever had these especially brilliant orgasms

with Miss Kim, and just one of them had been enough to make him unable to live without them.

Meanwhile, Rafferty was with Ghita. Neither of these eastern girls was a regular staff member at Pleasurehouse 13 which was, after all, for female customers. Miss Kim and Ghita were part of the small group kept there for visiting male dignitaries. It was a rotating team (except for Salkeld's Miss Kim!) and the girls would perhaps be on a training assignment or sabbatical from their usual post at a male pleasurehouse.

Ghita was on a refresher course. She'd spent the last two years teaching traditional dance to young girl Twos of Asian origin. There was quite a large Asian faction among the Ones, that race seemingly being a good source of the kind of intellect required to be a technologist, and so there was a considerable demand for the ancient formal entertainments as well as the more extempore sorts to be found in the pages of the Kama Sutra.

There was always a problem about what to do with the best Twos as they got older. The ordinary functionaries, the girls and boys who would never be anything more than sex workers, were simply destabilised when it became apparent that they were no longer considered up to scratch by their customers. For the women this usually meant a downwardly spiralling lifetime as a fuckbucket in a City brothel, and for the men something similar as an amusement arcade attendant. But the really excellent Twos, those who had trained and managed yet didn't quite have the nous to be a Twozec, inspired a sort of loyalty and gratitude in the establishment and so had to be found a better semi-retirement – which wasn't always easy.

Ghita was such, and she realised it. She supposed she could go on for ever teaching classical dance, but there were several others younger than her who wanted a chance at that. So she'd been sent as a temporary to the VIP team at Pleasurehouse 13 while minds were made up or while she discovered a new lease on life as a pleasure giver.

She'd known Rafferty for years – in fact, he'd given her her first promotion from the Rajah's Palace, a theme restaurant inside Pleasurehouse 10 where she'd been working as a waitress and upstairs girl. Rafferty had wandered up after a brilliant meal (he could still remember it) of Mutton Tikka, Chicken J'al Fraisi, Prawn Bhuna, Bombay Aloo, Bhindi Bahjia and Sag Gosht with Puri. He'd been looking for the lavatory but, having found it, couldn't resist a professional look down the corridor where he knew the girls would be.

A door was open, and inside a young girl was doing some bending and stretching exercises. She was naked except for her jewellery, masses of gold and precious stones, glittering and jangling as she moved, and a small gold coif to keep her hair in place. Joss sticks smoked in the corner of the shadowy room, and the lissom brown body twisted and twined to the quiet, almost animal-like sounds of sitar music.

She got herself into a near incredible position where one leg was up in a vertical splits with the other bent underneath her at the knee, and her arms seemed to be bent double in the wrong direction, and goodness knows where her head was. Rafferty coughed, and the girl unwound herself slowly and most gracefully. She stood before him, slim, medium height, neat. She put her hands together as in prayer, her elbows straight out to the side, and bowed her head to her fingertips. Then she looked him in the eye. Would he like a drink perhaps, or a sweetmeat? She had pillowbooks, would he like to see them? Or possibly . . .

Rafferty went for the possibly. He was quite an athlete himself. He'd started his Two career on the sports side, and became the youngest ever Junior Twozec when he got the chief coaching job to the Rugby football section after injuring himself badly in the England-Ireland game. Athlete he might be, but he'd never aspired to, nor seen anything like, the ease with which this girl could flex her body into impossible shapes.

On the exotic Persian-looking carpet with a fire flickering behind her, she put on a unique display presenting her brown quim to him from a fantastic variety of angles. Always, from his standing position, he could slip his madly vibrating cock into her without having to reach or stretch too far, but the constructions into which she put herself were mind-blowing. Legs, arms, torso, head, fingers, toes, neck, knees, every part of her did something outrageously demanding at some point as she folded and unfolded and folded again into living sculptures.

Each series of moves took about a minute. She would tactfully take hold of his weapon, withdraw herself from it, unfold into a simple lying or standing position, then go into a dramatic wheeling and whirling from which she would emerge entangled. She would then double-entangle so that Rafferty would never have known how to undo the knot if he'd had to, and the last move would be the sudden delivery of a wet, oriental spice-box into an area of space not far from Rafferty's eager sword.

As the quimlips opened during this last move, a wild wave of scent reached Rafferty, a deep animal scent, musky, violets, tigers, cinnamon, butter, old wine, all these things beckoned Rafferty, begged him to slide his Caucasian, northern, cold-weather cock into a mysterious, eastern, monsoon-weather hotspot.

On the fifth construction he had to come. She gripped him inside, pulled him further in, and how Rafferty pumped and spurted until his knees bent and he collapsed, taking the lovely girl with him.

Now he was lying on the floor, looking up at the kneeling beauty who was doing the same praying hands, elbows and forehead gesture as when he'd come in.

'I'm so sorry,' he said, 'falling like that. I might have hurt you.'

'This is not a problem,' said the girl. 'When learning my art, it was necessary to learn also how to fall well.'

'Could you teach others your art?' asked Salkeld.

'Oh yes, providing there are many of them, and they are no more than three years old. Out of such a group a person might emerge to take my place.'

Rafferty was disappointed but not deterred. 'But couldn't you teach some of the basics to other people? The principles of your flexibility, some of the simpler moves?'

'Perhaps. You are thinking then that more girls who provide for men could do it from more interesting positions?'

'No, I'm not thinking that at all,' said Rafferty.

And so it was that, eight or nine years later, Rafferty and his old friend Ghita could lie together in the white cotton sheets he preferred, laughing about the first time he introduced her at the rugby school.

'This is Ghita,' he'd said. 'She is beautiful, as you can see, and off limits to all players. She is going to teach you how to get more out of your bodies.'

'She's making my prick longer already,' shouted a voice from among the Scots lads.

'By the time she's finished with you, McIntyre,' responded Rafferty, 'your legs, arms and neck will all be longer. The only thing she can't help you increase the size of, is your brain.'

Thus was Ghita installed as special body coach to the Combined Squads, an organisation of about two hundred rugby-playing Twos who between them put on a full season of first-class matches for the telesat. The players to benefit most from Ghita's tuition were those who were in the backs, for she helped them with body swerves, feints and wriggling out of tackles. This in particular caused a sensation, for with Ghita's secrets learned it soon became impossible for any tackler to hold on to anyone he tackled.

Ghita had shown them how to move this limb that way and that limb this way then give a little jerk here and there – and they were free! There was a brief period when the only effective tackles were the heel-tap and the stiff arm, but then Rafferty brought in a few all-in wrestlers who showed the boys how to hold people so they couldn't move.

The crunch came when the leader of the wrestlers challenged Ghita. He would be allowed to put her in any hold he liked, and the bet was she couldn't get free. The winner would decide the other's forfeit, and the look on the wrestler's face told Ghita exactly what hers would be and how many wrestlers would be involved.

The challenge took place in the gym, on a raised platform. In came the wrestler, all silk cape and gold lamé, followed by a retinue of colleagues, to a huge cheer. In came Ghita, alone, dressed in a sari, to an even huger cheer. The wrestler strutted about, flexing his muscles, grimacing, grunting. He took off his cape and stood, menacing, a formidable mass of muscle and bone now dressed only in a black leotard and gold boots.

The silence was total as 200 rugby players and six wrestlers watched a slim young woman take off a sari and reveal herself completely. Her body shone with the oil she had dressed herself in, but this was all the dressing she had. She bowed with hands together to the wrestler, who blinked himself to recovery and gruffly offered his hand to shake. A small brown hand slipped itself inside a giant paw, and the man had the grace to feel sorry about the challenge which he could now see was in very bad taste.

But he would lose face with his colleagues and credibility with the players if he didn't follow through, and so on the nod he turned the girl round. He twined his legs around hers so that he was standing on her feet and her knees were pressed into the back of his calves. He reached under her arms and bent his arms so that his hands were on the back of her head. He bowed her into the full Nelson, compounded by the leg twist and the weight on her feet. He increased the pressure so that she would surely snap or submit.

Her left hand reached back and touched him on the neck. He stopped straining and relaxed a little. She wriggled her other arm free and reached behind her, inside his costume. Her hand was busy for a while, then those at the ringside could see that she'd got his cock stiff, and out, and was slipping it into herself, but couldn't quite tell which orifice. Keeping her touch on his neck, she made a few bobbing movements, a few bumps and grinds, and quite obviously the wrestler was locked into her like a dog in a bitch. She moved her touch to another part of his neck and pressed hard. His arms fell to his sides and his knees buckled.

With a sudden cry she let go his neck and went into a sideways wheel. She put her left hand on the floor beside her left foot. Her right arm came over, her left foot went before it, and now she was standing on her hands, her legs spreadeagled in the air. The wrestler had gone a pale shade of greeny grey as his cock was twisted and bent inside the girl. The noise was deafening now, as the players stood and clapped and shouted. Her hands walked a little way between the man's legs, and then she dropped onto her elbows.

The wrestler gave out a ghastly wail of pain as his prick, gripped tightly inside Ghita, seemed to be torn off at the root.

Ghita let go, took up her sari and walked from the arena. The wrestler stood, knees sagging, face turning from green-grey to a hideous dirty yellow-white, as he stared at the limp, distorted thing which used to be his pride and joy. Only those spectators on that side of the platform could see the same sight as he certainly wasn't going to turn and show everyone, but that didn't matter as the CLIT was on and they could all watch it in the bar that evening.

They couldn't congratulate Ghita though. She'd placed a call, Rafferty had sent someone to pick her up and she was then sleeping in Irish arms.

Which, back in the present, was what she was still doing. She and Rafferty had made gentle love, for old time's sake, and Rafferty was thinking. This Richmond woman was a dancer. Ghita was a dancer of sorts and a mover extraordinaire. Ghita could work with Richmond. The pair of them would make the most unusual espionage organisation in the history of the universe.

[5]

There was a two-day training course in City pleasure provision. The training officer could tell these young boys and girls about the difference between the aesthetic tastes of highly educated and motivated technologists, and the more earthy preferences of most of the decadent City dwellers, but really they had to experience it.

The idea was not for them to become expert in City entertainment, but rather to do their bit in the never-ending task of keeping the Cities satiated. A beneficial side effect was the broadening of the mind which naturally ensued from a City spell, helping them to cope successfully should they ever find themselves providing for the odd One who was less refined than average.

Brough and a girl student called Angela were detailed together, to go to City MK Unit 211, which was a combined strip joint and brothel. Brough was to run what was politely referred to as the theatrical side. Angela was a pro tem madame.

The journey to MK was not far, but they had to arrive at night since it was policy not to have the Threes witness any to-ing and fro-ing of the superior classes. It was likewise considered unsound to have predictably regular arrivals and departures, even at night, and so the pilotless All Terrain Vehicle programmed to drive to MK was also programmed for get aboard at 2200, knowing they might wait three or four hours before the ATV decided to go. Brough was never likely to waste an opportunity. Angela was a trainee he had not yet got around to meeting. The bunk loungers in the ATV were very comfortable.

He began by asking how she had become a trainee Two. Angela, a petite, wide eyed beauty with dark hair done in an elfin cut, a little turned-up nose and the most exciting rear end Brough had ever seen, told him about her background. She'd been the youngest of a brood of six, brought up by her mother in City HX. Fathers had been several and various and she hadn't been too bothered about that, nor about her mother who did nothing all day but drink gin and talk about the old days when she was an executive secretary for the managing director of a very large financial institution.

Come the Change and she'd been unable to prove any technological ability whatsoever, her main job always having been to accompany her boss on overseas trips and provide him with something to do of an evening. She was therefore dumped in the new walled City that went up around the place she'd lived in anyway, and her boss likewise. He hadn't been able to cope with the new life, especially since his hated and ugly wife had been made a One, so he fathered the first of the half-dozen kids then hanged himself.

Mother had lived from then on as if there were no tomorrow, a reaction common to many of the first generation of Threes. They felt doomed and, like the gladiators, ate, drank and were merry. Angela watched her older brothers and sisters do the same. The boys were drinking and drugging by the time they were nine years old, having been taught the facts of life by the two older girls. Mother and her two teenage daughters made a team of boozing, fornicating harpies, but there must have been some remnant of mother and sister instincts left because when little Angela arrived as the litter afterthought, she was brought up, as far as possible in that environment, to be protected from the degradation of the rest of her family.

Still she couldn't help observing it, and by the time she was old enough to draw conclusions, the first was that it was necessary to get out of the City. The only route was to become a Two, and the way to do that was to enlist as a pleasure provider for the Threes and hope that your superior looks, talents and enthusiasm would be sufficiently noticeable to get you out and off to training college. If you failed to make sufficient impression, you still got your perks as a pleasure provider, which was mainly two months' holiday a year at a monastery. You don't know the monasteries? Brilliant idea. On islands, like some of the Hebrides, there are cool, clean, airy places where you can be completely free of drink, sex, smoke, music, late nights, fat-bellied men, farting and filth. The opposite of the cities in fact. And the main privilege of being a Three-class pleasure provider was to have a holiday where you don't get any of the things you always thought you wanted. Fantastic!

But for the other ten months of the year you had a hard time ahead, screwing those drunken, smelly, foulmouthed, fat bellied men – mostly – or having to take part in the most advanced sado-masochistic exercises devised and demanded by those elderly Threes who, before the Change, had been ministers of the church, youth club leaders, theatre critics and other highly respectable types. It seemed that the more extremely virtuous you were before the Change, the more extreme your sins became when exposed to massive temptation after it.

Anyway, Angela told him, she had found herself a position in a Unit no doubt similar to where they were going now. These units had a strip-joint, a blue movie

93

theatre, several bars with hostesses, and suites of rooms upstairs. The girls were expected to take turns at all the jobs, but Angela never did a great deal of stripping since she didn't have the tits for it.

'They look nice enough to me,' said Brough, attempting to get his hand on the nearest but having it knocked firmly away.

'Nice they may be,' said Angela, 'but big and bouncy they are not. The audience in that place wanted big bazookas they could put their heads between. No matter what tricks I got up to on the stage, they never did any more than give me a little ripple of polite applause. If they were in a bad mood, they just booed and threw things. So I worked mostly as a hostess in the restaurant bar. This was the most up-market job in the place, because the customers actually preferred to eat a nice meal and have a couple of drinks before screwing you, rather than get their cocks hardened up in the theatres. Those bastards, the rough trade, they'd get so drunk and horny they'd just want you right there, wherever you happened to be, standing up against the wall. And they usually wanted it up your arsehole.

'So I worked in the nice part, making conversation with men who filled their time by writing, or painting, or making things, or gardening, rather than just swimming in beer. I would bring them something to eat, perhaps join them in that, and we'd have a few drinks together. Sometimes they didn't even want to screw.'

'I can't understand that,' said Brough, again making an attempt to stroke whatever parts of Angela he could reach.

'Look, fuck off, will you?' was her response. 'Anyway, I did that for about a year, then a Two at supervisor level paid us a visit. She was supposed to be checking up on standards, but really she was recruiting.

Anyway, she spotted me and took me straight to bed.'

'And you went?' asked Brough, more out of prurient interest than surprise.

'Of course I fucking went. This was what I wanted. This was my chance to get out of HX and into freedom, away from the lowest common denominator and up among the stars. And if some bull dyke wanted me to suck her clit for the privilege, then that's just what I would do.'

'And did she? Want you to suck her clit, I mean.'

'And the rest. You have no idea how much scope there is for novel activities between two women. At first all she wanted was to look at me. I would strip off and stand in front of her and do a few toe-touches, then I'd lie down and do some bicycle kicks, and that sort of stuff, while she sat on the bed and fingered herself. Then I'd have to kneel on the floor and give her a kind of medical examination, you know, a sort of passionless going-over, kneeling between her knees. Very weird. And then we'd get down to it.'

Angela was enjoying the effect her story was having on Brough. She quite fancied him really, but she had more important objectives to think about than a casual fuck with a handsome boy.

'Get down to it?' murmured Brough.

'I'd give her a good sniffing first, nose right up her pussy. She really liked that. Then I'd lick her, paying special attention to her little doorknob. Actually it wasn't so little. Sometimes if she was in the right mood I could lick it so upright that it stood out at me and I could get it between finger and thumb. If she wasn't in the right mood, I'd have to work that much harder to get her to come. This usually meant the warbler.'

'What's the warbler?' said Brough, trying to sit in such a way that she couldn't see his bulging member.

'It was a double dildo with a motor, and it made a cheerful, chirruping noise as it vibrated. She said she liked the idea of whistling while you work and so she'd had a synthesiser chip incorporated in it. You could program it to play anything. You just plugged it into the network, asked for Beethoven's Fifth, the network downloaded it into the dildo, and that's what you got coming from inside your cunt or wherever you'd put it. But she preferred this birdsong noise. Robin, I think it was.

'I had to turn it on and then jelly it up. She had jars of the stuff, various colours and scents, and each end of the machine had to have a different jelly on. So I would hold it in the middle, it would be vibrating and chir-ruping, she would be watching wide eyed, legs apart and fingers diddling, and I'd be dipping one end in the banana flavour and the other in the hot chocolate. Then I had to smooth it on, slowly, gently, just like I would with a man's cock if I intended suck it off afterwards.'

Angela stole a secret glance at Brough's bulge and noted with satisfaction that it was doing well. 'Then I had to put my end in first. I had to choose which end, and if I didn't get the same as she'd decided I should have, I had to take it out, have my bottom smacked, clean the machine and go through the whole business again. Sometimes, if she was feeling awkward, I'd get three or four smackings before we fucked.

'When I'd picked right, I would walk towards her like a man, with this whistling willy sticking out in front. I'd have to say "Open your legs, you fucking dirty bitch, and I'll shag your fucking arse off" – or words to that effect. She would moan and lie back on the bed and bring her knees up, and I'd get across her and there we were. The only problem was moving. If we both moved away at the same time we might lose the dildo, so she would mostly lie still while I made the running, but when she got near coming all hell might break loose.

'And by that time I'd also got the carrot up. You might laugh, it's true. She sometimes insisted on having a carrot up her arse at the same time. I had to get some fresh every day.'

'Every day? How long was this going on?'

'She was in HX for two weeks. As soon as she saw me she took me off regular duties, installed me in the apartment she was using, and that was that. Then when she left, I went with her. She left me on the training course and went off to her next City. And here I am. What about you?'

Brough told her about his career switch, and at the mention of Twozec Salkeld a change came over Angela. Brough wasn't subtle enough to notice when or why, but he certainly noticed the mellowing in her attitude as, at the end of the story, she pushed up close to him, asked him which part of the training he'd enjoyed most, and ran an index finger along his now slightly slackened bulge.

As he unzipped her outdoor blouson and put his hand under her shirt, he told her he'd enjoyed every minute of it the same, until now, when he thought the marks were getting better. She stood up beside him and with a few swift movements took everything off, then knelt on the seat. He could see her wonderful bottom reflected in the window as she extracted his rearing conrod and wrapped it in her mouth. Brough couldn't work out what she was doing at first, as the sensation was different to anything he'd felt before. Then he realised. What she was doing was the same as if she was tasting a wine, or using a mouthwash. She was doing that swilling motion, and it was out of this world.

97

Pleasure turned to pain as the ATV suddenly started and lurched forward and Angela gave him a reflex bite. After a few moments of apologies and nursing, Angela resumed by getting astride and gently easing herself up and down. Once again the ATV took a hand, as it ran off the road and headed across country. There were no longer any roads radiating from the Cities. The only roads there were connected the places where Ones and Twos lived. Supplies went everywhere from the distribution centres by robot transporters, which always went underground as they came to the Cities. The ATV therefore had some miles of rough country to cross to get to MK.

Just how rough was exactly apparent to Angela and Brough as they bumped along, she desperately hanging on to the seat and he hanging on to her. She was thrown off his cock a couple of times, and eventually he stood up, laid her on the seat and just gave her a straight-forward rogering in the simplest way possible.

'It's quite nice like that, isn't it,' she said, after getting her breath back from a great coming. 'I didn't think people did anything so basic these days. But tell me a bit more about Twozec Salkeld. I've seen him, of course, but I've never talked to him. I thought he might have given me a sampling, since I looked different from most of the girls in my class, but he only took every fifth girl in alphabetical order as per regulations, and I missed out.'

As they got dressed, Brough tried to describe Salkeld as best he could, which wasn't much, and he'd got on to the prick measuring with TwoAd Wilson when the ATV arrived at the City wall. It seemed to drive straight at it, and Brough and Angela were distinctly worried until suddenly a section of wall slid back and the ATV came to a halt inside. They were in a hangar, with

98

dozens of ATVs and people busying about. The PA announced that all Twostudents should proceed immediately to Exit F and thence to the third floor, and so Brough and Angela were soon in an elevator with ten other young people, all with good looks, charm, bright personalities and that life-joy which was the essential qualification for a young Two.

Six hoverbubble drivers waited for them. Brough and Angela slipped into the back of a vehicle, the driver pressed a few controls, the great picture window opened and the little car slid out through it into the night. They were on an elevated way for most of the journey – keeps us out of the way of the Threes, the driver told them. Threes weren't allowed transport of any kind except the autotrams which go everywhere and all the time. The hoverbubble stopped at a small platform. While the driver got their bags out of the boot, Angela and Brough looked out at the City, with its lights stretching as far as the eye could see – but where the wall was near enough to see, there was just a sheet of very bright white light and the occasional fizz and crackle of electricity. The driver saw them looking at that in some awe. All that crackling isn't really necessary, he explained. The forcefield would work perfectly well without it. It's just that the Threes might forget about their hopeless position if it wasn't there. Mind you, they sometimes turn the crackle off for a bit of fun, just to see how many Threes will walk into the bastard by mistake. They go off like Roman candles, they do.

Angela bit her lip. Brough said 'Really?', and they followed the driver down some steps. There was a door at the bottom. He put his hand over the identifier, said 'Twostudents here for Unit 211' and the door opened. They were in some kind of back corridor. It had that unmistakable air of being rarely used and then only on the quiet. The driver led them through various passages, with several identity checks on the way, until they came out into a suite of offices. He then disappeared back into the night and left the pair of them to examine their new home.

This was a large room with two workstations and a CLIT console above which were about twenty screens. They wandered over and had a look. Mostly they showed people looking straight back at them. From their reactions it was clear that they were audiences of some kind – these screens were for security, obviously. The others showed bars and people at tables and chairs, and a couple were blank. Angela pressed a button and said, 'Room 23'. Instantly a picture came up of a bed with a man and woman writhing on it. Angela said, 'Room 11', and a fresh picture came up. This showed, a rather haggard looking woman lying on her stomach, smoking a cigarette while a boy aged about twelve banged away at her from behind.

'And so on,' said Angela. 'That's my province. This is yours. Stage please.'

On a screen previously showing people's faces, a picture came up of a middle-aged, portly man, staggeringly trying to stand upright, with his trousers round his ankles. A semi-rigid cock was visible as he attempted with clumsy fingers to undo the piece of dressmaker's engineering which contained a vast pair of tits. The tits belonged to a very bored looking woman of about thirty-five, who nevertheless tried to smile and occasionally gave the man's cock a twiddle. Soon she got fed up, undid her bra herself, and the man fell on the released dirigibles with delight. Unfortunately for him, the combination of booze and being hobbled by his trousers meant he had to fall over, to a roar of appreciation from the audience, a member of which got up on the stage, kicked the man off, took his own cock out and wanked.

Angela said 'Stage off' and the picture reverted to faces. 'Just like the place in HX. Makes me feel quite at home.'

'So you've been in a Unit before?' said a voice behind them. 'Well, I suppose that will help a little. When I came I didn't even know such a place existed.'

The speaker was a blonde girl aged about nineteen, Scandinavian looking, tall, statuesque, everything about her was strong and well made. Brough thought she looked very, very attractive and just a little bit frightening.

'Fleming will be along in a minute. You'll be replacing him,' she nodded to Brough. 'We've got two days together for you to learn the ropes, and then we're off. I don't quite understand why we're being relieved by another pair of trainees. Usually they bring the regular management back, the people we took over from, but never mind. We can tell you all you need to know. It doesn't take long to understand everything about leisure provision for the fucking Threes. Ah, here's Fleming. Right. I'm Freda, you're called Angela, aren't you? And you're Brough. I've heard about you. They say you've got a premier-size cock. Is that correct, Angela?'

'What, that they say it, or he has?'

'I'll find out for myself anyway. Now, come with us and we'll show you your new kingdom.'

Angela examined Fleming and came to the conclusion he was an effete smoothie, the sort that some older women liked. She certainly didn't think much of him. She preferred Freda if anything, but they were both arrogant sods.

Everywhere in the place was viewable from a back

room or secret passage through spy-holes and two-way mirrors, as well as from the CLIT console. The thing you couldn't get from the CLIT was the smell of it all. It was not the combination of aromas a young Two was used to. Here there was sweat, and acrid unwashedness, and beer, and dirty ashtrays, and fried food, and more beer. There was also the smell of things put there to get rid of smells, and the strongly overlaid mixture of women's perfumes, vulgarly powerful.

A door at the end of the passage opened and two girls came through carrying a large, heavy black bag.

'Third today,' said the first girl as they went past.

'Third what?' asked Brough.

'Third bastard to die on the job,' replied Freda. 'They do it all the time. They're so overweight and full of a short lifetime's bad habits that heart attacks are as likely as not on the few occasions they're not too pissed to get their cocks up. I've introduced a bonus scheme – an extra day's holiday for every five dead a tart can produce. I think some of them are using methods which aren't strictly speaking in the spirit of the game, but who cares? The only good Three is a dead fucker.'

Neither Freda nor Brough noticed the black look that crossed Angela's face at that remark, but Fleming did, and Angela knew he had. Have to watch him, she thought.

As if to illustrate Freda's graphic observation, the next two-way mirror they looked through showed a fat, balding man who looked fifty but on closer inspection was obviously only about thirty. There were three girls working on him. The pale, hatchet-faced piece with the sagging tits was astride his pole and was going like the clappers. The middle-aged witch with the straggly hair was sticking her finger up his arse. And the very large lady with the folds of belly and tits like half-full flour sacks was sitting on his face.

At first she was hovering, allowing the man's tongue to explore her. Then, as hatchet face gave her a nod and grimly increased her pace, fatso lowered herself right onto the man's nose and mouth. Almost immediately he began kicking with his legs and waving his arms. The witch moved back and sat on his shins, hatchet face leaned forward and pinned his arms, and fatso squirmed herself more firmly onto his means of survival. In a couple of minutes it was all over. The women got up, put dressing gowns on, threw the man's clothes down the refuse chute and put him in a bag.

Brough frowned in thought. Angela turned away with a tear in her eye to find Fleming staring at her. Fuck it, she thought. I must be more careful.

'OK,' said Freda, 'that's enough for now. It's getting quite late and we have a busy day tomorrow. Brough, why don't you come up to my quarters for a nightcap?'

This was not a question expecting the answer no, and Brough didn't feel up to denying this girl anything. He was tired, it was late, he'd already had a bout with Angela, but he was quite sure that Freda would ensure complete satisfaction all round.

Angela went to bed. Before he did, Fleming got onto the communications network. Fleming was under cover for the Amenities Committee and had been sent to spy just like Rafferty had told a disbelieving Salkeld. After keying in a series of access codes which very, very few people knew, which gave him priority over almost everything else on the network and which scrambled his input to the extent that it would take all of Computer Centre NN five years to unravel it, he began his message.

'Re suspect Twostudent number 37. Seems over-sympathetic to Threes. Also unorthodox reactions to standard Two opinions. Suggest my stay here is extended.'

Fleming pressed the send key and waited. His reply was not long in coming. First it required him to enter even more codes to allow the screen to activate itself as a videoterminal. Whoever was sending wouldn't do it unless he could see Fleming there, alone. Then came the message.

'More evidence needed to confirm rebel status of suspect Twostudent 37. You will be informed tomorrow that your next post is not ready to receive you. Stay where you are until you have proof, in which case, eliminate rebel.'

Fleming went to bed, happy.

Meanwhile Brough and Freda entered a luxurious living room, went straight through that to the bedroom, and straight through that to the bathroom.

'We'll go in the shower first,' Freda informed him. She turned on the water inside the double-size cubicle, stripped the clothes off her miraculous body and got in. Brough was only a second behind her.

'Here,' she said. 'Me first.'

Brough opened the bottle she'd handed him. She turned her back, raised her arms above her head and put her hands flat on the tiles as if she was about to be searched. She was. Brough began rubbing the aromatic gel all over and under. She turned and put her arms out to either side, her legs apart. Brough continued until every inch of her was glistening. Then she did the same for him, pushing him into position and finishing with her hand cradling his cock.

'It is quite a biggy, isn't it?' she said. 'A bit more gel,

104

perhaps.' She rubbed it and stroked it. She bent it slightly the wrong way to test for hardness. She knelt, kissed it, ran her tongue down to the root, breathed warm air on it, flicked the glans with the end of her tongue, then swallowed it whole – at least, that was Brough's impression. He felt her sucking with her lips sealed tight round his cock, with the same power he used when trying to suck out something stuck between his teeth. He felt his cock getting longer and longer, and stiffer and stiffer. His cock was a metre long. Freda wanted him to fuck her from the inside. It was so hard now he could have broken bricks with it. It was still getting longer. Christ, it must be taller than I am.

All at once she released the mighty piece of plumbing from her vacuum-powered embrace. He looked down. It was harder and redder than usual and thankfully not a metre long. But it was trembling with a life of its own. Freda bent forward again and her tongue touched the shaft just where his foreskin was about to peel itself off for good. With the end of her tongue she tickled him at the very centre of all his sexual messages. Then she grasped her left breast and put it to the same spot. With the nipple she stroked that little place a dozen times, and he came. Some of it went on her majestic, muscular bosom, some shot over her shoulder and hit the shower door.

Freda got up, ignored him, and washed herself down.

'I've never been wanked off by a nipple before,' said Brough, admiringly.

'And you won't again, unless you do what I want. I'm setting the alarm for two hours' time. You sleep on the settee. I'll come and get you when I want you.'

She walked from the shower, wrapped a towel round her and left the room. By the time Brough was out and

105

dry, the bedroom light was off and he could hear the sound of deep, even breathing. He walked towards the light under the far door, found himself a sheepskin rug to wrap himself in, lay down on the couch and closed his eyes. Immediately – it seemed – he was being shaken awake. Here she was again, this Nordic goddess, this warrior queen from the sagas, naked, firm, long limbed, strong. She led him to the bed.

'I don't want anything fancy,' she said, as she licked his cock up to full speed. 'Just stick it in there, and pump steadily for fifteen minutes. I have never come in less than fifteen minutes. Don't stop, or vary the pace, or change the length of the stroke. Fully in, out as far as you can, once a second. That's it. Now, keep going, while I lie back and think of Norway.'

Actually, she was lying on her front, with her bum in the air. Brough was kneeling with his hands on her waist, wondering what *he* was going to think about. It wouldn't have to be anything too exciting or he'd fail to satisfy. But if he got bored he might suffer a collapse. He decided to count the strokes. He'd missed a few, but never mind. Sixty a minute, fifteen minutes, nine hundred strokes. He got as far as seventeen then remembered the episode with Ann when he'd pulled out and stuck it up her . . . steady on, old boy, or you'll be doing it again and coming far too soon. He had the impression that if he deliberately did something other than instructed he would be spending his Twotraining in Valhalla.

Was that time with Ann only a couple of weeks ago? His life had changed utterly in that time. He'd gone from being a technology student rattling his balls against the bum of a well-endowed redhead in a farmhouse, to an entertainments student rattling his balls against the bum of a well-built blonde in a brothel. Oh well, maybe things hadn't changed that much. He looked at the time read-out on the screen above the bed. 13 minutes to go. Maybe he should have put some delay-cream on. Never mind. Concentrate. All in, go on, right in, all out, well nearly, all in, right in, all out, well nearly, all in, right in, all out, well nearly. He was woken from his auto-doze by a strange sound. He kept pumping of course, but looked around for the source. Was there an electrical device shorting in the room? Was there water dripping onto a hot surface?

There it was again, a sort of hissing, spitting noise. Then he realised. It was Freda. She was making weird noises with her tongue and spittle. It was some form of self-expression peculiar to Scandinavians, perhaps. Did it signify approval, or the opposite? He soon found out because the spitting and hissing developed into throaty gurgles, and the hitherto immobile moon before him began to wax and wane most vigorously. Naturally he increased his speed. The noise stopped, the moon became still. He reverted to his one-second cycle, and like turning on the kettle again after it's boiled and cooled a little, there was a few moments' silence then gurgling started. The moon beamed up at him and once more moved in sympathy.

It required a great deal of control but somehow he managed to resist changing his rhythm as Freda got noisier and more violent. Soon she was screaming something totally incoherent in Norwegian, banging the pillows with her fists and whacking her arse against him with enough force to pop his testicles out of their bag if he was unlucky enough to get them caught.

With a final, heartfelt incantation to the gods of war and thunder, Freda collapsed in a heap, snorting and shuddering. Brough looked at the time read-out. Six minutes. He'd got the record. Got it? He'd smashed it. Except he hadn't come himself. His hand went to his handsome, high-performance prick. He smiled at it, congratulated it, gave it a flick of the wrist and watched the magnolia stream shoot out onto Freda's back.

In the morning, Fleming could not stop himself taking a careful look at Angela as he announced that he'd received a message to say he could not yet go on to his next posting and so would be staying here for a while as a supernumerary. If there was any way he could help, etc etc.

Angela saw the look, added it to the looks from the night before and made a spine-tingling conclusion. Fleming, whoever he was, was on to her. Well, nothing could happen here, today. They wouldn't arrest her or anything like that, because they could not admit there was any possibility of a reason for arresting anyone. So, tonight, perhaps, or tomorrow, Fleming would liquidate her. Even if they did that, she would still be safe for the day because she couldn't travel until night. She knew what she had to do.

By lunchtime Freda and Fleming had taken Angela and Brough through the administrative procedures and told them as much anecdotal evidence as they needed to get a feel for the place. In the afternoon they would talk about recruitment, and in the evening spend more time in the bars. Tomorrow Angela and Brough would take over, shadowed by Freda and Fleming, then the next day they would go solo.

They took their lunch separately, in their apartments. This gave Angela her chance. Taking a tiny radio transmitter from a hidden compartment in her luggage, she coded a message. Any rebels receiving it would know that their presence was required by a senior officer tonight at Unit 211. What they would then do would be to arrange a group to keep all entrances and exits under surveillance and sit out all night until something happened.

Angela finished her lunch and went back to the office. Brough would be looking forward to this session because it involved interviewing those who had been spotted as potential Twos while working in the Unit – young Angelas, in fact. Interviews were the norm. Angela had been sequestered by a senior Two and no questions asked, but that was definitely not usual.

Right then, Angela was hoping she would get through the afternoon without giving Fleming any reason to act sooner than tonight. In fact, she needn't have worried. There had been some trouble that morning with a couple of the girls hallucinating on drugs, which were banned for them, and Fleming had to sort it out so he didn't attend the meeting.

It was a rule of thumb that Twos had a second strength. With most of them, their first strength was sex and their second something in the entertainment line – which generally made their sex better anyway. Exceptional Twos might have so much sexual attraction and ability that they needn't have any other talent at all, and of course there were numerous Twos whose speciality – sport, or singing, or acting – was so highly developed that they needn't ever get involved in sex except perhaps later, in management.

But this afternoon, average Twos were expected – good looking, sexually flexible and eager, but with some extra ability to give them class above the ordinary tart or rent boy. The interviewees knew this and so would often arrange an event or opportunity to display themselves advantageously and – they hoped – to make them stand out a little in the crowd of would-be's.

Brough, Angela and Freda assembled in the strip theatre, closed for the afternoon. The interviews rarely resembled the across-the-desk kind of thing the word implied, but were interviewee-driven. In other words, the interviewers sat back and waited for a star to be born.

The curtains parted and a tall, well-built young man in strange clothes stepped through. 'My lords, ladies and gentlemen!' he exclaimed. 'The MK Pocket Music Hall is proud to present, at enormous expense, a positively theanthropic thaumaturgy of transvestite transubstantial Thespianisation – a costume drama. Yes, before your very eyes, here in this very temple of the arts, we shall take you back 150 years, to the time when the best mode of transport from A to B was driven by coal and water, and there was such a thing as a shortage.' With that he bowed and disappeared backwards through the curtain.

'What on earth was he talking about?' said Angela. Freda, who was a scholar as well as a beauty and a potential Twozec, told her that he had obviously done some research and was presenting something in a theatrical format popular in Britain in the last century but one. The long words were expected to get oohs and aahs from the audience.

So far, in just a minute or so, this young hopeful had made a big impression. Not only had he had the idea of doing his interview as a little play, he'd gone to the extensive but hardly used libraries and museums to make his costume and speech accurate – and of course he must have made the costume. As the curtains opened, they saw that a rather good set had also been made; it was small, but the entire thing was mounted on springs and was vibrating. Sounds accompanied the vibration – a wheezing, puffing sound and a regular metallic rhythm like diddly-dom, diddly-dom. The learned Freda told them that this was meant to repre-

110

sent the interior of a carriage on the steam railways, or at least the corridor and toilet of same, because that was all there was.

The man who had just made the introduction entered from the right, strolling along in frock coat and top hat, smoking a cigar. Occasionally he stopped to stare out into the audience and mimed wiping the window. A door in the back of the set opened and a small woman came out with her head down looking at something shiny which she then slipped into a small bag she had attached to her belt. Not looking, she bumped into the man.

'Hello to a fine gentleman,' she said. 'Wondering where to go and what to do?'

'Quite the contrary,' the man replied with a slight bow and raising of the hat. 'I know exactly what to do, and exactly where to go. I suggest the compact room provided at the end of each carriage for the purposes of bladder and bowel evacuation.'

'It'll cost you a guinea,' said the girl.

'But your last customer only paid you a pound. I saw you putting it in your dolly bag.'

'Very well then. A sov. You'd make a poor girl work hard, you would,' she responded. The pair of them went to the smaller part of the set, a cubicle with lavatory and wash bowl. She shook his hand as if to seal the bargain, then, turned round and bent over as far as space would allow.

'Go on then, in there,' she said. 'I ain't got no drawers on.' The man ignored her commands and instead lowered his trousers and undergarments to the floor. He produced a substantial prodder which he softly began to stroke. Within a few seconds it was up, and it was enormous. Freda and Angela looked at each other and then at Brough, who could only shrug his shoulders. He knew when he was beaten.

111

On stage, the impatient girl reached behind her with a 'Come on, hurry up'. Her searching hand found his tremendous cock and she gasped with surprise. She spun round, saying 'What's your game, mister?' only to change her suspicious tone to a whistle of awe and admiration.

'Behold the Maharajah of Bangalore!' cried the man.

'I bet and not half!' said the girl. 'It's real. I thought you was about to assault me with a peeler's truncheon. Some of them do, you know. They don't like your actual. They just want to do something nasty to you.'

By now she was fondling his artillery and gazing at it in frank and utter admiration. Her voice assumed a distant, almost dreamlike quality as she sank to a sitting position on the lavatory and examined, with a professional throughness, every millimetre, longitudinal and circumferential, of the peeler's truncheon and its appointments.

'I tell you what,' she said. 'I ain't seen nothing like this. You can have it free, and I'll put it down to experience. And I think it's going to be quite an interesting experience.'

She took off his coat, unbuttoned his shirt and took that off, then she stood on the lavatory lid and, not taking her eyes off the massive rod, stripped all her clothes, throwing them on to the small sink. She was a girl of good proportion, not in a refined, feminine way but like someone who is fit and physically active. She was reasonably well endowed – good, solid tits, firm and shapely – but her waist was very narrow and her thighs and calves were muscular. Freda consulted her notes. 'Athlete,' she said. 'Didn't know which to specialise in, fucking or jumping.'

With the much shorter girl standing on the low seat, her point of entry was about the right height for the tall

112

man's great poker, and the man indeed made a few clumsy attempts. 'Look here, old girl,' he said. 'My field piece has the approximate elevation but the range isn't quite right.' The girl raised an eyebrow and with complete assurance and no effort, she placed her left leg over the man's right shoulder.

The man placed his hands on either side of her, flat against the wall, and inserted about half of his length. It received a rapturous greeting. The girl then bent her right knee to get more in, and with a certain amount of wriggling and pushing, eventually the whole of the biggest cock even Freda had ever seen was in. Then the little actress went mad. She was hopping like a wild thing on her right foot, her left foot waving in the air, and the resonance of the bowl below the seat made every hop sound like a drumbeat.

From her breathing and little mewing sounds she was approaching the vital moment. With her body vibrating fantastically, she obviously felt that something was about to slip so she reached out with both hands for a secure object to hold on to. Her left hand found a chain with a porcelain knob on the end which hung from above the lavatory. Her right hand found another, shorter chain which hung horizontally in a space in the wall. As she came (or acted it, in which case very well) with a series of shouts which drowned the sound effects, she pulled both chains.

There was a mighty sound of water, like an elephant gargling, and the vibrating set went into juddering mode. Metal screeched. The erudite Freda whispered that the little horizontal chain was an emergency alarm which stopped the train. The porcelain knob operated . . . oh, they knew what that operated.

The actors struggled to stick together and they managed it. As the set came to a standstill and the water

113

stopped gushing, the man spoke. 'You, my dear, have completed your surge to ecstasy, but I have not. Will I be able to achieve this and have time to reassume my habiliments before the assuredly immediate arrival of the railway guard? He has a device in his van which tells him in which carriage the emergency alarm was generated, and so it will not take him long to check the compartments and conclude that the culprits are in the privy. Even so, I shall deal with him. I am, after all, the Mayor of Casterbridge.'

'Is you now?' said the girl. 'Well, I don't think any mayorship'll wash too many shirt collars with an official of the GWR, also known as God's Wonderful Railway. But he's on my payroll – commission, see – and if he causes any bother I'll see the right person gets to hear about it. So carry you on, my boy, and don't spare the horses.'

The man began the long strokes again. All was quiet except for the faint slurping and the girl's blissful murmurs in time with the in-stroke. Then, a voice offstage said 'Stand back, now please, ladies and gentlemen, well back now, thank you.' There were two footsteps and a sharp rap on the door. Anybody in there?' said the voice.

Without disengaging from coupling, the girl leaned sideways until she could get her head next to the door. 'Now you run along back to your van, George,' she said softly, 'and I'll pop up and see you later.'

'Ahem, thank you ladies and gentlemen, there's nothing here for you to see, now kindly return to your compartments while I continue my investigations in the next car. No need for concern, we'll be on our way shortly, thank you . . .'

As his voice died away the man's thrustings became more insistent and violent, and the girl began to vibrate

114

again. 'Oh no you don't, not again,' the man said as he pinioned her arms, lifted her off the closet seat, and came to fruition holding her in the air, her left foot still pointing skywards.

Finished, he placed her back on the seat. She withdrew her left leg to a more normal position and began dressing, picking her clothes up from the sink. He tidied himself up too, and felt in his pocket for something.

'No, I said, that's all right, dear,' said the girl. 'T'aint every day a girl gets to see a plonker as long as your arm. No, I'll dine out on this story for weeks. It'll be free meals in every pub and station buffet between Exeter and Paddington. No names of course. "An eminent kind of a gentlemen", that's what I'll refer to you as. An eminent kind of a gentleman. Very eminent.'

'Thank you kindly, Miss,' said the man, pressing a piece of paper into her cleavage. 'But I cannot renege on a contract. Now, if you'll excuse me, I have a few hands of canasta to finish in the bar.'

The curtain closed, the audience applauded, and there was absolutely no doubt that both of the applicants were successful. Compared to that, the rest of the afternoon was not and they were all glad when it was over. They went their separate ways to refresh themselves for the evening. Angela's way was directly to her bag where, beside the little radio, was a selection of weapons. These were extremely difficult to get hold of in the world of Twos and Ones. Nobody made weapons any more for open sale, but there were craft workshops in the Cities and nobody cared much what went on there. She selected a long, thin knife and slid silently out of her apartment and along the corridor to Fleming's. She knocked on the door. No response. She tried the handle. Open. Well, it would be. No Two ever locked his door. She stepped behind the door, closed it, and waited. It seemed like an hour but it was only ten minutes before the door opened. She checked for a fraction of a second to make certain it was Fleming, then from behind, slid her stiletto blade through his shirt and his skin and up under his ribs just a couple of centimetres.

'This knife is thirty centimetres long. Do precisely what I say,' she whispered, 'or it goes up the rest of the way straight into your right ventricle.' He just nodded. 'OK,' continued Angela, 'we'll walk slowly to the goods elevator and take it to the ground floor. We'll then use the goods entrance. Got me? Then let's go.'

It was cold, dark and wet outside. As Angela and Fleming appeared, they were alone. There was a moment which took its time passing. Angela had almost decided to give Fleming the remaining 28 centimetres and just dump him when a little group of men suddenly assembled out of the shadows. Angela glanced quickly at them. They looked right – young, not debauched but clearly a bit different. Some of the rebels came in for the excitement, some for the cause, and you couldn't always tell which was which. Angela spoke to a lad with long black hair, earrings, scruffy leather waistcoat and tattoos on his arms. She told him to take Fleming and see what could be found out, then slipped back inside.

Fleming's stomach was churning. When he was in charge of the situation he gave everyone the impression of being a soft, possibly bisexual charmer, and he had been chosen as a spy by the Amenities Committee because he appeared lightweight and therefore not to be taken too seriously. However, he cared very much about his own life and his high ambitions, and he was intelligent enough to realise that both now were in immediate danger of disappearing.

116

He decided not to say anything, but to watch for any opportunity of escape. Chances of that would be remote, apparently, because they put him in a sack, tied the top, then half dragged, half carried him for a short distance. He heard doors opening and closing, the sack was untied, and he emerged into what looked like a large kitchen. There was a girl sitting on the edge of a table, looking at him, and the men who had brought him obviously saw her as their leader.

'You know what this place is?' she said to Fleming. 'It's the kitchen of an old folks' home. Only there aren't any old folks any more. There were when you lot first put us in these cities. But not now. All play and no work, absolutely anything and everything you want, a life of complete indulgence. Doesn't make for old age, does it? So the home is redundant. Nobody comes here any more. Except us. Which makes it perfect for what we want to do tonight, doesn't it?'

'You cannot possibly get away with this,' said Fleming. 'They know where I am.'

'Oh yes. They might do. And if they don't they could find out. But the thing is, they can't admit that their ideal society has any cracks in it. Didn't they tell you? Whenever they lose a chap like you, they just close the book on him. He's never referred to again. No, your only hope is to tell us everything you know, then we can turn you to work for us. Become a double agent. Dangerous, because we won't help you either when you get in the shit. Can't ever quite trust you, you see. But better than being dead, wouldn't you say?'

'Go and fuck yourself,' spat Fleming, who was utterly revolted by the coarseness of these people. They were ugly. They dressed in a slovenly way. They even smelled, some of them.

'I don't think it will be necessary for me to fuck myself. You're going to do it.'

Hands grabbed him and ripped his clothes from him. He stood, naked, in front of all of them, degraded but defiant. Slowly the girl got up and walked towards him. Her hand went on his private parts. Her other hand rubbed her tee-shirt up and around her tits.

'I don't think he wants to play,' said the girl. 'Pity, because I like to fuck them before I finish them. It gives me a kick to think that I'm experiencing a man's last ever orgasm. But not you, then, sunshine. Probably a fucking woofter. In which case . . .'

The men took him, tied his hands together in front of him and led him to a long, wide, waist-high metal cabinet in the centre of the floor. They laid him face down on the aluminium worktop. They took ropes to his ankles and tied them to handles on the cabinet so his legs were spread wide, and fixed his hands the same way.

'This is what they call, in the catering trade, a hotplate. When we turn it on, you will begin to toast. But never fear. Because in case of fire, we're going to make sure you get wet. At least, part of you will be.'

A switch was clicked. Fleming then felt something being pushed up his arse. He tried to wriggle, raised his head, but got a crashing blow to his face. He blacked out for a few seconds, then came round to feel the metal beneath him getting warmer.

The girl waved a kettle in front of him. 'See this?' she said. 'It's a kettle. It makes water hotter. But you can heat anything in it. Thing is, when I think about it, if we pour boiling water up your arse, it'll cook your tubes as soon as it touches and then you'll all block up, and we won't be able to get any more in. So I think I'll heat up some cooking oil. Then you'll fry, but you'll still be

118

slippery. So I was lying about putting the fire out. It's going to be more of a case of being on the fire while we turn you into a frying pan.'

By now the hotplate was very warm and becoming uncomfortable. Fleming tried to raise himself off it, but whatever relief he got in one place was balanced by pain in another. In front of his eyes, the girl poured a bottle of cooking oil into the kettle. She walked away and he heard her plug it in.

He heard a male voice. 'I tell you what's always nice with a bit of fried meat. A drop of vinegar.'

'Good idea,' said the girl. 'But I tell you what. Vinegar's an acid, isn't it. Now you got that bottle of concentrated nitric acid from the electrical workshop, didn't you, for making a battery with? We could try that.'

There was the sound of a stopper being pulled out. Fleming felt the tube in his arse move slightly as they picked it up. He hung on by the thinnest coating to the last shreds of his loyalty and courage as he waited for the pain. It wasn't too bad when it came, just a stinging.

'You silly person,' said the girl. 'You've gone and given him the vinegar after all. So now we'll have to use the oil to fry him.'

The hot plate was burning him quite badly. He felt his skin beginning to stick to it. The girl showed him a jug full of oil with a touch of smoke coming from it. He felt the tube move again. That was it.

'All right, all right,' he sobbed. 'You win.'

They untied him, unstuck him and sat him in a chair. 'They suspect Angela,' he began. 'She's from HX. They think that's where the leaders of the unrest are. They don't know about you. They only think there may be some cells of rebellion in some of the cities but they

119

don't know which. Now, please, can I be taken somewhere to get my burns treated?'

'Oh yes, certainly sir,' said the girl. 'Take him!'

They put him back in the sack, and what followed was a nightmare. Every bump was agony and it went on for ever. When they let him out it was into open countryside, cold, raining, wind blowing. 'Big place, MK is,' said the tattooed man. 'Lots of parks and that. Plenty of places to hide bodies.'

Fleming felt the stab of terror and certainty that precedes capital punishment. But it wasn't to be yet, obviously, because they had all settled back with some bottles and cigarettes. 'She won't be long,' said Tattoo. 'She's just gone to report what you've said, and then she'll come to top you herself. Always likes to do it herself. She says after the revolution she's going to open a butcher's shop.'

Their attention wandered off him and on to an intense conversation about a gunpowderless gun which a small, dark, snaky-looking member of the group was trying to build. Explosives and their ingredients were difficult to get. You could make knives, even swords and axes if it came to that, but every revolutionary needs a weapon to kill at a distance. They were deep in discussion of the mechanical problems of air compression, and didn't notice Fleming gradually creeping away, every move a martyrdom.

When he was far enough he stood up. The cold wind and rain were having a numbing effect. His burns didn't hurt, not specifically, anyway. He was an entire hurt, a total weariness, but he had to get away. He stumbled through some woods, across a stream, through more woods, where every flicking branch and grasping bush was an enemy. Then he ran up against a wall.

This turned out to be a building of some sort, a

120

building which was partly brick and partly wood, with a big wooden door which opened. Inside it was black dark. Outside was therefore comparatively light and Fleming could make out a couple of small windows. By concentrating hard he could make out the way things were inside the building. There were some unidentifiable bits of old machinery in the corner, a few sacks of something, and a ladder going up to a large square hole. Climbing up the ladder he stuck his head over the edge of the floor above. Fleming could discern a near approximation to Paradise. Hay, lots of hay, and empty sacks.

He'd stumbled on a barn from the old farming days which no one had yet got round to doing anything with. Or maybe they'd just left it as a curiosity. He completed his ladder climb, out through the square hole, on to the floor and over to the sacks. He arranged a few sacks around himself like a shawl. After some extremely difficult knot untying, with trembling fingers and chattering teeth, he could burrow in between the hay bales and begin to get warm. He'd stopped shivering, and his burns had begun to hurt like hell again, when there was a thud outside and a simultaneous curse.

Fleming recognised the voice. It was the tattooed Three. It was indeed, and he'd tripped over something. He took a couple of large swigs from a hip flask and made a formal, thorough sweep of the outside of the barn by torchlight.

The steady probing movements of the torchlight through the windows seemed threatening to Fleming from his cowering position in the hay. Back and forth the torch went with a mechanical rhythm, covering every centimetre in neat order. They're taunting me again. They know I'm here. They know what I'm doing. They always know.

He crawled out of the hay in silence. Crouching – needlessly, because the angle from ground level outside through the windows only got Tattoo to see the roof trusses – Fleming scurried as fast as he could across the bare, dusty, hay-straggled floorboards. His body was warm so he moved well, but he felt every one of his burns, plus the scratches, bruises and bashings received from the forest god's army.

He also felt, as he ran, the agony of stubbing the toes of a foot against the slightly raised rim of the great square hole in the floor, the pit of darker darkness which marked his way to freedom. For a fraction of time he concentrated more on not letting his pain escape his lips than on his forward movement, or his balance, or where the steps were.

Fleming tipped. He thrust his arms out to catch hold of something, anything, but they only met the dark. He fell, like a bad diver doing a very, very careless belly-flop into the pool, head up, arms and legs all over the place.

His hands and arms went first into the hole. They passed just beneath the floor level, under the rim-frame of the great square. His head, his forehead that is smacked against the rim with all the momentum generated by a running, falling, diving, full-size man. The head of the six-inch nail, four and a half inches of which were sticking out of the frame ready to hang a coiled rope on, perhaps, or a shepherd's crook, or whatever it was a Bedfordshire farmer used to hang on a nail – the head of the nail caused no impedance whatever to the general speed and thrust of projection through bone.

The metal went straight into the brain and for a moment Fleming was bridged between the front edge of the hole and the stairs. His head was pressed against the flat vertical surface of the wood. Slightly above and behind, his feet, the tops of his feet, rested on the floor, the edge of the hole. His arms dangled down and slightly to the front. Then, his head staying where it was as the pivot, Fleming's feet dragged down the stairs, the skin being stripped from the knuckles of his toes as the rest of him swung forward, unconscious from the impact of braincase against stout wood.

The nail, hammered in well and angled to take weight, was like a coat hook and Fleming was like a coat. Speared through the front centre of the head, he swung with his feet clear of the stairs, arms by his sides.

Tattoo had heard the clodding thump, the muffled crack of bone against wood. He didn't hear the nail going in because that was a very small noise. As he came through the door torch first, seeing Fleming swinging there, not a care in the world, he at first assumed that the man had hanged himself.

Looking closer he saw no rope, just a seemingly magic ability to hang by friction which reminded him of a man he'd once seen in the pub who could keep a dessert spoon on the end of his nose. Tattoo also saw a pulse still working in the neck, and then two or three drops of blood squeezing past the forehead skin where, he deduced, there was a nail and where, he deduced, the swinging of the body had worn the puncture slightly larger.

Tattoo didn't know how long Fleming would live up there. Even less did he know what would happen if he tried to get him down. He decided to take a short walk to think things over. A mistake now could prejudice the entire revolution. He, like all the rebels, had no illusions about keeping nobly silent should they be ever tracked down and captured. There was no way of keeping anything back from the Amenities Committee.

Fleming never really came to. There were a few seconds of semi-awareness immediately before he became officially dead, when a confused sequence of pictures played across a dark screen inside his head. There was a fat woman, naked, sitting on his face while Angela conducted an imaginary orchestra. There was a row of black bags, all of which suddenly opened as hideous tattooed figures leaped out and surrounded him. There was Angela again, smiling, laughing, as a witch with long black hair stuck pins in him. Now she was sticking one right in the middle of his forehead . . .

Fleming's body was still when Tattoo came back. He went halfway up the stairs, wiped off the last drip and fundament from the legs with a handful of hay, then put his arms round the thighs in a bear hug. He lifted. Nothing. He pulled backwards. Nothing. Shit. He went up onto the floor above and, with heel of his hand as he knelt on the floor, pushed Fleming's head back off the nail. The body fell all the way down the stairs to the floor below. Shit. Now I'll have to carry it all the way back up again. Which he did, then arranged the bales of hay around it. He put some more bales down below, so that when the wooden floor collapsed the conflagration would continue and, with any luck, the walls would fall in too and complete the cremation.

There was a tin of motor spirit in the corner downstairs. He splashed that around, threw down a lighted match, and fled.

And nobody ever knew where Fleming went.

[6]

'This is Twozec Rafferty.' Salkeld introduced his old colleague and mutual survival expert to Ann Richmond in the splendidly antique dining room of Pleasurehouse 13. Rafferty's recommendation yesterday, that Ann should be brought in without delay, had been easy to implement. She'd already primed her husband – and he wouldn't get too worked up on his objections anyway – and the ATV had arrived to pick her up just as she finished packing. Rafferty had also put to Salkeld the idea of bringing Ghita in, and that was fine too.

Ann flashed her very best smile at Rafferty, shook his hand and smoothed her thin sweater over her waist. The effect of delineating Ann's fabulous bosom in perfect detail was noticed – as was the calculation which led to it.

'And this, Ann, is Ghita. She is an authority on movement and on ancient Asian dance.'

The two women hit it off well from the start. Ann was older, ampler, more imaginative and more extrovert; Ghita was a more experienced professional, perhaps shrewder and wiser. So between them there was potentially an excellent combination.

'We'll have some lunch now, and I have to tell you Ann that since we last spoke there have been developments which mean that working only as a choreographer, with the theatre company, will leave you too isolated to get right inside what's going on here. What I'm going to suggest is this.'

Anthony arrived with the first course at that moment, so conversation ceased for security and gastronomy's sake. Anthony announced the food as 'Thousand Sided Soup'. On a platter were numerous little piles of delicately sliced vegetables – spring onion, cucumber, bamboo shoot, plus sweetcorn, the thinnest potato chips imaginable – very well done, as were the thread-like onion rings – and chicken. There was a small bowl of something bright, shimmering red, and a large chafing dish, on a burner, of clear liquid with shreds of greenery in it.

'It's not actually got a thousand sides, of course,' explained Anthony, 'but then size isn't everything, is it Mr Salkeld?'

'Did you see that little note on the screen the other day, Rafferty, about a shortage of pinball machine polishers?' asked Salkeld.

'Yes. Something to do with high levels of wastage. No sooner do they get the hang of it than some of the customers bugger them up.'

'Yes, well dears, that sounds very nasty, so different from our own home life, don't you think? Now, what you do is this.' And the nice boy Anthony showed them how to put a bit of this and a bit of that from the platter into the bottom of a Chinese bowl, add some of the fiery sauce if they wished, then ladle the boiling soup liquor over it.

They bent to their bowls for a while, but Ann couldn't wait for the rest of what Salkeld had started to say. So it was come on, Salkeld, spill the beans.

'The beans are as follows, my dearest Onewife Richmond. Must stop calling you that. You are either Ann, or TwoCon Richmond, or should we change your name entirely?'

'Toucan? What do you mean toucan?' asked Ann.

126

'Consultant. Two Consultant. It's just a token title, but it gives you a roving commission. How about if we call you Lucan? Then you can be Token TwoCon Lucan.'

'You're the only Con around here, Salkeld. Get to the point, will you?'

'Quite right, Missus,' interrupted Anthony as he swept in with the next course. He placed the dishes on the Sheraton sideboard and cleared away the soup. 'Mr Salkeld is a proper caution. He's forever pulling my . . . leg. Aren't you, Mr Salkeld?'

'I don't know why I should, Anthony, I'm sure. From what I hear, you pull it quite enough yourself.'

'Thank you madame, sir, madame, sir,' Anthony sniffed in mock offence as he put out the clean bowls. 'Now what we have here – ' he placed half a dozen rectangular porcelain dishes on a small hotplate and a large bowl of rice next to it – 'is Kok Plong Dong Fong Dik. Or something like that, it's Korean anyway, which Mr Kim tells me translates as "Fishes and Birds Lie Together at the Magician's House". So there you are, then.'

After tasting the various fish, poultry and vegetable blends provided by Mr Kim they agreed that this was indeed the Magician's House. Salkeld then got back to the point.

'Where was I? Ah yes. The position as adjusted. You see, Ann, we need you to get involved in the mainstream of the goings on here. So we've installed Ghita, with the manager Spencer's full agreement, as another TwoCon with a brief to try and introduce novel and more athletic body movements into the daily services provided here. The notion is that with the knowledge that Ghita has of movement ancient and modern, some of the young Twos here could begin offering a more interesting service to their clients.

127

'So where do I come in?' asked Ann.

'You can help her. You've been in the same sort of line, theatrical dancing. And she could help you with the choreography for the show, so you'd have more time for, er, getting involved with what happens here.'

'OK. Sounds fine. Phew, that was delicious. Couldn't eat another thing. So now what happens?'

'I'll show you round later – the others know it well enough already. But what nobody knows much about is the new kit we've just had installed here, the Dreambox.'

'You've got a Dreambox here, have you?' asked Rafferty. 'How come? That must be the first in the country. I couldn't get the damn thing, and all my Twos who've heard of it are clamouring for it.'

'This is the first Dreambox to be released. I made a special case for 13 as being the only Pleasurehouse where there appeared to be some dissatisfaction at the moment. Maybe the Dreambox will help to put it right, I said, not believing a word of it.'

'Will somebody tell me what a Dreambox is, please?' said Ann.

'And why the Twos should want such a thing?' asked Ghita.

'Ghita,' answered Salkeld, 'you should appreciate this. You know how tiresome it can get, dressing up for Ones who need fantasy around their indulgences. They want you to act the part of Florence Nightingale, or they want to re-enact a scene from *A Midsummer's Night's Dream* but in a real forest with a real donkey. Well, all you have to do now is programme the Dreambox and everybody in it can do whatever takes their fancy and it seems like a real forest with a real donkey. Or whatever. It's like a sort of four-dimensional CLIT system of the imagination – the

128

fourth dimension being that you are right there in it and being it.'

'Can you have dual illusions? I mean, can I be seeing you as a Viking, raping and pillaging, while you see me as your nanny, spanking your botty?' inquired Ann, trying to appear interested only from the professional point of view.

'Yes and no. They've only just got this machine working. It could cope with supplying you with images of a Viking while I had images of a nanny, but not the different actions simultaneously. So you would believe you were a Saxon village woman being raped and then spanking a Viking's bottom, and I would be a small boy in school clothes raping and pillaging a nurse who would then turn round and beat me. But they're working on it. Meanwhile, I suggest we agree on an outline scenario, get inside the thing and give it a whirl.'

Ghita suggested mud wrestling. Ann thought that was too basic. How about the Amazons versus Hercules? The others wanted to know who won before they'd agree to that, and Ann couldn't remember except she thought the Queen of the Amazons gave Hercules something he wanted. This was thought to be not community minded enough for a group of them, so eventually they settled on a scene belowstairs in a grand house in eighteenth-century England. This would test the Dreambox's capabilities with costume, setting, realism such as the smells – cooking on the kitchen fire and so on – and it would also have to prompt the plot along, because none of them had the slightest idea about what went on in an eighteenth-century kitchen.

Salkeld, ever the pro, wanted someone to stay outside the Dreambox to see the actuality, so they could compare it with their own, machine-induced experi-

ences. Ann was deputed for this, since the rest of them –
who included a couple of the girl Twos from the Pleasurehouse to make up the numbers – were in the business, as it were, but Ann was, strictly speaking an
outsider. Rafferty volunteered to keep her company,
because of professional interest, they understood, but
also because he was anxious to get to know Ann a little
better.

The Dreambox entrance looked like any other door,
but heavier. There was a small lobby, like an airlock,
inside that, and then they were in a square room, white,
featureless, with the floor and the ceiling looking identical with the walls. There was an opalescent glow from
every surface, which began to change as soon as the
door closed behind them.

Outside, Ann and Rafferty were looking into a small
window which gave them a fish-eye view of the whole
room. What she saw was a group of people at first
standing about, then sitting in mid-air on non-existent
chairs, then they took their clothes off and got closely
involved in what her husband used to call rumpty-
tumpty.

Inside the Dreambox it was altogether more
remarkable. Within a few moments of the door closing
and the opalescence beginning to pulsate, Salkeld,
Ghita and the other girls were sitting in front of a great
fire against which a spit was turning. On the spit was a
hare. They could smell the honey and herbs as it
cooked, and the fire spat and made a noise, and the
smoke gave the atmosphere a comforting feel.

'I followed that receipt in that there book the mis-
tress give me' said the auburn-haired girl. 'That book
of Mrs Glasse, *The Art of Cookery Made Plain and Easy.*
I don't know about easy, I'm sure. It ain't no easier to
cook dinner for them upstairs since I read that book

130

than what it was afore. 'Cept now I know I got to skin a hare afore I cook it, bless my soul.'

'What are you prattling on about, Esther? Can't a man have a drop of ale and a pipe in peace without your drivelling?'

'That's not drivel, Mr Montgomery. That's what she says in her book. Take your hare when it is cased. As if I would put it to the fire with its coat on.'

'As if you would, Esther,' chimed in the other girl. 'I never did know anyone could cook a hare like you. I'm sure that little beauty there does make me hungrier and hungrier.'

'God's teeth and nails!' exclaimed Mr Montgomery (né Salkeld). 'Esther! Rebecca! Stop your twining or I shall have to give both of you a sharp lesson.'

'Oh, Mr Montgomery,' said Esther. 'Would that be a lesson like you gave us yesterday, and the day before that? I seem to have been through several of such lessons, but I can't be learning much because we have to keep doing it again.'

'Is it school time right now, Mr Montgomery?' whispered Rebecca, as she took the pipe and the glass of beer and placed them on by the hearth.

'Can I join in this time, please?' said the dark-skinned girl who sat in the corner and hadn't spoken until now.

'Why not?' said Mr Montgomery. 'I suppose it must be possible to educate the oriental into our own homely ways, eh girls? Now just you clear that table of all that clutter, and give me somewhere to lie down.'

And so he did. He just lay there, fully clothed, on the table. 'What do we do next, Mr Montgomery?' asked Esther. She was instructed to take off all her clothes, and then his boots. Esther revealed was a magnificent sight, with long auburn hair cascading down over a jutting bosom. Her waist nipped in sharply, then out came arounded pair of hips which looked like comfort personified. While she struggled with the boots, her plentiful flesh vibrating with effort, Rebecca was told to remove her clothing likewise and attend to his jacket and shirt. Rebecca was out of the same mould as Esther, full, curvy, buxom, but with blonde hair.

Ghita, referred to in the Dreambox only as 'You, the dark girl' had to deal with trousers and undergarments, but she was not allowed to touch anything she might find in there until instructed how to do so by her betters.

Mr Montgomery was now lying naked, his pole stuck up and bent towards the north. Esther took it in her hand and massaged it gently. 'Is this right, sir?' she asked.

'That's just right, Esther,' he replied. 'Now you have a go.'

Esther said to Ghita. 'Just gently. There. Don't it feel warm, and sort of soft and hard at the same time? Oh I do like that, look, how nice the black hand looks holding the white, er, the white, er, Mr Montgomery.'

'Now, girl, you hold it steady for me,' said Rebecca. She put her hands on the table and leant forwards and sniffed the reddening end. 'Why, Mr Montgomery,' she said, 'that smells good enough to eat. No, keep hold, girl, I'll tell you when to let go. Now just hold it up straight, that's it.'

Rebecca's mouth opened a little, and she kissed the very tip of Mr Montgomery. He squirmed with pleasure as she opened her lips a little more and slid the great hot rod a bit further into her mouth. 'You, the dark girl,' commanded Esther. 'You see those hairy balls. Now you get your head down and take those in your mouth, all of them. And be careful of your teeth!'

132

As the previous incarnation of Ghita did as she was bid, Rebecca straightened up and climbed on the table. She swung her leg over and was soon trotting, then cantering. 'Tally ho!' shouted Mr Montgomery. 'Well now sir,' smiled Rebecca. 'If you're after a fox, I can tell you where there is a one, but he's gone to earth surely.'

Esther joined in the action. She was kneeling face to face with Rebecca, her knees by the man's ears, her hands on either side of his waist, her neat little quim brushing his tongue while her nipples lightly scratched and swept up and down his stomach.

'You, the dark girl' was standing on the floor with her head to one side between his thighs. While Rebecca raised her canter to a gallop, Ghita sucked in on his balls while somehow contriving to put a finger up his arse and another, as he could clearly feel from his privileged position within, up Rebecca's.

Esther raised her haunches, taking her honeypot away from Mr Montgomery's flickering tongue as she leaned over in an attempt to get her tongue to the base of his cock. Not only did she manage that, she also got a slippery centimetre of it in her friend's fanny alongside the mighty Montgomery marmaduke.

For some while now, with faces together at the fish-eye window, Rafferty had had his hand down the back of Ann's waistband. He had gradually insinuated his hand through the warm tightness of her crux and got a finger to her most influential spot. At first she gave him no help. Then she loosened up a little, then she began, unable to help herself, pushing back and forth on his fingers. She reached to remove his hand, turned, put her arm around his neck, looked into his eyes, and put her other hand on a rigid development near his thigh. 'Can we get in the Dreambox, now it's

133

started?' she asked. 'Or do you want to wait that long?'

'Nothing wrong with both, I'd have said,' replied Rafferty, undoing a row of buttons down the front of Ann's blouse, finding a front catch on her bra, undoing that, then finishing off the blouse buttons. 'They are just too beautiful,' he sighed, weighing Ann's truly wonderful tits in his hands, then kissing each.

'You're not so bad yourself,' said Ann as she succeeded in extracting his cock into the open air and ran her hands up and down it. She stood on his feet to try to get herself on a level. Rafferty bent his knees. She fell backwards, her skirt riding up as she hit the floor, her magnificent breasts spilling and bouncing. She opened her legs as wide as she could, and Rafferty dropped on her. Deeply he thrust, as hard as he could, no pause for gentle introductions. In 30 seconds Ann was coming, her body bounding and rebounding as Rafferty gave her everything he had. In 33 seconds Rafferty was coming too, and they both yelped and rattled in a single climax.

After a minute or two, Rafferty got up and helped Ann to her feet. Just as they were, clothes in disarray, he offered her his arm. 'This way to the eighteenth century, madame.'

As they walked through the second door they saw Salkeld apparently levitated on his back, with Ghita eating at his crutch while the blonde Two sat astride and the auburn Two, her hands under his bum, was trying to put her tongue where his prick was. As they stepped forward into the opalescence the rest of the scene appeared, the kitchen, the fire, the table, the heaps of discarded clothes.

The scene was still basically the same, but not only did it look different, in a new context; Ann found herself thinking about it in different language. She saw

134

the back of a servant girl's head giving the suck to her butler's testicles and wagging her tail like a lamb going for its first feed of the day. She saw the back of the second kitchen maid going like a winter's morning with the Quorn over the Leicestershire countryside. All she could see of the other maid was the very top of her upside down posterior as she grovelled her way towards the point of conjunction.

'Why, Montgomery!' Ann heard herself saying. 'What is the meaning of this?' At her voice, the other three women leaped aside and assembled in as near to apologetic and submissive propriety as they could get with nothing on. Montgomery stood to attention and bowed his head. 'Good afternoon, my lady.'

'Montgomery! Get to the harness room. And you girls too.' This was Rafferty speaking, cast by the Dreambox in the role of master. And so they seemed to walk, up some stairs, along a corridor. They reached a room with saddles and all kinds of horse-connected articles in it, including several whips. A powerful aroma of leather and polish hit them, with a thread of sweat and animal exertion running through it. Here men worked and lords and ladies called on their way to recreation. Here men had rubbed and sewn and shaped and cut. You could sense it in the air.

There was a saddle with a sheepskin cover on it, and it was strapped on to a wooden contraption as it would be in proper use. My lady ripped off her clothes, mounted the saddle and began to urge the 'horse' forward with her body. My lord handed her a longish whip and told Montgomery to get on all fours in front. My lady could just reach him, and was soon giving him a few stinging little switches as she cursed him for a profligate and a corrupter of innocent maids.

The maids by now were partly dressed. Rebecca had

135

on a pair of boots, and Ghita a pink jacket. They writhed together on the floor, their hands and tongues exploring every part of each other. My lord on a stool, encouraging my lady, swigging at a leather-bound silver flask he'd found, and occasionally thrusting forward to meet Esther's eager mouth as her head bobbed backwards and forwards on his cock. He put the flask down to his side as he felt the seed rise within him. He clasped his hands behind Esther's head and held her hard in as he clenched and unclenched his coming muscles. She swallowed frantically and moaned.

The butler had by now had quite enough of my lady's chastisement. He jumped up, grabbed the whip from her, flicked her arse with it so she scrambled off the saddle, flicked her again to chase her across the room, then pinioned her against the wall. She lifted a leg and curled it over his hip, stood on tiptoe of the other foot and put her hands on his shoulders. He grasped a mighty tit in each hand and whammed his unbending bough right in at the wet and welcoming joypit. He thrust roughly, a servant giving my lady what she wanted, something a little less refined than she was used to. Her fingers dug into his shoulders as she began to thrust back, her mouth was open, her shuddering grunts and groans gave a kind of raw musical accompaniment to the pig-fucking, ball-wrestling, arse-banging war dance which soon reached a loud and violent climax. They collapsed, still standing.

Rebecca and her mate were also fulfilled and were snoozing on each other. My lord was lying back in his chair, his plonker limp on his thigh, swigging from the flask. Esther sat on the floor beside him, her head on his knee, her eyes closed. The scene was played out. What did they do now, wondered my lord Rafferty. His answer came in the form of a scent, a rich, sweet aroma

136

with an acrid streak to it. Abstract sounds came from somewhere. The lighting changed and the scene began to dissolve into pink and red, then purple, then black . . .

The Dreambox had sensors which told it when an episode was over. It emitted a light drug into the room, played soporific music, and then sent for its operators.

These were middle-ranking Ones, technologists, as the Dreambox was still in its development phase. When it was perfected and had completed its field trials, it would be operated by Twos. But now the summons went out and in walked some of the men who had been working on the Dreambox for a couple of years. They noted with satisfaction the replete attitudes of the six naked bodies. They, of course, had a screen which showed the scene as being played, rather than the fish-eye window which showed it without the Dreambox's contribution.

They felt reasonably satisfied, but knew that the capabilities of their wonder machine had not been tested anywhere near its limits. 'What we need,' one said as he lifted the superb, recumbent body of Ann Richmond onto a stretcher trolley, absent-mindedly giving her left tit a squeeze, 'is for someone to try to change themselves, not just change the surroundings. Then we'd see if the D-RAMs can cope.'

'I'd be more bothered about the power transistors,' said another, carefully untwining Rebecca and Ghita. 'Surely we've put enough D-RAM in. I mean,' as he put a hand behind Rebecca's neck, another under her pussy and lifted, 'sixty-four chips, each the equivalent of 128 megabytes of random access, with 32 communications processors to run them, shit, this black girl's a beauty, look at those muscles, I mean, if anyone is going to get that lot to capacity there'll sure as buggery be some traffic through the power circuits.'

He ran his hand thoughtfully up and down Ghita's stomach. 'May I remind you gentlemen that we have just four minutes to clear our participants?' said a sharp voice. It was the One in charge of Dreambox development, a stocky, peasant-legged woman who could be described by her very best friends as plain. She was carefully arranging Salkeld's cock to lie nicely alongside his inner thigh and was ready to go. They pushed the trolleys out and into a side room, collected the dayclothes which still littered the Dreambox, and left the players to recover.

Which they soon did. The girl Twos who had been recruited for the experiment had duties to attend to, so Rafferty, Salkeld, Ann and Ghita went to the management's private lounge for a drink. Salkeld felt the Dreambox was quite good but no better than a good stage production would be. Ann thought a good stage production would be better. Rafferty pointed out that actors hit with whips and dug into by fingernails would have reminders on their skin. They had none. He also thought they hadn't pushed the machine enough. 'Suppose, for instance,' he said, 'we tried to give it more to do than just dressing the set, giving us costumes and writing our lines. Suppose we asked it to make changes to our physiques, or our personalities.'

'I'll volunteer to be ten years younger,' said Ann.

'OK. And I'll volunteer to – well, I think I'll keep it to myself, and then we'll know I can't have suggested it to you' replied Rafferty. But first, let's have a little something to eat. All that exercise, you know. I wonder if roast hare is on the menu.'

A couple of hours later, they'd agreed a setting. Ann had recently read Waugh's *Brideshead Revisited* and

138

fancied a transatlantic journey on a great ocean liner. The time would be the early 1900s, when women wore long dresses and the men doffed their hats and had whiskers.

The couple walked into the Dreambox and found themselves approaching a dining table in a large room with chandeliers. It didn't matter that they'd just had an excellent meal of chicken satay and Singapore rice sticks, courtesy of the magic Mr Kim. They sat down to dinner with relish. They also completely accepted that they were sitting with other people! This caused some astonishment afterwards when they retold the tale, until they realised that the Dreambox had memorised the people from the previous adventure in the kitchen, modified them and replayed them. The mature woman sitting on Rafferty's left was, they worked out, an older version of Ann. The girl on his right was the younger version, an eighteen-year-old – Ann had increased the age reduction without telling Rafferty, and the machine had got it just right.

The ladies introduced themselves as the Cavendishes, Miss and Mrs, on their way to New York for a holiday with relatives. Rafferty was Grogan, an Irish newspaper owner who wanted to start up a few titles in the land of the free.

He flirted with Madame outrageously during the soup. She responded as he knew she would, and at one point, between the fish and the entrée, he had to knock over a glass of wine in order to cause a diversion. Had he not done so she would have had his pogo stick in her hand and the entire plot would have been blown. Also to take into consideration was the avid notice which was being taken of every move by the lovely Miss Florence Cavendish, whose long dark eyelashes were perfect disguise for the sidelong glance.

She saw what her mother was up to, and she must have realised that he upset the wine on purpose. What she did not yet realise was the reason for her mother's fascination with the contents of Grogan's trousers to the exclusion of everything else including normal discretion. She just couldn't believe what she was feeling. She ran her fingertips along the cloth-covered pikestaff and her brain refused to credit what her nerve-ends were telling it.

But Grogan needed to ascertain if the girl, Miss Florence, was perceptive of his intentions for the rest of the evening. He wanted the filly, not the mare, and wanted proof that she was going to ride willingly – otherwise the mare would have to do.

He was weighing in his mind the relative virtues of the direct and oblique approaches in the case of Miss Florence when, between the pudding and the savoury, she said to her Mama that she would not be going on to the dance afterwards as she felt a little uneasy at the slightly increased motions of the ship. Nevertheless, Mama should have no reservations about going to the dance herself, as Florence would be quite all right with bed and a glass of hot milk.

Mama obviously thought her daughter would indeed be quite all right, because at that news she again put her hand beneath the tablecloth and measured the length of the protruberance in Grogan's trousers with several spans of fingers and thumb. He watched with some concern the proprietary smile on her face as she imagined what would surely be the night of her life. His concern was shared, for as she rose from the table Miss Florence, she of the bright eye beneath lowered lashes, whispered a few words in Grogan's ear.

Grogan, experienced seducer though he was, had to be more than a little surprised by the words of a gentlewoman of no more than eighteen years old: 'All her lovers say I'm a much better fuck than she is.'

His coughing fit caused Madame Cavendish to stop speculating upon the powers of his pronger, and he managed to continue it sufficiently long to make important a visit to the deck outside. Refusing all her offers of assistance in the most polite way possible when fully committed to a coughing fit, he left Mama disappointed at the table and retreated outside.

The Dreambox provided a moonlit night at sea, with a freshening wind which was beginning to verge on the strong. Grogan stepped swiftly to the private apartments of a certain Cavendish, Florence, Miss.

His light tap on the door swung it open – she had left it ajar. Inside all was quiet, then he heard the first few notes of a popular song. 'Come into the garden, Maude, For the black bat night hath flown. Come into the garden, Maude, I stand at the gate alone.'

Maude is not a name to which Grogan normally answered, but since the singer was Miss Florence, the garden was her bedroom and the gate was her bedroom door, at which she was standing now dressed in nothing but a silk shift, he could not have cared if he was addressed as Mary from the dairy.

He marched across the room, about to catch her in his arms, bear her to the bed with many kisses, and so on and so forth. She simply put out a finger, placed it on his chest and stopped him dead. She undid the buttons on his waistcoat, likewise the buttons of his trouser suspenders, and swept the dependent items to his ankles. She repeated her expertise on the buttons of the John L Sullivans which were also made to descend, and she took up his shirt tails and tucked them around his waist.

There he was, naked all below, with his Member of

141

Parliament standing up to make debate completely unnecessary. It was at this point that the young Florence realised what had so diverted her mother – or, had she not been subject to the illusions of the Dreambox, what changes Rafferty had decided the machine should make to him.

His cock was absolutely massive. It was, Florence guessed, ten or eleven inches long and with girth in proportion. She sank to her knees before it, her eyes wide, her mouth slightly open. For an eighteen year old girl, Florence was thoroughly experienced (as the real Ann had been). She had seen, touched and incorporated a wide range of male organs, but she had never been given a clue that such a terrific thing as this existed.

The ship gave a lurch, the first proper warning of bad weather to be given, which movement took Grogan hard against the kneeling girl and they fell to the floor together.

He was on his back. Florence removed her shift to reveal quite the finest piece of the good Lord's work Grogan thought had seen for many a year. She had a fine long neck and a proud bosom which was quite large; certainly each partner would require the cupping of both hands to encompass, yet they kept their shape as she moved. And move she did.

She swung a leg over his body and waddled on her knees until her sweet little mons veneris was over his lips, then she lowered herself gently. His tongue sought her vital part and found it without difficulty. She sighed as she swayed slightly back and forth, agitating the quite erect little miniature dandy across the end of his tongue.

He took it between his lips, but she was hot now and like lightning she wriggled down his body and placed

142

herself full on the end of a dandy to which the epithet 'miniature' could never be applied.

Wet from her excitement she had no trouble locating the end in the right place. From there, however, she was in doubt. Should she, or should she not, impale herself on the Land's End lighthouse? She desperately wanted to plunge the entire thing into herself, but she wondered what the cost might be. At one moment, Florence would decide 'yes'. She would lean forward, her hands on the carpet on either side of Grogan, a faraway look in her eyes as she thrust her torso downwards. With another inch or two inside her, she would hesitate again. Now the 'noes' had it.

He watched her quandary with some little amusement – it was not the first time that Grogan (supplied with a fully equipped memory by the Dreambox) had met this problem. Indeed, many women, having heard the reputation, had refused point blank when they saw that nothing was exaggerated.

He allowed the delightful Miss Florence to continue thus, hovering in blissful purgatory, and meanwhile he untied and unbuttoned and unstudded whatever remained of the many and various fastenings required to accoutre the top half of a gentlemen in evening dress in 1902.

Then, with a suddenness which opened wide those grey-green, lustrous eyes and brought them hastening back from faraway land, he sat up. He shrugged off what he could of his clothing. He hooked his arms around her back, his hands on her shoulders from behind, and gave a mighty pull downwards to her body as he gave an equally mighty thrust up with his hips.

The motions combined to push home the tackle. She gave a curious wail of wonderment and fainted on his neck. This caused a slight difficulty with removing the collar and tie, but he achieved total nakedness in this position. There is no future in shagging a dead sheep, as an Irish farmer friend of his had once said, and so now he had somehow to awaken the damsel. There was water in the ewer, but that was on the far side of the room.

Once more the ship did him a kindness as she gave a combined roll and yaw. The motion took the locked bodies over onto their sides and gave him the idea he needed. Over and over he rolled, with Florence fully glued the while, until he got to the wash stand. The ship went again and rolled them back a yard. He rolled, the ship rolled, and he began to feel careless of Florence's lack of active participation. One more roll and the sensations in his loins were such that he would not be able to stop himself.

On top of her now, he gave her – as he remembered the English Bard has it – the stuck-in with such a mortal motion that it was inevitable. What with the see-sawing of the ship his thrusts did not need to number many and he came with a gush and a gasp, and the realisation that it was the first time he had reached a climax with an insensible partner who nevertheless would not stay still.

He withdrew, picked up the girl, lay her on the bed and mopped her brow with a little water. Her eyes opened, saw him, closed again, opened again to make sure that this was reality (which sort!) and then, to make doubly sure, her hand reached out for his pendulous column.

'Oh,' she sighed. 'I've missed it'.

'Not at all, my dear,' he assured her, since the gentle fondlings of her fingers were quickly bringing back the earnest rectitude so necessary to the successful burglar. (The Dreambox could make cocks seemingly inex-

144

haustible as well as infinitely extensible). He also calculated that the lubricious evidence of their immediately previous engagement would make entering possible without breaking, and so the lovely Florence would this time be able to stay awake.

So it proved. She laid back on the pillow, pulled her heels up to her bottom, and opened her knees to the widest. Grogan was tempted to dive into her pussy with his tongue again, but this was not what she wanted. She wanted Long Tom and she pulled him towards the eternal entrance. In he went, up went her heels to clasp behind his back, locked were her arms around his neck.

Once more the ship heaved. This enforced push seemed to give Florence confidence, for she began pumping like a little good 'un. Grogan soon caught her rhythm, and together they did the *amour ordinaire* with the equipment extraordinaire. That distant look returned to her eyes and he began to worry that she might faint again. He could just reach the damp cloth with which he'd bathed her head, and slipping that under her and applying it to the small of her back, at the same time biting the fine edge of her ear, he brought her to full sense as his pumping took over from hers, faster and faster until he gave forth to the accompaniment of Florence's squeaks and cries which were, fortunately for decorum's sake, inaudible beyond the bedroom as they were overcome by the creaks and groans of a ship now properly in a storm.

'How are your sea legs, my sweet?' he enquired shortly afterwards of the young lady who was gazing up at him in thanks and admiration. 'I am never seasick,' she replied. 'I take after my mother in that too.'

He sat on the edge of the bed and took a long draught of the wine which stood on the small table beside. While his head was in the air he felt a movement beside him and then the gentle brush of hair against his thighs. Florence sat with her legs under the bed. This brought her pretty head to just the right height, for she could bend slightly and take the now somewhat limp Sir William between her lips. At first she just kissed the end, occasionally sweeping the tip of her tongue across the slit which a few moments before had been making the letter 'O'.

As her ministrations began to take effect she opened wide her mouth and took in the diameter if not the length. Had she not started thus, with the member at its smallest, she would probably never have attempted the exercise, but as it grew she found it more possible to cope than she would had she started with it fully up. At any rate, she kept a good three or four inches in, and gave what suction she could to that portion.

There was still room for both her hands on the shaft, and so with a series of combined movements, sometimes syncopated, sometimes synchronised, she was able to raise Grogan to his full majesty and soon to bring about the expectations of a third coming.

He took another draught of wine. Florence looked up as if to enquire if she might have some too. He smiled and patted her on the head, silently recommending her to continue with the job in hand. Her head began to bob faster as she sensed the gathering finale. Wine was now out of the question as Grogan too had all his attention turned to the crux of his body, that temple where now were worshipping fingers and thumbs clasped in prayer and a mouth about to take communion.

Grogan, not unnaturally for someone of his proportions, was an expert on fellatio. He had found that some females like to swallow at these moments, as quickly as they can to prevent the great surge forcing an escape of a single drop. Other ladies – and he generally believed that the more aristocratic and superficially frosty they were, the more likely this was to be – prefer to pull back and spray their face and neck with the stuff, for all the world like a young under-gardener on a hot day turning the hose on himself.

It may be, Grogan conjectured, that a lady may believe in the nutritional value of semen, while another believes it to be a cosmetic to prevent the onset of wrinkles. Or it may be that the dirty little hussies just like to swallow it or luxuriate in it. This hussy, this beauty of the dark bobbing head, was clearly a swallower. Her determination was exemplary. He lunged forward, trying to get every tenth of an inch he could between her lips. The ship swung and wallowed as she fought her way through the tail end of the storm. Miss Florence hung on for dear life, her arms around his thighs, her head tossing like a small buoy as she sucked and swallowed while the tide flowed. With the last droplet brought out and taken down, she wiped her mouth with the back of her hand, looked up at him, smiled, and said, 'Pass me the wine, will you?'

[7]

For Brough and Angela, the secondment in City MK
was over. Brough had been, and Angela had seemed to
be, disturbed by the lack of official concern over the
disappearance of the young Two, Fleming. There was
little in the way of a command structure for the Twos
when they were in the City – there being no need – and
so there was only the screen to ask. It remained unper-
turbed, eventually putting out the line that Fleming
had been called away suddenly and had left in a hurry in
an ATV without having time to say goodbye.

Brough and Angela struck up a good working
relationship, but there was no repeat of the incident on
their night of departure from training college. Brough
in particular had plenty to do anyway, since almost
every stripper, tart and hostess in the place was anxious
to make a good impression. Several did, and they had
been recommended as Two applicants.

The best and most vividly recollected incident had
been when he went upstairs to his rooms after a long day
and found a pair of identical twins in his bed. He had
half a mind to chuck them out, but they were very
pretty blondes, about seventeen years old, very buxom,
and they did look charming sitting there in their little
nighties. As she got out of the bed to make room for him
in the middle, Twin A bent over to pull back the duvet.
Under her frilly babydoll nightdress, which came just
low enough to cover the vital spot, she had nothing on.
Her rounded moon looked very inviting, and Brough

wasted no time in stripping to his underpants and hopping in.

The twins snuggled up beside him. 'Hello,' said Twin A, putting her delicate hand gently on Brough's bulging pants. 'I'm Sarah, and this is my sister Suzie. We're twins, you know. We do everything together. Everything.'

'I had rather gathered that,' replied Brough, his voice shaking ever so slightly as the cooler hand of sister Suzie slid inside his pants and grasped his cock while sister Sarah fondled his balls from the outside. 'We were hoping you might be able to recommend us for Two training,' said Sarah, pulling his pants down. She dived under the duvet to push them right off, and then returned, her bright smile and blonde curls looking up at Brough from under the sheet.

'We think we'd make very good Twos,' said Suzie, pointing his prick towards Sarah's nearby mouth and massaging the shaft while Sarah kissed the nut. 'We're so obliging, and anything we lack in experience we can make up through imagination and effort.' Sarah now had as much as she could get of Brough's cock in her mouth and was slurping it slowly. 'The other thing,' said Sarah, taking the meat out of her mouth, wiping her lips with the back of her hand and swallowing the saliva she'd generated, 'is the looks of us both. We thought that being twins and looking the same, and quite pretty really, would be an added interest. Don't you think?' She went back to her sucking.

'And, from the back anyway, you can't tell which is which,' added Suzie, swinging a leg over Brough. Sarah lay with her head on the bed and, looking carefully up, guided the prick into her sister's quim. Once Suzie was settled she reached for the hem of her nightie and pulled it over her head. She leaned forward and massaged

Brough's shoulders as she slowly ground his cock around. 'What about from the front?' asked Brough. 'Is there any difference there?'

'Judge for yourself' said Sarah, pulling her nightie over her head and taking her own left tit in her hand and, reaching round her sister's back, Suzie's right tit. She weighed them, pulled the nipples forward, and squeezed them. Then she took Brough's hands and put them in the same places. 'Close your eyes and spot the difference,' said Suzie, writhing her arse in circles. He closed his eyes and couldn't tell which was which after both sisters had mounted and dismounted three or four times. He didn't know if it was the same sister getting on and off, or if they were taking it in turns. Their hot, wet, tight little pockets felt exactly the same. Wonderful.

'OK,' sighed Suzie in a mock seductive voice. 'You've got to say which of us you think it is next, and then open your eyes.' There was a withdrawal and an insertion. Brough said 'Sarah!' It was Suzie. 'Now we're going to give you another examination.' said Suzie in the same low, breathy voice. 'Close your eyes.' Brough felt the girl get off, and there was a shifting of bodies, and then he felt warm breath. In quick succession his prick was licked and sucked by different mouths, at least, he assumed they were different, although for all he knew it could have been the same mouth every time. 'Any better?' they asked, in unison.

'Still can't tell,' said Brough. 'Is there no way of guessing which of you is which?' 'Close your eyes, then, and we'll try again.' Now he felt his cock having to try a little harder to win its way inside . . . what? A little arsehole, that's what. 'Right,' a voice said. 'Now this is Sarah . . .' and he felt the girl lift off him. 'And this . . . ummmmph . . . is Suzie.' So it was

151

Suzie who was speaking, and Suzie's delicious bum he was currently piercing. She lifted away, and another came down on him. 'Now then, big boy, who's this?' The closest glove-fitting in the universe gave several swift stimulations to his red-hot knob which by now was very nearly bursting.

'I don't know,' said Brough breathlessly. 'But who-ever it is, is going to get a hot enema any minute.' 'Oh,' said a voice. 'But we agreed. You said I could have the first come and you'd have the second.' 'OK, but be quick then.' A girl – might have been Sarah, could have been Suzie – unglued herself and another – might have been Suzie, could have been Sarah – speared herself onto his pole. Now she galloped. Her arse bounced up and down as fast as she could make it and within six or seven bounces Brough was coming so hard he must have sprayed right through her system and up into her throat.

Brough had not been able to keep his eyes closed during this. Suzie had – for it was she who was riding him, her head back, her blonde curly hair flying as she walloped his cock up her bum just as often as humanly possible in the shortest space of time. Her nice-handful-sized tits danced madly with her violent movements, and her sister, the equally lovely Sarah, watched avidly, her hand straying to her own private cubicle with fitted carpet surround.

As the dervish slowed and eventually stopped whirling, Brough turned his face to the watcher. 'That is Sarah, isn't it, sitting unconscious on my cock?'

'No, that's Suzie.'

'Ah. So that means that it's Sarah, viz, your very own good self, who is to receive my second offering.'

'Correct' said the girl. 'Are you ready?' she continued. 'Because I am.'

Wow. That seemed a long time ago. It wasn't, of course, it was just a week or so, but they were back in training now, City MK was in the past, and graduation day was upon them. They looked forward to that, not just because it symbolised the beginning of their careers, but because it promised to be the most monumental piss up. Having been tutored and practised in every form of sexual activity during their courses, the grad-night celebrations didn't begin as a sex orgy. They didn't want that. They wanted to relax and be as juvenile as possible before the onset of serious responsibilities.

By watching CLIT recordings of previous grad nights, the Twostudents realised that there was a traditional game to be played by everyone. They asked the tutors about it, and got the details. But where, oh where, to get the main item of equipment, a contraceptive condom? Such things were unknown among Ones and Twos except as special stimulators. Venereal disease had long ago been totally eradicated from all classes, and pregnancy in Ones and Twos was only possible if permission was given and facilities provided to reprogram the electronic spermatazoa neutraliser that all females had implanted.

A tutor let it slip that such things were available from the small stores kept at Pleasurehouses to provision the very occasional trip abroad which senior Ones sometimes made. This information was deliberately planted, it being part of the course to see who would emerge as the leader and members of the inevitable gang to be set up to rob the store. Nobody was surprised when Angela came up with the stratagem and Brough developed it into action. It was impossible to break into the store itself. Electronic security made the place impregnable, and inside it was all locked, robust compartments accessed only by robot. No, they had to get a One to request some condoms for a trip, and then rob him, or her.

All the other students were entertainers; only Brough had a technical background. He was deputed by Angela to hack into the communications system, imitate the authorities and put a false commission for an overseas trip into somebody's private pigeon hole (as the electronic message-dumps were still called).

Brough knew that this was not possible for him without a powerful front-end processor to work on the access code combinations, but said nothing. Instead he went on his night off to the nearest Pleasurehouse, number 8, which was installed in and around the old Warwick castle buildings. It was a house for females, and he wanted to know which was the most insatiable One in the area. She being identified by popular vote among the male Twos who worked at number 8, Brough now needed to know her technical speciality. This was easily found out on low-level access to personnel records: food processing systems. Brough now had to take several chances, the most important being on the greediness of this One for new experiences.

Instead of attempting the hack, Brough put a message on the ordinary, open communications system addressed to the One. Would she please make the necessary preparations for a week's trip to Jamaica, where the Agriculture Department of the United States of PanAmerica had developed a new process for preserving fresh fruit. The ATV would pick her up tomorrow, apologies for short notice.

Apart from a few industrial installations around the islands' agriculture, the whole of the West Indies had been turned into a sunset home. There were many ladies of a certain age there, widows of the PanAmerican economic system which still forced its menfolk to work themselves to an early standstill. To serve the ladies with their spiritual requirements there were, it was rumoured, large numbers of highly proficient gigolos, young men who had dropped out of mainstream PanAm or dropped into Jamaica from parts of the world such as tribal Africa where the men were poor but big.

The food-processing specialist had heard these rumours and requisitioned a good supply of condoms, a couple of the anti-viral, anti-bacterial capsules which were always placed into orifices just in case, and a bottle of the gargle containing the same compound.

Brough had now to hope that she wouldn't check out her instructions with anyone, or check back with the communications system. He had deleted the message as soon as he sent it, so that once she'd called it up on her screen at home it would vanish. If anyone ever bothered to chase it back they could find out where and when it was sent and by whom, from the indelible trace code attached automatically to every transaction on the system, but it would take some doing. No, the main risk was whether the One would get suspicious and not take possession of her condoms.

Brough made sure he just happened to be passing by the gate of her Regency town house in the fully restored town of Leamington Spa, just as she was coming home from work. He smiled appreciatively at her tiny, elfin-like figure and she crooked a finger. Brough was in. She said she always took a swim at the end of the day. Brough said that was fine by him. She said she always swam in the nude. Brough said that also was fine by him.

At the back of the house was a long, narrow space where a garden used to be. Now there was a glass-roofed swimming pool, with palm trees growing in pots and a table with umbrella and chairs. She pushed some buttons on the service communicator and the robot brought them champagne. She poured, toasted, stripped, and dived. Brough followed. They swam for a while, then she came up to him, put her hand on his balls and looked straight into his eyes.

'Listen, boy,' she said. 'You know you shouldn't be in here. You're a Two, aren't you? Should be in a Pleasurehouse, doing your official job, shouldn't you, not moonlighting in a One's private swimming pool? Never mind. I won't tell. Providing you lick my cunt until I'm quivering, then fuck me until I faint. OK?'

She gave his balls a squeeze and swam to the side. She sat on the edge of the pool and spread his knees wide. Brough swam over, stood in the metre-deep water, and lingually examined the inside pocket so liberally exposed. He noted that there was no correlation between size of body and size of quim. Here was a wisp of a woman, a woman who could be broken in half, you would have thought, by the average man. When standing she hardly reached Brough's breastbone. She couldn't weigh 40 kilos. Her figure was like a young girl's, beginning to develop – everything there, but in its first stages of growth. The barest swellings for tits, the hint of fullness in the hips, only a few hairs on the prominent mound – but there was nothing young girlish about the space allocated for poking. Brough began to have doubts about himself as he tried to cover all the ground with his tongue. He had a large prick, no doubt about it. Everybody said so. But it would flap around inside this woman like the last frankfurter in the can.

She grabbed hold of his hair and began to make grunting noises. Between her teeth the words became hardly decipherable, but he could make out a few words like 'You cunt' and 'Bastard fucking bastard' in among the gutterals and glottals. She was bashing her minuscule hips against his face as he strove to keep his tongue moving fast enough for her. She had a powerful, animal smell coming through now that the freshness of the pool had gone, an insistent, primeval smell of mating. As she gripped his hair tighter and shook his head and smashed his face again and again into her crutch, he felt her spill. Groaning and gurgling she knocked his nose against her pelvic bone the last few times, then slid into the water beside him.

'Anyone would think you'd had lessons,' she said. 'Now, let's have a glass of that champagne, and then I want you to stick your fucking brilliant megacock right up my cunt so far that it meets the champagne coming down. OK?'

Brough just had time to take a sip and a half before she was on her knees in front of him. His loosely expanded organ soon hardened up in the back of her throat, and she gestured to a sun-lounger. He lay on his back, and she hovered over his straining post. As she grasped it and was about to put it in, she felt it slacken. She looked at him.

'Sorry,' he said. 'I've never had any lack of confidence before. If you don't mind me saying, it's . . .'

'. . . the size of my hole you're worried about. Well don't be. It's adjustable. I can wrap it around any cock in the universe, even a little boy's, and I have, I can tell you. So you'll be no problem.' She slithered down, sucked him up to full standing height again, and swiftly jammed him in. She was right. Brough felt as if he was inside a totally different tunnel from the one he had previously explored. He checked with his hand to make sure – no, it wasn't her arse. She did have an adjustable quim.

157

By this time she was bouncing like a maniac. Brough pushed up to meet her. He put his hands under his hips and lifted. She went even faster. There was that animal scent again, he thought. How could he recognise what it was when he'd never smelled it before? But he did know. It was the smell that called prehistoric man across the cave floor to ask which of his mating brood was so obviously without a headache. It was a smell which had evolved out of most of the species homo sapiens, as unnecessary as the third eyelid and the appendix, but which had somehow sneaked through the genes to this tiny woman, who was now going berserk on the end of his cock. She jiggled so fast it was a drum roll, than she fell, exhausted and satisfied, on top of him.

In a minute she came to, felt his rod hard in her, lifted off, swivelled round, and slipped it carefully into her bum hole. Her actions were quite different this time. She took long steady ups and downs, taking his prick very nearly out, then sliding it in smoothly as far as it would go. It didn't take many of these to make the warm stream gush up into her, whereupon she dismounted, announced her intention of going for a shit and told him to dress and leave. This was his chance. He was alone for a short time, enough to rifle her case and take the condoms. By the time she came back, he'd gone.

Back at Twocollege he proudly displayed his trophies. When graduation was celebrated next week, the traditional game could take place. The other necessities were easy to obtain – extra hot chilli con carne, cream-filled chocolate eggs, and black stout beer from Ireland.

Came the day and the party was going flat out. Every Two who had passed, and the three or four who had failed and would be destabilised, was as drunk as a

158

skunk. Angela stood on a chair. There was a chorus of Strip! Strip!, and when she'd obliged she called for silence.

'Right. You all nozeroolz. Litre of stout, down in one. Nob'diz allowed to spill, not even a teeny weeny drop. Teeny weeniestest. Then diving forward roll over my bum, which will be stickinin . . . the air. Thasswot it'll be stickinin. The air. No stopping for anything. Nosir. Not even for abitov, you know. Forward roll. Over my bum, no touching. Then, gotter eat . . . the yegg. Choccy egg. Very, very nice. Stuff it all in at once, suck it, chew it, and swallow it. Very, very nice. Then, gotta forward roll over Erica's bum. Whichizbiggeran mine. Sorry, Erica. Sorry. Whichiz not biggeran mine at all. Jussat mine's smalleranhers. Then, nother litre beer. In one. No spillin. Teeny weeny. Then, forward roll over Janice's bum. Whichiz biggest of fuckin' lot. Much, much fuckin' biggerer than mine. Even biggeran Erica's. Then, isser beans. Chilli beans. Hot. Hot hot hot. And you know what we've done? Meen Erica? An Janice? We've taken all the joossy-woossy out. Iss solid. No joossy-woossy at all, whatsoever. Dry. And cold. 'Cos we put it in the fridge as well. Then, when you've doner beans, iss nother litre beer. Anner boy who's fastest, he can fuck Janice's bum. Or anything. He can fuck anything. Right. Ready? Steady? Go!'

Hardly any of the contestants in this ancient ritual of juvenile male domination got as far as the beans. This had been forecast, and the girls were quite sanguine that six condoms filled to bursting with ice-cold, dry and solid chilli con carne, super hot spiced, would be enough, and so it was. More than enough. Only Brough and three others got as far as the beans. Only Brough and one other managed to eat the chilli, squeezing the inelegant bulges of utterly undesired meat and beans into open mouths and desperately trying to swallow it before they either seized up or threw up. Of these two, only Brough managed to down the last litre of stout and so, without the need for faster times, Brough was the winner.

It took about 30 seconds for the girls to get his clothes off. He begged them not to sit on his stomach. They poured advocaat on his famous cock and tried to lick it erect. Eventually Angela pushed them all aside. She got Janice to squat over his crutch while she, Angela, lay down to lick his stem and tickle the end with Janice's bum hairs. At last it began to stir. It got harder. Angela rubbed the end along Janice's quim lips, and tried it against her arsehole. It was in. Janice began to move, luxuriating in the feel of Brough, biggest cock in the class, winner of the chilli race, sounding her depths. Angela meanwhile stood astride Brough, with her quim to Janice's lips. Erica stood the same but behind Janice, facing Angela. While Janice tasted Angela's juices, Erica and Angela kissed. Janice's hand reached up Erica's thigh. Her fingers met Angela's at the top, and together they began to bring out Erica's favourite feelings.

There was a cough. Everything stopped. Everyone looked round. 'I'm very sorry to interrupt your party,' said Twozec Salkeld. 'I can assure you it's the last thing I wanted to do. But I need the services of a particular male and a particular female graduate, and I apologise again, but duty calls. Angela? Brough? Follow me please. The rest of you, carry on.'

Outside the door, Salkeld spoke. He was brisk and businesslike. 'Something most unusual and untoward has happened in City HX. You, Brough are well equipped to deal with the problem, and you, Angela will be his second. You have been selected for this task because of your special knowledge of HX, and because the pair of you make an exceptional partnership. Go and shower and change, and get some caffeine down you. I'll be in my office. There's a hoverbubble waiting to take you.'

Half an hour later they were sitting, listening to Salkeld. 'Last night a body was found beside a fountain in one of the main piazzas in City HX. Drowning was the cause of death. The body was naked, trussed up and covered in cigarette burns. This in itself might not cause very much comment or interest from us. Except that the body was that of Twozec Mulholland, newly promoted to be in charge of North-central Region, who had decided to go himself to HX to sort out a decline in recruitment of girls to work in the Units. Strictly speaking HX is nothing to do with me. But they've put the problem on my plate because North-central has only an acting Twozec in charge, I'm now the most senior man in national operations, and I once spent some time in HX. It was a fair time ago. But I can tell you, I have reason to remember it. And the name of a certain woman of no inhibitions, called Pam the Pram. You've heard of her too, Angela?' Salkeld had noticed a slight frisson running up the young Two's nervous system.

'No, I don't think so.' Angela was in turmoil. So, the revolution is beginning. And I'm going right into it. Are they using me? Do they know I'm on the other side? 'No, I was just wondering why you were sending such inexperienced people to such a problem, and whether we would end up in the fountain too.'

'Well said, Angela. My thoughts precisely,' added Brough.

'OK, boys and girls, I could pull rank and tell you simply to go off and fucking do what you're told. But I won't. I've picked you, Brough, because you are a

161

rarity. You are of potential Twozec quality, you have not yet been coated with the varnish we Twos all acquire after a certain amount of time providing limitless pleasure for the Ones, you have a technical background, you have proved that you are willing to take risks and do the opposite to everyone else, and you work extremely well with Angela. Angela I have picked for the aforementioned; you make a good team. But also because she is the most intelligent Two in the country – didn't know that, did you Angela? You scored four more IQ points than me, and the same as Mulholland, who was the youngest ever Twozec to take charge of a region. Which goes to show that IQ isn't everything.

'Angela also has the advantage of coming from City HX. She knows the score there. She knows what lurks beneath the green slime. So, you are being posted as the new managers of HX's biggest Unit, number 436. There will always be Twostudents there, so your only duties should be to take a couple of days every so often to train them as they arrive. You will have plenty of time to track down Pam the Pram and whatever it is she's mixed up in, because I can tell you this, unofficially, unrepeatedly and totally deniably by me. Pam the Pram is not just a homicidal maniac. There is more going on than crime. Rafferty and I have concluded, from instincts and observations rather than hard evidence, that unrest approaching violent revolution is a possibility.

'Nobody on the Committee would acknowledge this to be true, but I'm telling you so you'll have a better chance of surviving. I will also tell you that it is my prediction, if you fail to return or indeed fail in any way, that all Twos will be withdrawn from HX and it will be liquidated. On an evening in the coming winter, it will cease to exist. It will become a small cloud of slightly

162

radio-active gases, to be dispersed by the breeze. The Amenities Committee will then expect the matter to end, but I would not. I would expect whatever is going on in HX to be going on elsewhere, and sooner or later, there would be a savage revolt with bloody consequences. Of course I haven't mentioned this interesting prognostication to the Committee, nor have they mentioned anything to me other than the death of Mulholland, its manner, and my responsibility to clear it up. You might say I'm merely giving you the benefit of my considerable experience and my friend Rafferty's considerable nose. Any questions? Brough, you don't look well.'

'I have a slight stomach upset . . .'

'Ah' said Salkeld. 'This could be a circumstance not unconnected with stout, chocolate eggs, chilli beans and so on? You have my permission to go. Get yourselves packed and ready, and call to see me before you depart, which is in 100 minutes' time.'

Brough raced to a bathroom, took a quick-acting emetic from the machine, and felt much better shortly. He met up with Angela in the communications room. They spoke their requirements and the robot back at college began gathering them together. Extra things they got from stores, and an ATV was dispatched to pick everything up. They still had an hour to kill.

'How about a nap?' Angela suggested. 'Come on. Let's go to the rest room.' They were exhausted, by the party and by the thought of what was to come. They showered together, soaping each other gently without feeling more than a tremor of fleshly excitement, asked the bed to wake them up in an hour, and curled up together to sleep.

Four hours later, which included another nap – on the big hoverbubble this time – and a quick look around

Unit 436, they were sitting, dressed in Threestyle clothes, in a pub in City HX. It was about 2200. After his earlier excesses Brough hadn't fancied a beer, but it would have been noticeable for him to have anything else. The large glass of ice-cold fizzy, almost tasteless lager stood, still full, on the table in front of him. 'This is probably the worst lager in the world,' he said. Angela offered him some of her whisky. 'No thanks. Now, you know this place. Where are we going to go?'

Angela was in some difficulty. She had to look like she was doing the job, yet minimise the risk of meeting anybody who might, unwittingly, give her away. It didn't matter about her family, or any of her old customers from the Unit, but there must be forty or fifty rebels here who knew her, and it only needed a careless glance and she would be done. It was even possible that her friends, the rebels, might think she had turned her coat – now that would be nasty.

'It's our first night, Brough. We're not going to solve the murder and put down the revolution in ten minutes. So let's just have a wander round the main streets. You can get the map of the place in context and I can see what's changed and answer your questions. OK? Now drink your pop like a good boy.'

As they were rounding the corner into the piazza where the body had been found, they heard the empty echo of a discarded drinks can rolling along plus some groaning. They glanced about them nervously. Anything unusual was making them jump. There, in the open square, under a street light, was the answer.

It was indeed a drinks can. It was caught by the sharp edges of its opening in the folds of a girl's dress, which was almost entirely unconnected to its owner – a slight, dark-haired girl – except that it was somehow still looped over the end of a toe. This toe, on the right foot,

164

was like the left foot standing forth on the end of a black-stockinged limb which was horizontal to the floor. The limbs were through the arms of the other participant and resting on his hips. He was a very large man of about thirty, hairy, bearded, ugly, with a chest so big that you almost didn't notice his vast stomach.

The slip of a girl faced the lamp post, he had his back to it, his trousers round his ankles, his hands beneath the girl's buttocks, supporting her without any effort at all. Somewhere in the midst of the tails of a brightly coloured check shirt and a black suspender belt, there were flashes of bare flesh and, no doubt, there was a strong connection.

As they heaved and swayed, the dress was pulled back and forth across the ground, taking with it the can. The very large man was emitting some very small groans. As Brough and Angela watched, the tempo changed from that of a steady walking speed to something more like a woodpecker going flat out. The young girl's head went back as she drifted into space, and his face was buried in her neck as he devoted himself with utter concentration.

Suddenly she came to her senses in more ways than one. With a deft struggling movement she released herself from him. As he stood in blank amazement she knelt down, took his cock between her lips (it was a cold night in late autumn, and they could see vapours rising from it) and with three or four forward movements of her head brought him to climax. That he was in this state was apparent from the cries he made and the trembling of his enormous body. All that bulk reduced to a quivering wreck by a feeling in one of the bulk's smallest components, thought Angela.

The girl was clearly a practical sort and not at all new to this kind of pastime. She simply swallowed his offering, wiped her lips on a small handkerchief which she drew from inside her underclothes, and said 'Well, we don't want to get pregnant, do we? Same time tomorrow?'

She pulled her dress on, accepted a small packet of something from the man, and clipped swiftly away on high-heeled shoes. Brough and Angela strolled on, past the man, who took no notice of them as he pulled up his trousers and tucked himself in.

'What did she mean, pregnant . . . oh, of course, they're not fitted up like you are unless they work in the Units, are they?' Brough was a little puzzled by what he had seen. 'And what did the man give her?'

Angela's first hurdle. She thought it was probably ingredients for explosives, but had better not reveal such foreknowledge. 'There's a black market in quite a few things. Drugs, mostly. And there's no money, nobody wants anything, and so sex is the only currency.'

'Drugs?' asked Brough. 'But I thought they were all freely available.'

'So they are,' replied Angela. 'But not pure. The Ones' drug production facilities are programmed for volume, not quality. They don't care if a Three stupid enough to take drugs kills himself from the impurities they've left in. So some of the Threes reprocess the stuff and let it go at a price. Such as someone's daughter. She'll be doing that for her mother or father. Or both. She'll do it every night until the big moron gets tired of her and wants something different. Such as her sister.'

'Shit. Well if that's typical, why don't we just liquidate the place? What's the bloody point of carrying on? Sorry. I know you come from here. But you must admit it's human activity at its most worthless.'

'If you give people everything except something to

166

do, this is what happens,' replied Angela with a certain crispness in her voice which Brough took for loyalty to home. 'Seen enough for your first night? Then let's go. And if you want someone to fuck later, pop down the Unit elevator. Don't come tapping on my door.'

'Sorry, Angela, sorry. I didn't mean . . .'

But Angela was away, walking quickly in front of him. She was annoyed with his ignorance, but that was not the main reason for her pressing on. Out of the corner of her eye she had noticed a shadow, a looming shadow, of a rather shapeless but substantial person, probably female, pushing in front of her some sort of a trolley.

Angela's return to City HX had been noted by the underground movement. The rebels couldn't know why she was there. It could be coincidence that she'd come back to run the Unit she used to work in as a Three tart desperate to get out. Or it could be more than coincidence. At any rate, she would be watched.

Pam the Pram had given notice that she intended to expand her campaign against the Twos. This was not a well-dovetailed element of the revolution, since Pam was more of an anarchist/sadist psychopath than a freedom fighter, but the movement had asked her to leave Angela well alone. She probably would, too. But that young man with Angela, he hadn't been given any special protection. He looked exactly the sort of victim Pam would enjoy. As she watched him catch Angela up and talk earnestly, Pam the Pram decided that Brough would have to be hers.

In the morning, Angela and Brough had a planning meeting. Brough was anxious to discuss how they proposed to carry on, because he felt that if they just drifted, they would fail and that would be that. Angela didn't want to fail either, although she was damned if she could see how she could save her revolutionary friends and save City HX from the vapouriser at the same time.

'Look, Angela. Let us suppose for a moment that there is some kind of an underground, a resistance movement, a swelling of discontent. I mean, I've read *Animal Farm*. I know that there will always be people who prefer freedom to plenty. So, if there is such a movement, it must have leaders. Now, where will the leaders come from? Will they be bandit chiefs, forcing themselves to the top by their physical prowess and daring? Or will they be intellectuals? Or will they be tub-thumping evangelists, getting everybody on their side by their oratory? Or what will they be? If they're not bandit thugs, they most probably will come from the more, er, what you might call upmarket Threes, those with their roots in the old artistic and business classes. Threes still have their class distinctions, don't they?'

'Oh yes,' replied Angela. 'City HX is the same as cities ever were. You've got the scum and the slime, you've got hoi polloi, you've got petit bourgeois, and there are the superior types. Maybe they really are superior, because they can paint or philsophise, or maybe they just think they are because great-grandfather was a Sir something. The only difference between then and now is that all members of all classes have the same amount of everything – all they want. But you can't change people. There will always be some who would rather eat fish and chips than smoked salmon, and some who would rather sit silently in an empty pub than read a good book. There are even people who dig up a bit of waste ground and spend their time gardening, when limitless supplies of the best fresh produce are available for no effort. Yes, there are classes. So I suppose there are the potential groups of intellectuals and free thinkers who might supply political leadership, and I've no doubt at all that there are the low-life adventurers who could supply the muscle for the sake of a bit of excitement.'

'We'll start by looking at the areas of HX where the upper classes live. I assume there are such areas?'

'Everybody has the same standard of accommodation, with the same level of services. But people do gather together with their own clans. Come on, we'll go and take a look. But let's have a bit of lunch first.'

If they hadn't had lunch, they would have been too early to see what they did see that afternoon. And things would have turned out very differently. But they did have lunch, and while they were having it a certain lady with aristocratic pretensions was also eating. What she found so delicious was a huge, hot, hard cock. It smelled fairly powerful, since its owner didn't believe in bathing over often, but this lady was excited by that. She was repelled, too, because her sophisticated upbringing had naturally refined her sensitivies. But she was excited more than she was repelled. She was driven to embrace the beast, to put its head in her mouth, more than she was frightened by it.

That this lady had the option at all was due to her beauty more than her education. She was a handsome woman, about thirty-five years old, with a fine, full figure. She dressed immaculately, her hair and make-up were perfect, everything about her made her look totally and utterly superior. And so she was able, when she felt the need become so strong that she couldn't resist it, to gather together a group of four or five rough, tough, hairy monsters who stank of beer and cigarettes and armpits. She would contact a certain man she knew, and the word would go round. They would

169

arrive at her door, and she would invite them in for morning coffee, or tea, or cocktails, depending. There they would sit, their dirty fingernails scrabbling on the plates for the last cake crumbs, their oily, ragged jeans and mucky boots leaving evidence on the chair seats, their gap-toothed mouths opening wide with guffaws.

When they'd had their coffee, or tea, or cocktails, this lady would say she had a broken curtain rail in her bedroom, or a dripping tap, and could they look at it for her? So much more convenient than sending for the service robot, since they were right here. So they would all troop upstairs, and then the short, beefy lad, balding on top with a back curtain of dandruff bespattered hair, the leader, would say he didn't think she had a broken curtain rail at all. He thought that what she wanted was a fucking good screw. No no, she would protest, please, don't. They'd just laugh, and start to rip her clothes off her.

She would try to escape. They would catch her and throw her on the bed. Then the short, beefy, balding lad would take off his belt. 'Turn her over!' he would shout, and then give her three or four larruping slashes with the leather. She would cry and wail, and be told to keep her fucking gob shut. Then they would turn her face up, and sit on her arms and legs, and the short man would push his jeans down and wave his cock at her and then stuff it in her. He would shaft her as hard and fast as he could. He hadn't the slightest concern about whether she would come or not, or whether she needed stimulation. He just wanted to come like a dog.

When he'd finished, he'd get up as from finishing his dinner, and another would have a go. The lovely lady had lost the last shred of her clothes by now. Her proud, marble breasts were red from the mauling they were receiving. Her lips were sore from the hard, inexpert kisses. But she was having what she wanted.

There were five of them on this particular day. As Angela and Brough were sitting down to cold chicken with potato salad, the man with the waist-length hair, high-heeled boots and leather bracelets was bucking and broncoing on top of the elegant lady, while the man with the shaved head, barrel chest and tattooed knuckles was kneeling on the bed trying to stick his cock out of the back of the lady's throat.

When Bronco had come with a wild cry, the silent, cold eyed man with the broken nose said 'Gizyer belt' to the short one. With Knuckles still occupying her mouth, he pushed her left leg up and back and tied it with the belt to the bed head. Then he took his own belt off and tied the other leg. Then he too knelt on the bed, and took out his cock, and banged it up the larger and wetter of the two holes facing him.

The lovely lady was gurgling. She could feel Broken Nose whamming away, and she was trying to gobble down a stream of come which was filling her throat from Knuckles. Broken Nose's thrusts got faster and faster. His balls were banging against her arse cheeks. The fronts of his thighs were slapping against her flesh, wet with all the spunk she'd already taken and which was squeezed back out of her by the next intruder. Broken Nose came with a grunt and got off her. 'Got any fucking beer?' he inquired. She shook her head. 'You better fucking have, or you'll suffer.' She shook her head again. 'It'll be in the cooler, as usual,' said Knuckles. 'What, you mean she's lying?' said Shorty. 'Go and get the beer. And when you come back, we'll show her what happens to dirty fucking little liars with big tits, eh?'

The final member of the group was never allowed to

171

touch the lady. He was fat, with a face like a paving stone, and his real idea of fun was to be sucked off by small boys. Not many small boys thought this a worthwhile pursuit, so he resorted to watching Bronco and the rest with their naked arses bouncing up and down. He would stand there, fully clothed, with his dick in his hand, wanking. He put it away when the beer arrived, and sat with the rest of them.

They left her with her feet tied to the bed above her head while they drank cans and smoked. They discussed what they might do to her when they were ready. They could fuck her with a broomstick, except there weren't such things these days. They could flay the fucking skin off her arse. They could stick their cocks down her throat one after another and choke her with spunk.

What they actually did was untie her. Knuckles turned her roughly on to her face, spread her legs apart and went into her up the back. He put his brown, scrawny arms around her neck, held her to his chest and, while still shafting into her innards, rolled over on his back. He gripped her tightly. She complained he was hurting her. He told her to shut up, fucking bitch, or he would really fucking hurt her. He gave her some more hard pushes up the arse. She watched with anxiety as Shorty got on top of her. Now she was the meat in a writhing, squirming sandwich. Shorty pushed his prick in at the front. She could hardly speak.

And now she certainly couldn't speak at all, because the evil-smelling Bronco had filled her mouth with cock. 'Suck that, you dirty shitter,' he said, 'and it'll do you good.' He laughed. Fatso was idly wanking himself. Broken Nose felt a bit out of it, so he took the lady's hand and placed it on his column. She did her best to oblige, but the commotion in her crutch and the

172

whacking great rod ramming against her tonsils were not good for brain-to-hand coordination.

Knuckles made his final jerks and came. Suddenly feeling the weight of the lady and his short mate, he rolled them all off him. Bronco complained because he'd been bitten in the maneouvre, but Shorty didn't mind now he had the lady on top of him. Broken Nose took his chance and, kneeling behind her, found her smaller but now well-lubricated hole.

Bronco got back into her mouth, and they all drove like madmen. Even Fatso was getting excited now, and at the same moment as Broken Nose welled up inside her back avenue, he came and sprayed his spurts on the lady's face. 'You dirty cunt!' shouted Bronco. 'Some of that went on me. Go on, you bitch, keep sucking, keep sucking, keep sucking, that's it.' Shorty was last, thrusting upwards into the usual spot. With Broken Nose off her and getting dressed, Shorty pushed her to the side and did the same. With a last look at the satisfied, sweating beauty, streaming with come from every possible place, they waved goodbye and left.

They went down the street, thumping and pushing each other. Brough and Angela, lunch finished some time ago, were walking down the same street. Brough concluded that the only reason five such horrible men could be in such an obviously nice street was that they were rebels who had come to see their leader. Angela didn't think so at all, but she readily agreed. At least it would keep Brough diverted for a while.

While Angela went to check on whoever lived behind the door they'd just come from, he followed the men, unobtrusively. The short, bald, barrel-chested man was seen to be the main inspiration. They decide to wait outside his apartment, or at least, Brough would wait. Angela would go back, see if she could find out anything about these men from the girls working in the Unit, and return. If he'd gone, she would wait for him in the nearest pub.

About half an hour later, Shorty emerged. He made straight for the pub in question. Brough followed him in, got a pint of lager from the robot and sat in the corner. Bronco and Broken Nose came in also. When Broken Nose walked past to go to the gents, Brough couldn't stop himself looking, almost staring for a few seconds. Broken Nose picked him up by his shirtfront.

'Ere, what the fuck are you lookin' at, cuntface?'

Brough just shook his head and, without too much difficulty, feigned sheer terror.

'Well then, just fuckin' watch it. Don't fuckin' look at people.'

Brough's subsequent determination not to look at anyone meant he didn't see a huge mound of a woman walk past the window pushing a trolley. He didn't see her park it outside against the wall, come in, get her pint, notice him, and sit down round the corner with a grin on her ugly fat face. She spent a minute or so having a think, worked out that as the boy was alone now was her chance, and tried to conjure up a means of getting him, vulnerable, into a place of her choosing.

Pam had always been a mean and vicious character, but she'd got methodical and dedicated as well since her friend Irene had been killed. Irene had got drunk, suppressed her usual high principles and gone into a Unit. She'd demanded service from four girls at once and had more to drink. That much Pam had been able to find out. Knowing Irene she'd probably taken some stardust as well, but at any rate she'd never been heard of again. She'd gone upstairs to get her oats and somebody had turned her into porridge. Pam blamed the Twos. Bastards.

She got up and walked over to where Broken Nose and the rest were sitting. 'See that cunt in the corner?' she said. 'He's a fucking Two. I know he is. He wants getting, that bastard. Spying on us.'

'Why'd he spy on us?' said Shorty.

'Maybe he wants to know where the lady lives,' said Bronco.

'What's it fucking matter?' said Pam. 'He's here, he's dressed like us, so he's a spy. So he wants fucking getting.'

'Well I'm not snuffing no Two,' said Shorty. 'There's no future in it.'

'You don't have to,' hissed Pam. 'Just get him where I can snuff him, and you can piss off out of it.'

'Where d'you want him, then? Under the bridge, by the canal, I suppose.'

Pam nodded.

Broken Nose got up and went over to Brough. 'Here, fuckface, I thought I told you no looking.'

Brough stammered something.

'Come on,' said Broken Nose. 'Outside. We'll settle this all right.'

Brough didn't mind the challenge too much. Outside, out of the pub, he was at least the equal of Broken Nose. He would have a chance. But he didn't. Arms grabbed him from behind, fists thumped into his stomach, and everything went even blacker than it already was on a dark winter's evening.

As he came round he was first aware of the pain under his ribs. Then of the cold and wet on his back – he was lying on the ground, face up. Then there was the smell, an indescribably acrid smell, bad fish, bad eggs, dirty washing, shit, ammonia, what the hell was it. Then it rained. Hot rain. He opened his eyes. Above his face was a mouth. It was spitting hot water at him. It had very bad breath. It had hair round it. Fuck no, it wasn't a mouth. It was . . .

Pam got up and pulled her clothes up. 'Fucking good job for you I didn't want a shit,' she told him, confidentially. 'And the other good news is I've run out of fags. So I'll have to go and get some. So I'm going to hide you in here, and I'll go and have another couple of pints in the pub, and then when I feel all mellow and well disposed towards the world, I'll come back and see you. That'll be nice, won't it?'

She pulled him by his feet into an old shed. He was trussed hand and foot and gagged, so he could do nothing. She closed the door and left him, ice cold, in the dark, trying to compose himself for the ordeal he was sure was coming.

Angela, meanwhile, had made a discovery. She discovered she cared about Brough. When she saw he wasn't in the pub, and she saw who was – Shorty, Broken Nose and Bronco – she knew something had happened. She went outside, feeling sick, and saw, coming towards her, the dreaded pram. She almost threw up in fear, and ran. She ran to a house she knew. She passed a short message, knowing it might be too late, knowing that whatever happened now she'd made her call, she was blown as a Two.

When Pam returned, half drunk, with plenty of cigarettes and matches to her hut, she was amazed to find it empty. She couldn't work it out at all. She was sure she'd left a night's entertainment here. Sure she had. How much fucking beer have I had tonight? Oh well, fuck it, might as well go and have some more.

Her night's entertainment was sitting up and rubbing his wrists and ankles in an apartment not far away. He wasn't gagged any more, but he was blindfolded. There were people round him he knew, but they wouldn't say anything. Then a door opened.

'Lance,' said Angela's voice, 'you were on the menu for Pam the Pram tonight. You were saved from that. But unless I have your word, I won't be able to save you from another, less painful death.'

'Angela? My word? My word on what?'

'Listen. Brough. Tomorrow morning they will find Pam the Pram hanging from a lamp post. We hope that will persuade them that the problem is solved and they won't vapourise the City. But just in case, we're going.'

'Going? We? Who's we?'

'The revolution, Lancelot. And if you don't give me your word that you will come with us, out of the City and into hiding, without causing trouble or trying to escape, you will be hanging beside Pam.'

'Revolution? Then you must be part of it. All this time. And you want to hang me.'

'No, Lance, I don't, you bloody fool.' Angela was finding it extremely difficult to maintain the air of military command expected from her. 'But I will have to order it if your living endangers our work. Don't you see? I'll have no choice.'

'Order it,' said Brough. 'So you won't be stringing me up yourself, then.'

'Lance, please. Can I have your word?'

'Yes. I suppose so. Yes. You have it. And fuck knows where I'm going next.'

At Angela's nod the others, the men who had pulled her from Pam's shed, filed out of the room. Angela took the blindfold off and kissed Lancelot Brough. It was the first kiss he had ever received that had all love and no lust in it. It was quite good.

'Listen to me, Lance. This is imperative. By saving you I have blown my cover. I can't be anything like as useful to the movement now, so I'm going to get shit from the rest of the high command. The only thing I can say is that I've recruited you. You've got to join the revolution. You've got to come with us. My commanders would never trust you back among the Twos as a double, so we're both in the shit together. We'll have to leave the City, leave everything. Go to the hideout. I think it's pretty wild up there. Not the sort of thing you're used to. But we'll both be there.'

By this time tears were falling. Angela couldn't remember crying since her mother died, but she was crying now. Weak, weak woman. Blast the man.

Brough was holding her. 'I don't care a stuff about your revolution. I don't know what the hell you're revolting about. But if you want me to join it, I'll join it. I mean, Salkeld saved me from being an agricultural robotics engineer, you can save me from being a Two. And now I suppose I'll be a Three. There can't be many people who've gone and done the bloody lot. So why not? I just have a tiny little problem with all of this. How the bloody shite do we get out of a City without being turned into crème caramel?'

'There are ways, dear Lancelot, there are ways. Meanwhile, how do we get out of this apartment tomorrow morning without sleeping together all night?'

[8]

It didn't take very long for the new choreographer to
get herself well and widely known in Pleasurehouse 13.
She was that sort of person anyway, and having been
frustrated in a dead marriage for so long she could
hardly restrain herself. She and Ghita began holding
movement and body-articulation classes for the
working Twos; the Ones who came to Pleasurehouse 13
for their rest and recreation heard about this, of course,
and demanded their own classes.

Ghita immediately acquired the highest reputation as
a contortionist and a beautifully exact formal dancer.
Ann, whose dancing was a bit rusty, became known as
the ideas and fun person, so when the thirtieth birthday
of a senior Onezec came round, it was predictable that
Ann would be asked by the Onezec's friends to dream
up a special evening's entertainment. They discussed
the kind of thing the birthday girl might like. She
herself wouldn't want to be made to look a fool, so
nothing participatory – as far as she was concerned,
anyway. She also liked sport, so a competitive activity
might go down well. When the birthday organisers had
gone, Ann looked up the records on this particular
Onezec and found that she was not into any kind of
bondage, bestiality or bull-dyking – the three Bs as the
staff called them. She liked plain sex, preferably two or
three on one, and she was known among the male Twos
as the best oral stimulator of a tired prick in the whole of
NN Computer Centre. Ann went to work.

The audience assembled in a small threatre-in-the-round, a luxurious cockpit with a sunken stage in the middle. Each seat was a double, a deep settee, so that watchers could lounge in Roman style as they looked, or invite a Two to come on the couch with them to assist in their enjoyment. Drinks and food could be summoned from the communications panel in the chair arm, where also were small CLIT screens (with soundphones attached) on which close-ups of the action could be called up. This was the ultimate theatre, the theatre designed by its patrons.

Tonight there were Ones filling all the couches. An excited full house watched as twelve of the best looking and most vigorous young male Twos came onto the circular stage below, dressed in Tarzan-style waistcloths. Whispers and giggles and knowledgeable comments ran round the audience. The dozen young men bowed inside and out to all the four winds, then gathered in groups of three.

In came the four contestants, wearing silk dressing gowns. These were handsome, even beautiful women, all in their late twenties and early thirties selected by Ann out of the numerous volunteers from the more extrovert, competitive and carefree of the Ones. They waved to their friends and the audience in general, then went over each to a group of Twos. They seemed to be having team talks, involving gentle squeezes of greeting for the team's members.

There was a fanfare, and in came Ann wearing a full-length red evening gown, backless and slashed to the waist in front. She looked stunning. 'Ladies!' she began. 'Tonight we have a contest of one round, three submissions – or, more properly, e-missions – the prize to be your congratulations and admiration. The four contestants you probably know. In the east we have

180

Ingrid!' At this Ingrid took off her dressing gown and spun around to reveal a neat pair of small, sweet, pear-shaped breasts and a purple G-string.

'In the west is Maria.' Maria slipped off her dressing gown slowly to make the most of showing, centimetre by centimetre a pair of tits of which the most highly specialised Two would have been jealous. Maria had a soft, light brown skin, set off wonderfully well by the shocking pink G-string.

'In the north, give a hand please to Prudence.' Prudence said she'd prefer a cock to a hand any day, and gave a nervous little laugh as she pirhouetted and dropped her gown. Prudence was almost flat chested, like a young girl, except for very high profile nipples. The space between her inner thighs, however, covered by a bright green G-string, showed that what she lacked above she made up for below.

'And in the south, please welcome Natalie.' Natalie, dark of hair and eye, tossed her head back like a Flamenco dancer and stamped her foot. She swept her gown off, threw it in the air behind her, and pushed her chest forward as she struck a pose, one arm up with hand extended back, the other bent elegantly at her waist. She looked very fit, slim and smooth. Her body was what every woman – although not necessarily every man – would regard as the ideal. Nothing big or small; all evenly in proportion.

'As you are about to see, ladies, tonight's entertainment is a balancing act. These four contestants have to balance stimulation with caution, excitement with calm, in their attempt to achieve simultaneity. The rules are that the boys are not allowed to touch themselves, the ladies must do the driving, and quills must be kept out of both inkwells. Those are the only rules, of course. And you must judge if they succeed. There

181

will be a CLIT recording of tonight's performance, with action replays to help you decide –' cheers, 'and four angles on the stage are projected on the big screens' – she gestured, they were all around – 'so you needn't miss a thing. You must watch carefully, and there can only be one winner. Thank you.'

Ann bowed to the audience in four directions, and the connoisseurs and AC/DCs in the audience were most impressed by the revealed scenery en route to her navel. The contestants stood, facing inwards, with their three male assistants behind. There was a buzzer, they all turned out to face the audience, the twelve men all whipped off their loincloths and the game began.

Each of the women had a different approach. Natalie knelt in front of her three, sucking and wanking alternately and furiously. She had decided that her best way of getting them all to come together was to go for it as quickly as possible. She reminded the onlookers of an entertainer they'd seen recently who did a musical juggling act, so that he would be spinning plates and throwing balls in the air while playing a tune on a set of rubber-bulb klaxons.

Prudence had a different idea. She laid her assistants down, then sucked just one of them while the others watched. She took great care to aim her rear end so the boys in waiting could examine this particularly exemplary part of her anatomy, with the gap at the top of her legs ever beckoning. When she was satisfied that the first subject was nearing the point of no return, she switched to the next.

Maria had her boys lying down too, but closely side by side. She took off her G-string – to cries of 'Cheat' from the audience. But she just smiled, shook her head, and bridged herself across all three boys. She took the far lad's cock in her mouth. She rubbed her record-breaking tits against the middle cock, and rubbed her pussy along the third. The disadvantage of this method was she couldn't really tell what was going on with 66.6% of her team, but her idea was to provide some entertainment for the crowd before bringing up the triple climax.

Ingrid meantime was taking a much more relaxed line. She had obviously decided that the others would confuse speed and activity with promptness, and was willing to let them all shoot off as they liked, leaving her the only contestant still in the game. She would take all the time she wanted. At the moment she was having her sweet little pears kissed and cooed over by one of her boys while she lazily scratched the balls of the others. Occasionally she would rub her hand up and down a shaft, just to check it was on yellow alert, but otherwise she would lie and soak up the atmosphere.

The atmosphere in the north was getting hot. Prudence had got excited and conceived a daring plan which was doomed to failure. She got two of the boys to kneel facing each other with their pricks alongside and touching. She then straddled them, there being plenty of room in her crotch for four pricks side by side, never mind two. She squatted, gripped the members between the soft skin at the very top of her inner thighs and rocked to and fro while taking the third in her mouth. What she had failed to realise was that the same stimulation would not necessarily produce the same result in different cocks, and sure enough the boy from the back shot off all over the boy in front, more or less at the same time as she took the prick out of her mouth to look at its state and saw it coming in close-up. Oh well, she'd lost, might as well make the best of it. With a quick word to the boys who'd just come, she lay down, opened her legs and threw aside her bright green G-string. The just-comers lay alongside her and took a giant nipple each on the otherwise level plain of her chest and sucked and tickled it. The third boy took a tube of something from a pouch in his discarded Tarzan cloth, rubbed some of its contents on his hot, stiff weapon, presented it to madame for her approval, then pushed home. Presumably that was delay cream he'd put on, because Prudence clasped her hands behind her head, closed her eyes and settled down for a nice, long, steady screw.

Also in deep water was Natalie. Her frantic attempts at instant success had led to one of her boys coming in her hand. Another's highly reputed stylus, previously pointed to the sky, now looked like a dead caterpillar on its way down from leaf to ground. The third's erection was getting more and more adamant, until the lad thought his cock would explode, but come he could not. The more Natalie tried, the harder it got in every sense. She too decided to salvage something from the evening, so she too put herself in repose while the hard man worked steadily. Once inside her he began to feel more comfortable. When she took hold of him and placed him at the rear entrance, he gave a heavy thrust and was all done in a matter of moments. The sight of all this had energised the flaccid caterpillar and he too was beckoned to continue where his colleague had left off. She got herself up on her knees, put her elbows on the floor and her chin in her hands, and offered a radiant sphere. He knelt behind and, finding the correct tangent, gently pumped his way to heaven.

Interesting though this was, the audience hardly gave it a glance. They were watching the increasingly close rivalry developing between Maria and Ingrid. Maria had abandoned her bridge-crossing tactic in favour of the simplest method of all. The three lads lay down close together on their backs. She sucked the middle one and wanked the two outside ones with her hands. She left off sucking occasionally to check the relative progress, and by means of a secret and quite unsporting code of communication they'd worked out, involving the slight raising of fingers, she was looking like she might get a reasonable result.

Ingrid was still taking the long way round. She'd brought some props on with her, and was now smearing her pert little pear drops with what looked like lemon curd on the left and strawberry jam on the right. The boys took it in turns. Boy A would kneel and lick a breast. Boy B would kneel on the other side while Ingrid lazily reached up, skinned his cock a couple of times and gave it a swift razzle with her tongue. Boy C meanwhile was putting the index fingers of both hands inside her purple G-string, and to good effect it would appear from her cosy little wrigglings.

The crowd was getting noisy now. They'd had a few drinks, they'd seen third and fourth, now they wanted a grand finale. Maria lay on her back. A lad got across her, put his cock in her cleavage, pushed the mountainous flesh in from either side and fucked her like that. She had the other two on the point, and as the tit-fucker began to speed up she too accelerated her hand-jive. The tit man came first, a huge spout that shot in her eye and across her forehead. Almost at the same time the left hand got its reward, and four or five jives later the last boy came – that was all three in the space of maybe three or four seconds. She curtsied gracefully to the applause while wiping the spunk off her face, looked enviously at Prudence and Natalie who were still getting some, then turned and sat to watch Ingrid.

Ingrid thought Maria was stretching the rules with that tit-fucking business, in that the boy was pacing the job rather than the contestant. So, what was OK for Maria . . . Ingrid took a chair and sat on it. She put some lubricating jelly in each armpit. The tallest of her three boys stood in front and put his cock in her mouth. The other two frigged her armpits. In contol of their own destiny, and able to nudge each other without anyone noticing, they were able to come up to a climax together. At the same moment they all withdrew and shot all over Ingrid's face. Three lots of come dripped down her nose and off her chin. She licked in what she could, wiped her eyes, and smiled in triumph.

Seated on the back row were three couchfuls of Ones who thought this show was the best thing they had ever seen. They had hardly been able to contain themselves during the performance, and each of the half dozen had been stimulating herself and her couch partner throughout. Now they decided they must go and thank the producer, so they trooped out to the manager's suite where they guessed Ann would be that night. They were right. She was sitting in an armchair, sipping a gin and tonic and reading the libretto of the show they were putting on. She rose to greet them.

They didn't say anything at first, these six Ones. The tallest of them went up to Ann, put her arms round her and kissed her on the lips. Ann felt the tongue in her mouth, searching and twisting, and felt obliged to return the gesture. She felt hands on her dress, gently tweaking at the deep V-neck which barely enclosed her nipples. There was no bra, as the hands soon discovered. With her glorious bosom out in the open, other hands were at the fastenings at the back. There were hands everywhere, and all Ann had to do was step out of her stockings and shoes.

She took a breath. 'This is all very nice,' she said 'but

slightly irregular. I hadn't realised I was appearing in the second half.'

'We just wanted to say thank you,' said the tall One, her fingers at the fastenings of her own outfit. 'Now why don't we go through to the rest room?'

Ann strode to the rest room door, opened it, walked in, and lay on the bed, on her side and one elbow, a knee up and a knee straight. She watched as the giggling, busy mob of six excited women stripped themselves and each other. They came towards Ann, who just laid back and closed her eyes. It was impossible to trace exactly what was going on. Tongues were in every possible orifice – ears, quim, mouth, bumhole, everywhere. Hands and fingers roamed likewise. Ann was a mass of warmed-up erogenous zones. Initially expecting to remain distant from this strange thank-you present, she felt herself starting to slide. All the girls had different perfumes, they all had different ways of using their fingers and tongues. Some made little noises as they worked. The constant slither of flesh changing position and the endless variety of touch were getting to Ann's core. She began to touch back, but was firmly put in her place. Later, darling, maybe.

So she relaxed, legs open, arms wide. She opened her eyes. Two heads were busy in her crotch, two on her tits and one was licking her tummy button. The sixth had the fingers of one hand up her own fanny and the other in Ann's arse. She leaned forward and kissed Ann, a long, exploring, wide ranging kiss. Ann felt herself approaching the moment. Her pelvis began pushing up into the faces of the girls who happened to be down there at the time. She groaned as the tongues worked harder and quicker. She felt fingers pulling her quim open wider, and more fingers and tongues delving in deeper. Quite out of control she thrashed and heaved

187

while her accolytes hung on, until she gave a little scream, bridged herself on elbows and heels, and came in a series of rhythmically spaced jerks.

She fell back on the bed. The tall girl ran her index finger up Ann's body from clitoris to nose. 'Was that nice?' she asked. Ann nodded, unable to speak. 'Well,' continued the One, 'we're going to go now and leave you to rest. If you want another happy time, all you have to do is ask.' She gently squeezed Ann's right tit then, with her hand flat, rubbed the very end of the nipple lightly with her palm. Ann sighed, closed her eyes, and was asleep before they'd dressed and left.

She awoke in the middle of the night, the book of the show on the floor beside her. She looked down at it. It had been considered an old show when she was on the stage. This lot here would never have heard of it, probably, unless they'd come across the music somehow and asked the network to put up the old film with Howard Keele and Ann Miller. Now, there was a dancer. Legs went right up to her armpits. And for the 1001th time, Ann wondered what had made her pick *Kiss me, Kate* for the bumper special show at Pleasurehouse 13. Of course, some of them would know the Shakespeare part of it, *The Taming of the Shrew*. But would they like the music? She kept telling herself that Cole Porter was class, and class would always be appreciated.

She'd thought of spicing it up a bit. There were plenty of opportunities. The whole thing was about sex. But she decided in the end to do the show straight and let it stand up for itself. So she put her request into the communications network for a theatre company consisting of actor/singers who preferably could dance, plus some speciality dancers, and some more musicians to supplement the regular orchestra.

There were some very good songs – 'Wunderbar!' for

instance, and 'I Hate Men', and 'Where is the life?', and some great comedy – 'Brush Up Your Shakespeare' – and brilliant dance numbers – 'Too Darn Hot' and 'Any Tom, Dick or Harry'. It was a great show. She would need an excellent cast, and she would need to be pretty red hot herself. Crises of confidence occurred daily as she worked on the script and the dance steps, but once the cast assembled and they got to work, Ann was so busy she forgot to lack confidence. In fact she had been very lucky with the company. The man who was playing Petruchio was really good, a fine singer, a good actor, tall, dark and handsome. At first Ann thought he must be a queer, since he took no notice of the tits and bum which Ann took every opportunity of showing him – subtly, of course. But the lack of interest was apparently due to overstimulation elsewhere, since he was suffering from the excessive attentions of the girl playing the Ann Miller part, Bianca, who was a famous nymphomaniac. Like one of the old Presidents of the United States, Ann couldn't remember which, Bianca needed a fix of sex several times a day just to stay normal.

That problem was solved when the musical director arrived, a suave, sophisticated, arty-looking man who was clearly a musical genius. Bianca decided that she had to have him wave his baton in her direction, and so Petruchio was off the hook. Within a few days the colour had returned to his cheeks and Ann's little hints began to get some reward. He asked her up to his dressing room for a drink after rehearsals. They were sitting, chatting about the theatre before the Change – Petruchio was no spring chicken either – when they heard strange noises coming from the dressing room next door. At first Ann thought it was water going down the plughole, then maybe somebody with hiccups, then possibly someone being smacked.

189

'Who's next door?' she asked.

'Oh, that'll be our dear heart Bianca. Under the supervision of the Musical Director, whom God preserve, she has been working her way through the strings and is now halfway along the brass section. Want to look?'

He got up and went to a framed poster on the wall, advertising a movie of *Henry V* starring Lawrence Olivier. He took the picture down and put his eye to the wall. 'I say. She's doing a step-shuffle-hop all right. You'll have to change that number of hers, Ann. It's not a maid who would marry any Tom, Dick or Harry. It's a tart who would click with dick after dick. May I present, through this peephole thoughtfully provided by a previous incumbent, Bianca, the Conductor, and the French Horn?'

Ann put her eye to the hole in the wall and saw that the noises she'd heard must simply be those issuing from Bianca, the naked, beautiful, long-blonde-haired, pertly titted Bianca, as she lost her cool while riding astride the horn. They always said the brass section contained the biggest drinkers and had the biggest cocks, Ann mused, and obviously they were right. This brass player was on his back on the carpet with his feet towards the wall. Ann could see his huge, pale column with a fuzz of red hair at the base as Bianca reared up and down on it. She was rocking and bumping as if she was trying to break a wild horse, and every time her arse got high enough into view for a clear swipe, the musical director was giving her a crack with a short riding crop.

'Fancy that!' said Ann. 'They're using one of your props. What a cheek.'

'What a cheek indeed,' murmured Petruchio, his hand now down the waistband of Ann's rehearsal two-piece and gently cupping a large handful of buttock.

190

'You shouldn't be doing that,' whispered Ann. 'I am your director, and I direct you to stop immediately.'

'Shan't,' said the actor.

'Typical,' said Ann. 'Spoilt, temperamental. Must have his own way. You lot are little boys, all the same, I suppose I shall have to humour you, or no doubt you'll just up and walk out of the show.'

She shifted her position at the keyhole slightly while saying this, so he could slip his hand more easily around her bottom and his fingers into her waiting slit. As he reached his target, Ann wriggled appreciatively and put her own hands out searchingly behind her. She found what she wanted, and apologised for calling him a little boy. While he pulled down her pants, she undid his fastenings and brought him out into the open – and that's how they did it, the first time. Ann was facing the wall, her eye on the hunting scene next door, and her male lead banged her in the quim standing up, from behind.

Ann watched the French horn make his top note while the actor was sliding in and out of her. Bianca dismounted, bent down to touch her toes, took a couple of good thwacks from the musical genius, and then took the whip to him. He fell backwards to the carpet in mock terror and she passed the whip to the horn player whose big white soldier hung limply now from its hairy red hiding place but still, even at ease, looked to Ann to be twice as big as some she'd come across when fully at attention.

Petruchio was accelerating now, and Bianca in the next room was mounting the musician's face. She gurgled and moaned and hiccupped the equivalent of Yoiks! and Tally Ho! and was soon fairly flying over vale and hill, slapping herself on the backside. This was not to complete her impression of a horsewoman but rather to remind the slack horn that it was his turn to whip her in. She seemed to enjoy her ride all the more when it was helped along with a few light slashes across her roundest parts, and she went into full gallop as Ann felt her partner enter his final phase. Ann pushed her bum out to meet him as he went home, and felt the warm fluid spurt inside her. She hadn't come herself, but there was still time for that.

The sights next door had made her increasingly randy anyway, so just the single fuck wouldn't have done even if she had come. She needed some more. She stripped off her rehearsal clothes and stepped into the shower cubicle. He stepped in after her, but she barred his way. 'Wait a minute,' she said. 'Don't be impatient.'

She was lavish with the perfumed shower gel, letting it run down her breasts and across her tummy and into her crevice, and luxuriated in the sensuality of foam and hot water. She massaged more gel around her body, pushing her breasts upwards, feeling the plentifulness of her ample bottom, cruising slowly towards her own private pleasure parlour. With the index fingers of both hands, as the hot water cascaded down her and through the scented foam, she pushed her quim lips apart and felt for the sanctum sanctorum. There, inside the temple, was the idol, the little statue that came to life when you stroked it. With her left hand she reached for the gel, and squirted herself with more of it as she orbited then came into land on the most sensitive strip. With her left hand she massaged her tits, her arse, her tits again. With her right she rubbed herself into that state approaching climax when every other aspect of life is temporarily suspended. She put both index fingers back again, a finger tip on each side of her clit, and twirled herself to coming.

She felt better now. And maybe, with the rest, Petruchio would too. She left the shower. 'Your turn,' she said. 'Don't be long.' Ann searched through the wardrobe to find something flimsy and comfortable. The nearest thing was a towelling dressing gown, but draped tastefully across her as she lay on the carpet with a knee bent and her head on a couple of cushions, she was quite sure the effect would be good enough. It was. Petruchio never took his eyes off her as he towelled himself dry, and his cock was doing its best too. He knelt beside her face. She took his warm, clean, soapy smelling prick between her lips, gently bit it, then sucked it in. She felt it harden and rise. A few more squelching sucks and it was up as far as it would go. She pulled the dressing gown off her body, opened her legs invitingly, and guided him in.

'We'll leave the foreplay until later,' she breathed, and the actor responded with steady thrusts. Ann lay back on the cushions, her eyes closed, her mind blank, her body wanting a really good, long, slow, satisfying, total screw. Petruchio put his prick on autopilot and began to examine the luscious bounty beneath him. He could easily support himself on one arm while the other hand traced the tremendous outline of the finest pair of tits in British theatre. Admiringly he caressed every square millimetre of their surface, and saved his softest touches for the very tips of her nipples, which were standing out now like a pair of termite nests.

She was moaning slightly, just under her breath, as the combined stimulation of touch and fuck began to excite her. Petruchio took over the driving from the autopilot and banged a bit harder. He squeezed her bosom and pumped her hole. He tickled and thrust. He twiddled and rammed. Her arms went round him and pulled him close. Her feet locked round each other behind him and drew him up as far as possible. In he went, and in, and in, penetrating her to her core, lunging for her centre, stabbing for her heart.

It was next door's turn to hear funny noises, as Ann began mewing and wailing in her glory. She didn't care who heard her, and she certainly didn't notice the eye at the peephole as she began doing little bicycle kicks, drumming with her heels on the actor's buttocks and yowling as she came in a great rapidfire orgasmic volley. Petruchio kept going for a few more seconds then he too was grunting with joy as his seed burst out into the secret world of Ann's within.

They collapsed into each other's arms and lay there, at peace, for maybe fifteen minutes. When Ann awoke she was still lacking. She didn't feel replete. 'How are you doing?' she asked the great Thespian. 'Ready for more?'

'My dear lady,' he replied. 'You ask much. At my advanced age of very nearly forty, you cannot expect the vigour of youth. I may need a little extra stimulation,' he smiled.

'Well there's a thing,' Ann said. 'I could quote Cole Porter, you know. The first number. There is, as he so rightly says, "Another Opening, Another Show."' Ann turned over and offered her perfectly round, perfectly wonderful rear to Petruchio and, without realising it, to the musical director whose eye was glued to the peephole almost as hard as his hand was fastened to his own cock. He was thinking of dashing round when he saw Ann reach under her crutch towards the kneeling actor, take hold of his prick and rub the end of it up against her puckered little bumhole. It expanded immediately, and was soon hard enough to effect an entrance. Once inside it firmed up completely, and Petruchio, despite his protestations, was into his third fuck in an hour.

This was what Ann needed. She'd had a quickie, and

a wank, and a long heavy screw, and now the slightly illicit thrill of a big prick in the wrong place would do just nicely. The tightness of the skin around his tool was far too stimulating for Petruchio to last long. As he realised he was on the way he went for it hard and fast. He reached forward and under, took a lovely tit in each hand, and threw himself at her arse until, for the third time, he spilled his spunk into her plentiful body.

They stayed, locked in that position, for long enough for the peeping conductor to bring himself up to boiling point. Had Ann been able to untie herself and go to the hole in the wall, she would have seen the conductor comically and anxiously looking for a place to call home. While he'd been occupied with his peeping, Frenchie had got stuck into Bianca. She was underneath, wrapped around the man like an octopus and with her face buried in his shoulder as she heaved and cried. None of her orifices was available for selection by the conductor. He was never a man to worry about the niceties when necessities arose, so he knelt behind the charging arse of his French horn and drove his cock in there.

There was a wrathful roar but so entwined was the brass player that he couldn't throw off his boss. He did the next best thing and carried on regardless, feeling the gush of genius behind as he himself blew everything he had into the talented singer and dancer beneath.

[9]

'Get me Rafferty.' Salkeld spoke abruptly to the servile screen, and waited with tapping fingers for his friend's face to appear. 'There you are, you old bastard. I thought you'd be out sacrificing young maidens with your witches' covens under the greenwood tree.'

'You may laugh, Salkeld, but it has been mentioned. Some of the more, er, gamesome Ones seem to think I can get post-pubic virgins of both sexes out of the cities by the cartload, just so the mad fuckers can stand and wank while somebody slits them open. What they don't realise is that there is no such thing as a post-pubic virgin these days in the cities. Every girl has been fucked by her father, her brother, or the next-door neighbour before she's 10, and every boy's been sucked off by his mother and shown where to dip his wick by his sister. You see, dear man, this is what happens when the ancient Irish virtues of temperance and restraint are abandoned in favour of free everything.'

'To be sure, bejabers and pyjamas, you fucking Irish tarts are all models of sobriety. Now look, leprechaun-bollocks. I'm due some leave. The unfortunately double-length saga of woe at Pleasurehouse 13 seems to be in suspension, thanks to the activities of the very wonderful and accommodatingly breasted Onewife Richmond, and so I thought how about me and my old emerald-green chum doing a spot of fishing? Just a couple of days?'

'And why not indeed? There is but a single

drawback. Despite the holy traditions of thieving, poaching and sporting so beloved of the Irish race, I have never fished a fish in anger.'

'This does not matter, oh bog-trotter. The English gentleman will teach the Irish peasant how to persuade a salmon to leave its preferred milieu for the hotter water of the fish kettle. We shall go to Whitby and fish the River Esk, and we shall go the day after tomorrow. OK?'

'Sure, OK,' said Rafferty. 'I haven't been to Whitby since before the Change. Very nice too.'

'It's even nicer now the Ones had all the modern buildings demolished and that god-awful flyover. It's just the old town now, on the east side, every old fisherman's cottage converted into a One-standard holiday home. It's Whitby as it was the day Captain Cook sailed. Your screen will let you know as soon as residential arrangements have been finalised in this connection. I remain, over and out.'

Two mornings later, a fine wintry sun shining and a keen breeze blowing down the dale, Salkeld was in full flood of enthusiasm. He simply had to teach Rafferty how to catch a fish. First, he had to teach him how to cast. 'Right, keep the line moving, forward and back, until you can feel the full weight of it in the rod tip. You will know when you've got it right. You will know when you reach the point where there is enough line out to make a short cast because there will be a change in the tempo of the rod. Which, incidentally, is no robot-made article machined out of a redundant space-rocket's arsehole, but an extremely decent piece of equipment, hand made many aeons ago by Northumbrian gnomes out of split cane, silk and spit.

'Now, careful when you change from back-cast to forward . . . ah, pity. Never mind. Flies are easy to crack off if you push into your forward movement too early. Create a sort of whiplash at the end of the line, see, and the weakest link goes – which is the cast with the fly on. Never mind. Try again.'

With a new fly tied on, Rafferty managed to get a fair amount of line out then, in attempting a cast, he tried to put some more effort into it instead of letting the line do the work. 'Look, you stupid Irish twat. Remember Archimedes. Give me somewhere to stand and I will move the earth, or whatever. Pivots. It's all about pivots. No good setting up the system to run in a certain way then chucking something new in the last minute. Here. Watch my elbow.'

Salkeld reeled in the line which was lying in a foolish coil here and there, waved out about 20 yards in half as many seconds and then put his left arm across his chest and cupped his right elbow in his left hand. He cast, beautifully.

'See? The pivot is still. The arm is straight. Now, when you've got that, and you can keep your right elbow still on its own, you can use your left hand to shoot a little line at the last moment so that you get a bit further and your fly lies down with a gentle sigh rather than a big fat flop.'

Rafferty got the hang of it enough to try some serious fishing, so they left the practice water and walked to a fine run of river which Salkeld considered would have some good fish in it. 'Water temperature above 50F, air temperature above that, which information indicates the smaller type of fly, fished near the surface on a greased line, as opposed to the cold water tactic of a large, two-or three-inch fly fished deep on a sinking line. Don't ask me why, because I don't know. No one knows, not really. Left alone, salmon hardly feed at all when they're in fresh water, so why they should prefer one form of fraudulent snack to another, depending on how warm they're feeling, is one of the mysteries.

'Also the light is not so bright as it was, now it's clouded over and we've missed all the fucking sunshine due to your ineptitude at learning the simplest things. Therefore we shall forgo the Silver Blue with which I intended to flog the undeserving stream this morning, when I was under the illusion that it would be easier to teach an Irishman than a mentally retarded kangaroo, and transfer our allegiance to Hairy Mary. You will notice that she is on a small treble hook, which will give you as a beginner a better chance of hitting the mark with your strike. Mary herself consists only of a few bits of hair, wrapped around a small plastic tube which will move up the line out of the way when Salmo salar is seduced.

'Over there please mark a part of the stream where we have two different rates of flow – a quicker channel with slower water on either side. I'll make one cast to show you how to fish the fly in the water, then it's up to you.'

Salkeld waded in, not far in this narrow river but enough to give him the angle he wanted to the patch of dark quick water. He cast into the slow on the far side and mended the line by rolling a loop around it with a flick of the rod end. The line now bellied upstream of the fly, which he fished across the current with slow and steady drawing movements. He had another cast for luck, then waded out.

'Right. There you are. Pay especial attention just as your fly moves into the quicker water, and just as it moves out. Drop a few paces downstream with each cast so that you work the whole length of that current. Then we'll find you another one.'

'Aren't you going to fish?' asked Rafferty.

'Only if you get a salmon, or prove to be utterly hopeless.'

Rafferty did as he was told, and ten minutes of silence later a swirl of water brought voice to the excitement. 'Damn it, I missed him!'

'No, you didn't. Reel in and stay exactly where you are. You didn't miss, because he turned away before he got to the fly. Decided he didn't want it after all – so we'll try something smaller.'

'Smaller? But it looked like a big fish.'

'Not relevant, and probably not true. It was a moderate fish, I'd say, but we'll see. And the preferred size of snack is more to do with how you feel than how heavy you are, yes? There. Now try that.'

Salkeld finished tying on a smaller Hairy Mary, Rafferty sent it back to the same spot, or as near as he could get it. Not near enough, try again, blast it the line's all coiled up, keep my left hand still, that's better.

The old friends and allies in adversity watched in the most intense and co-operative quiet as Rafferty's fly slipped from slow water to quicker, around in an arc. Surely the fish must have been put down by whatever nervousness had caused it to turn away the last time. The line stopped.

The fly, less than three quarters of an inch of bedraggled nonsense that couldn't fool anyone or anything into believing it was delicious, nevertheless had struck a note in the instincts of a fish. He was hooked and Salkeld was shouting at Rafferty to get ashore.

'Let him have some line. Get on the bank. Quieter now. That's it. Follow him down – keep your rod end up! It's there to take the strain – good, don't let him go anywhere without working for it, steer his nose away from those weeds, slow him down, he's tiring, agh!'

The salmon leaped from the water in a magnificent

last attempt at freedom. The in-born urges which had forced it to grab at imitation food it didn't want also compelled it up and out of the water in a soaring, eye-stopping curve that transfixed Rafferty and allowed Salkeld no time to issue instructions.

The salmon fell, smack, onto the taut line. Fourteen pounds of muscular, royal fish from that height were too much for the cast. One party to the encounter now had a hook in its top lip with a few yards of thin nylon trailing from it. The other party just had a very empty feeling.

'Should have dropped the rod end, old man.' Salkeld actually felt uncomfortable. The maestro had forgotten to tell his pupil one of the basic rules. 'Standard practice. Soon as he leaps, you drop the rod end so the line goes slack so it's less likely to smash if he lands on it. Sorry. Should have told you. Anyway, he'll live to fight another day. Wish we could all have that chance, eh?'

There was no more sport on what later became a cold and wet day, and so when they walked back to the riverside inn where they were staying, they felt they deserved a little comfort. The big fire was alight, the bar looked inviting, so they had a large gin and tonic before they went their own ways to bath and dress for the evening.

These olde-worlde pubs and inns had been kept going for the Ones and off-duty senior Twos. Usually they were run by female Twos who had gone past their most attractive years and preferred the idea of running a pub to destabilisation. Typically you'd have a landlady, chef, waitresses, barmaids, all good looking and bright eyed but all of a certain age. They had robots to do the cleaning and the rooms, so it wasn't at all a bad life.

Of course Rafferty and Salkeld were of a certain age too, and being Twozecs as well meant that they attracted a fair bit of attention from the staff. The woman who brought them their first post-bath drink bent down right in front of them as she placed the glasses on the low table. Rafferty could see her navel and Salkeld, from his angle, claimed he could see her knicker elastic. The woman who brought the menu leaned over Salkeld's shoulder and pushed her left tit into his ear. The woman who took their order asked if there would be anything else the gentlemen might require later on.

Rafferty and Salkeld thought there might be something better on the go than a couple of has-been knocking-shop professionals, and they were right. As they were finishing their main course a pair of female Ones came into the restaurant. They were about twenty-nine years old, and despite the ancient rural charm of the Eskdale wayside inn they were dressed for the razzle. The little dark One had a minuscule mini skirt of dark brown leather, fishnet tights, a skin tight thin sweater of red cotton which showed every detail of her proud young bosom – and she had plenty to be proud of – and lipstick to match. Her companion, a tall, elegant girl with bleached white hair cut very short, had on a trouser suit – but there was nothing underneath the jacket, which had only a single button, and guessing by the movement revealed by the very close-fitting trousers, nothing under them either.

They smiled graciously at the older but still wolfishly handsome Twozecs who, as they left, invited them to the bar later for a drink. When they'd finished their meal they came over with a bottle of wine each. The talk was light and amusing, and obviously the four of them were going to get on very well together. Rafferty and Salkeld had long ago become used to beautiful young female geniuses who understood the depths of microphysics and psychorobotics when, to look at them, you could have thought they only understood how to dress to kill.

The small dark miniskirt, name of Roxy, happened to mention she'd been rooting around upstairs and found a small lounge cum games room, and in it an ancient box containing various board games and the like. How about if they go and try some out? She knew her friend – tall, white-blonde, name of Ophelia – liked games, 'don't you, Pheel?' Pheel agreed that games were a favourite of hers, so they all trooped upstairs to a cosy little room with a couple of chairs, a table, a bookcase full of old children's books, and this box. 'Compendium of Games' it proclaimed on the lid. The girls had never seen such cardboard relics before, but the men remembered them. They even knew the function of the little blowpipes, the plastic ball and the goals.

'Ah, now then, this is the thing,' said Rafferty. 'You put a goal at each end of the table, like this, and you place the ball in the middle. Now, you Ophelia, you bend down with this little pipe in your mouth, and try and blow the ball towards my goal while I try and blow the ball towards yours.'

'Ophelia, you've never had a pipe as small as that in your mouth before,' giggled Roxy.

'You've never had such a tiddler up your arsehole either, dear, but that doesn't mean you're not going to get it sometime,' responded Ophelia crisply, giving the ball a few trial blows and Rafferty a clear view of her swinging bosom inside the loose-fitting jacket.

'Inappropriate, isn't it?' said Rafferty to Salkeld. 'What is?' came the reply. 'How they call those jackets single breasted' said Rafferty.

'Look, you guys,' said Ophelia. 'Suppose I score a goal. What then?'

Salkeld gave them the rules. 'Whoever scores a goal can name an item of clothing, and the person scored against must take it off. If the scorer already has items off, he or she can put one of them back on again.'

'Hey, that's not fair,' complained Ophelia. 'I haven't got as many items as you lot.'

'Then you'll just have to blow that bit harder, won't you?' said Rafferty.

They bent over the table, pipe to ball to pipe. Salkeld gave them the off. Ophelia gave herself a little shake, and while Rafferty's gaze was diverted down the front of her jacket, she blew the ball past him and over the edge of the table. Goal kick. Ophelia came round to contest it, and a savage duel ensued. Out of the corner of his eye Rafferty saw Roxy with a leg up on the chair, adjusting her suspenders. Ophelia easily rounded his distracted pipe and blew into goal.

'Brilliant!' she cried. 'Right, Rafferty. Knickers off.' Rafferty's protests were overruled. Nobody had said clothes had to come off in sequence. So off came shoes and trousers, down came underpants to much whooping and cheering from the others, and back on went the trousers. Rafferty thought it was time he evened things up, so at the kick-off he sucked the ball hard onto the end of his pipe, stepped swiftly round the table and dropped it into Ophelia's goal.

'Trousers' was his only utterance.

Ophelia turned her back, knowing full well that her bottom was an exceptionally fine example. She slipped the trousers down, taking her time and making sure the men had every opportunity to appreciate the best points of a truly terrific arse. She turned, and they saw her other hair was dyed to match her head, and cut by the same hairdresser. Rafferty was determined now, and

205

with a surge of power blew the ball straight from the halfway line into the goal. 'Jacket,' he said.

Ophelia came over to him and put a hand on his shoulder. With the other, while she looked him directly in the eye, she slowly undid the single button. The jacket fell open. She put both arms around Rafferty's neck as his hands went inside the jacket, firstly round her back, to feel her firm young flesh there, and then around the front to find those elegantly shaped little grapefruit he felt he already knew so well.

Salkeld and Roxy seemed happily engrossed in a game of tiddlywinks. Roxy had Salkeld lying on the floor with the cup on his forehead. She was trying to flick the winks into it by using Salkeld's stiff cock as a catapult, but they were going all over the place.

Ophelia's hands were busy now, unfastening and pulling and unfurling, so that Rafferty was as naked as she was. She wanted him there and then. She backed him onto an armchair, so that he was astride one of the arms, his left foot on the floor, his right leg doubled on the seat, his balls and cock ready. She walked onto him, slipped his cock into her in an easy movement, put her hands on his shoulders, looked him in the eye again and slowly began writhing and gyrating.

Rafferty was able to pay full attention to her little pearls now, those perfect, champers-glass measures of malleable flesh which attract irresistibly and inexplicably. Her nipples rose up like soldiers. She put her hands on top of his hands and helped him squeeze harder. She groaned, and called on the gods to help her as she hurtled to oblivion, wriggling and pushing until she collapsed against Rafferty and the chair back in a rushing mixture of noise and movement. Rafferty let her stay for a while, but he hadn't come yet. He sat her in the chair and put a knee on each chair arm. He swung his prick towards her mouth like a battering ram. She opened and took in the sour-tasting eager beast.

She was only part recovered from her recent ordeal by pleasure, so she didn't take much active part. Rafferty held her head and just fucked her mouth until he felt the charge being loaded. Then he pulled out and put his cock in her hand. She made a ring with thumb and forefinger, brought him off and, as he guessed she would, he directed the creamy stream half and half onto the tips of her lovely little tits. She smiled up at him. 'Rafferty,' she said. 'Get me a drink.'

Roxy had given up on her tiddly winks by now and taken the rest of Salkeld's clothes off. He was still lying on his back, reading the instructions on the inside of the game-box lid while she, fully clothed, pulled her crutch gusset aside and sat on his cock, facing his feet. Salkeld cast the lid away after a while. He didn't want to miss a turn. He couldn't do anything about the leather mini-skirt and the frilly knickers, but he could about the sweater, by sitting up and pulling it over her head. Roxy had a brown, shiny skin and big, hanging tits with huge dark aureoles and long purple nipples. Salkeld grappled these from behind while she continued to screw in her own time. She'd bounced there for several minutes before suddenly dismounting, ripping her skirt and panties off, then walking away with her fingers busy inside her quim. She reached a chair and bent over it, offering her arse to Salkeld. This was fine by him. He got up, went over to her, and brought a grateful 'Oh yes!' from her as he speared her through the back door.

Her fingers were rocking and sawing like a fiddler's elbow now, as Salkeld went for it. She was an arching jiggling wreck by the time Salkeld began to spurt, her brown jugs bobbing like basketballs in a fast dribble,

207

her long, indigo nipples pointing frantically in every possible downward direction. He went home as deep as he could with each surge of come, and her fingers brought forth her own spasms as the pair of them locked in a near-airborne passage to Nirvana.

As they relaxed, Rafferty brought them a glass of the dry and sparkling. They sat about, sipping, not needing to say anything. It was Roxy who moved first. She took her friend's hand and led her to the centre floor, where she lay on her back. Ophelia knelt above her, her perfectly coiffed white rug hovering just over Roxy's red lips. Roxy could smell Rafferty, a faint whaft rolling down Ophelia's body, a few smudges of spunk still visible on the underside of the tall, pale girl's neat breasts.

Roxy's tongue flickered out, and Ophelia lowered herself slightly so the tip could part the folds of delicate skin guarding the entrance. A finely poised sensation developed as Roxy beckoned to Salkeld. He was to kneel behind Ophelia and enter her alongside Roxy's tongue. His prick was hard now, and it easily curved around and under, and into the front pocket. Roxy licked his balls and the root of his cock as she watched it at the closest of quarters, slurping in and out. She heard mumbling and murmuring and presumed, rightly, that Rafferty was getting a good sucking from Ophelia. What she couldn't see was the gallant, gentlemanly pose as Rafferty stood, casually, a glass of champagne in one hand and a thin cigar in the other, while the long upper body and neck of the gorgeous blonde reached up to his meat, thrust out at her in abandonment.

Salkeld was moving faster now. Roxy watched anxiously, wanting to make sure she got her timing right. She was very close, the thrusting rod going into the tidily bordered quim right in front of her face. She saw the final acceleration begin. She reached up, grabbed the cock on its out-cycle, and pulled it down into her mouth. It tasted strongly of Ophelia. She knew the taste well enough. The warm liquid fountained into her throat as she tried to push the source of it past the back of her tongue. She had trained to stop gagging and could pour a drink down her as fast as it would fall from the glass. Now she pushed her head onto Salkeld's spending nut, and he had the feeling of being eaten and swallowed.

They stayed in this tableau for minutes, the only movement coming from Rafferty as he off-handedly pushed his cock in and out of the lovely Ophelia's grasping lips. But his glass was empty. He threw his cigar on the fire, gestured Ophelia and Salkeld off the prone body of Roxy, and lay on top of her. He grabbed those long, bottom-heavy tits and banged his cock hard into her. He sucked on the purple nipples and gave her a good, old-fashioned fuck, orthodox position, on the carpet. There was too much imagination going into fucking these days, he thought, as he powered his way to a climax and took delight in noticing that the grunting, gasping Roxy beneath him, with her arms and legs now grappling around him, also appreciated the old ways occasionally. Her teeth were fastened painfully in his ear as his come burst out of him and she went into wet vibrations at exactly the same moment.

After they'd finished off the champagne the girls picked up their clothes, slung them over their shoulders and swaggered out of the door and along the corridor. If they met someone, so what. They were Ones, they were what life today was all about. Salkeld and Rafferty, brief holiday over, dressed more or less and went back to their rooms and so to bed. Salkeld had some tough problems to solve when he got back to his office tomorrow.

No such worries affected Roxy and Ophelia. They showered, dressed again in different outfits, and went back to the bar. There would be no other customers, but there was a barmaid they fancied. Roxy put on a shiny red plastic miniskirt this time, and a thin white lace blouse through which every detail of the colour and shape of her ample breasts was clearly visible. Ophelia tied a brightly patterned silk scarf around her perfect little pair and put on some white silk pyjama-type trousers which fitted closely and left plenty of bare midriff.

They swanned up to the bar, draped themselves on stools and ordered more champagne. The barmaid leaned over to reach Roxy's glass and felt Ophelia's hand cup one of her tits. This barmaid was about thirty-five, a pocket Venus, short, narrow waist, well-rounded hips and big, big tits. She had been a working Two, of course, and had had to do all sorts of things she didn't especially like, and the main thing she didn't like was being used as a sex toy by women. She did it because it was her job. In a sense it still was, because although she was no longer attached to a Pleasurehouse there was no doubting the expectations of any One, male or female, who came to stay at the old inn by the River Esk on the edge of the North Yorkshire moors.

The barmaid finished pouring and resumed her normal stance. Ophelia's hand stayed on the bar, palm up. The index finger crooked and made a couple of small movements. The barmaid understood what was wanted and came, resignedly, around the other side of the bar. She smiled as best she could at Ophelia. The long, slim, white-haired beauty seemed to grow arrogant, even slightly cruel, as she reached out a finger and pushed the barmaid's nipple as if it was a button to start something. Which is what it was.

Roxy got lazily off her stool and stood behind the barmaid. She ran her hands up the woman's thighs, inside her skirt, and reached for the thin material of her panties. The woman winced as Roxy tore them off and threw them on the fire, and then began fingering around her bum hole. Ophelia stood too. She pulled the woman's blouse out of her skirt top, reached up behind and undid her bra clasp. Then she put her hands up the front of the blouse, squeezing the massive knockers as hard as she could.

Roxy's fingers left their intimate exploration and found the blouse. That was ripped off too, and cast aside. The skirt wouldn't tear, and nor would the suspender belt. But the stockings would. What wouldn't rip off was roughly taken off, and the woman, still magnificently shaped even though slightly past her best, stood naked in the bar.

Ophelia whipped off the scarf she was using as a top, and Roxy took off her blouse. The topless women led the naked woman to the chaise longue beside the fire. There they laid her, face down, eyes peeping to see what they intended to do next. Ophelia went to the counter and brought back the glasses and the champagne bottle. While Roxy examined a collection of riding crops displayed on the wall next to a fox's mask, Ophelia filled the glasses and then trickled some champagne onto the rounded, white, exposed arse beneath her. Some went north to the small of the woman's back. Some filtered down through her hairs and into her orifices. They're probably going to lick that out, she thought, but her mind changed on the instant as she felt the first lash of the riding crop slash across both cheeks.

Years of training and experience came to her rescue.

She didn't move or make a sound. Instead she concentrated on her options. If she objected she would be reported and destabilised. If she took it, she would have to act as if she enjoyed it, or hated it, or whatever she could perceive it was these bitches wanted. She felt the stock of the whip under her, urging her to turn over. Then they made her pull her knees up to her chin, so she could still display her arse but she could watch what they were doing.

At the moment they were kissing each other, their tongues visibly roaming inside each other's mouths, their hands on each other's breasts. They parted, gasping, and Ophelia took up the whip. 'What's this?' she said. 'A Peeping Tommette, a voyeuse, looking at me and my friend here while we engage in intimate pastimes. She will have to be punished.' Another painful slash arrived. The woman hadn't quite made up her mind about the role she was expected to play, so simply maintained a look of willing submission.

More champagne, and a little dribbled this time into the barmaid's navel, from where it spilled gently downwards. 'Have you ever seen tits like that?' said Ophelia. 'They are just fantastic. I think they deserve something special, don't you, Roxy?' She went back to bar and took up a bottle of Creme de Menthe. This she poured all over the gigantic tits, then licked a little off so the nipples were clean. 'I shall be drunk at this rate,' Ophelia slurred. 'Mixing my drinks. Very bad.'

'Very naughty,' said Roxy. 'Have to be punished.' But it was the barmaid who got the punishment – three hefty whacks across the thighs. This was beginning to get very painful. The woman desperately hoped they would stop soon, fall over drunk, or something.

'I think I'll have another drink,' said Roxy. 'Here. You. Get your cunt in the air.' The barmaid swivelled round on the chaise and put her legs over the high end and supported her hips with her hands, so she was doing a kind of assisted bicycle stance, legs wide apart. Roxy carefully poured champagne into the woman's vagina as Ophelia held the lips open. Then she bent down and licked some out. 'Oh, fuck this, I'd rather drink you, Pheel.'

'So would I,' said the other. 'Turn over, you. You are not satisfactory. Me and my friend here, we would rather lick each other's arseholes and play with our toys than play with you. You're just not good enough. Give me the whip, Roxy.'

Ophelia gave the barmaid six this time, six huge arcing lashes across the buttocks. The woman could not help whimpering. 'Go on,' muttered Ophelia. 'You can fuck off.' And the pair of elite citizens put their tops back on and lurched upstairs, stopping every so often to give each other drunken, deep-throat kisses and urgent fondlings. By the time they got to the bedroom the drink had so affected them they were too pissed to do anything. They fell on the bed as they were, and slept.

But the angry barmaid wasn't asleep. She put her clothes on hurriedly but very carefully, and went up the back stairs to the attic. There she kept a torch. She flashed a series of long and short flashes up into the dark fastnesses of the moors. There was an answering flash. All would be well. With no one else up and about, the barmaid went wearily to her room to anoint herself with healing ointments and contemplate happily the certain fate of a small, dark, big-titted bitch and a long, white streak of dyed shit.

The barmaid was sound asleep when they came. Five men dressed in black checked the register with a hooded torch. They went to the first room listed. It was empty. The second room had females in it, draped across the bed. Moving with professional speed and precision they gagged the women, then tied wrists and ankles. The girls were both awake now, eyes almost popping out of their sockets as the totally unbelievable happened. They were Ones, for fuck's sake. Nobody could possibly be doing this. But they were. The men hung the women from poles, like dead animals, and carried them downstairs and outside.

'Which is your hoverbubble?' hissed a man. Ophelia shook her head. 'Listen, bitch. Either you tell me which is your hoverbubble, or I slice one of your friend's tits off and make you eat it.' With her eyes Ophelia indicated the vehicle. The man went over, got in and drove it off. It would be found, crashed, miles away, far enough away to make sure there was no connection between the girls' disappearance and the barmaid of the inn.

The four remaining men carried the poles, women slung below, for about ten miles. They were right up in the moors now, among trackless bogs and hidden valleys. There they came to a camp, in darkness. The women were dumped on the ground without any care, covered with blankets and bracken to make sure they didn't freeze to death, and the men went off somewhere to sleep.

In the grey murk of dawn the women were dragged in front of a young man who seemed to be in charge. 'We don't usually take you Ones' he told them. 'Causes too much fuss, usually, so we don't. But occasionally we get a cry for help. Some of you bastards are going too far, and you have to be snatched. We have to let your Committee know that we're still around, and the odd little bit of One-snatching does that. But we need an excuse. We need to know that the Ones we take are especially arrogant shitehouses. Like you.'

Even Ophelia had got the message now, and resisted er natural instinct to tell these ignorant yobs to release er immediately, because didn't they realise who she as? The only tiny chink of hope was her sexuality. Look,' she said. 'When we're cleaned up we're very resentable girls. Couldn't we take a turn with you, you now, be your, your, girls?'

'Oh, you'll be that all right' said the man. 'There are hirty men in this camp. No women, because we're a nobile operations unit. No mixed sexes on ops. The vomen have their units, and we have ours. So it's six veeks since any of these men had a woman. And they're ll going to stick their cocks up every orifice of both of ou before the day is out. And then we've got to move n. We can't take you with us, so we'll have to leave ou.'

'What? Out here? On our own?' Roxy cried.

'Don't worry,' said the man. 'You won't know a ning about it.'

They made some sort of breakfast then, porridge, read and tea with no milk. Roxy and Ophelia, feet still ed, ate little and talked less. This cloudy, cold, miser-ble day might be their last. But there was still hope, so ong as they were alive.

When the men had all finished they strung the girls ack on the poles and plodded another few miles to an ld stone barn. Inside there was hay and straw and a ortoise stove with a metal pipe going up to a hole in the oof for a chimney. They clearly considered themselves fe here, because they lit the stove, sat on the bales, lit garettes, and looked very hard at the girls.

The top man cut their bonds. They stood, trying to nafe some circulation back into their wrists and ank-s. A bucket of water was heated on top of the stove, id the man with the big red beard produced some soap

out of his pack. 'Here,' he said. 'You told us you wer
presentable when you were cleaned up. Well, clean up.
Ophelia looked at Roxy and shrugged. If they wer
going to go down, they would do it with bravado. Thes
dirty, unshaven, ugly outlaws weren't going to mak
cowards out of the cleverest couple of Ones in the whol
of network maintenance.

Ophelia took off her brightly coloured scarf fron
around her smartly peppy little tits and bent to the bow
the water had been poured into. There were murmur
of appreciation as the men saw her tits dangle and swin
sweetly as she rubbed her face and neck. Then sh
stood up and soaped her chest, and handed the soap t
Roxy to do her back. Roxy gave the soap back and too
off her white lace blouse, not so white as it had been
The men already knew what was inside, since th
blouse was hardly opaque, but they still chortled wit
delight when they saw Roxy's dark nipples and heavy
aggressively pointed knockers. Ophelia soaped them
trying her best to look luxuriously sexy, and then slip
ped off her trousers while Roxy did her best taking o
her stockings, suspender belt and red plastic mini.

The girls, naked, soaped each other, and finished b
splashing the water down each other's bodies. The
turned, struck a tart's street-corner pose – they'd neve
seen a street-corner tart but the pose came naturally
and waited. The top man indicated a couple of his band
and they came up to the girls, unbuckling themselves
They threw the girls back onto the straw and wit
absolutely no ceremony stuffed their smelly, smokin
cocks unerringly into the waiting quims.

The next hour was a maelstrom of men, sweating
hairy, unwashed men, stuffing cocks into holes, some
times three at a time. Occasionally a man woul
demand a girl to himself, and would take reasonabl

216

care to fuck her properly and with some respect to her person. These were the men the girls asked about their future. Were they really going to be killed? They got yes, no, and don't know. If yes, how and when? Don't know. If no, what else would they do? Don't know.

The girls were draped over hay bales and poked from behind. They were made to kneel down and suck prick after prick. They had orthodox sex in every position, and unorthodox sex likewise. By the time they'd got through to number 30, numbers one and two were ready to go again, and so most of the day passed before the men had had enough and it was time to move on.

Ophelia was still more or less compos mentis. Her legs were running with spunk. She felt sick from the amount she'd swallowed, but she was still hanging in there. Roxy was less good. As a result, some of the men had left her alone and Ophelia had had to do some double duty.

Ophelia held Roxy up with her right arm round her as they were made to kneel in front of the top man. Ophelia looked him smack in the eye as he spoke. Roxy couldn't. Her head hung down. She was far away. 'In some ways you don't deserve all this punishment. You've been brought up in the system. You've always been a One. Probably, being young women, you've never been in the cities to see how the Threes live. So why should you question the way of life, where you have everything, and the Threes have everything except freedom?

'Around you is a gang of filthy rapists. They have treated you like inanimate baggage, with little or no respect for you as people. Rather like you've always treated the Twos, and exactly like you treated a certain ex-Two last night. But this gang of filthy rapists isn't justifying its behaviour simply by tit for tat for your

217

being cruel to a fat old tart. These are dedicated men. They are mostly Threes, but some are Twos and we even have a couple of Ones. I myself am unique in this organisation. I am the only member to have been both a One and a Two. I was in agricultural robotics, then I trained as a Two and was taken by the underground in City HX. I joined up quite happily. It's a hard life. You now have the opportunity to join us. You have behaved nobly and strongly. Your friend, unfortunately, has not made the grade. She is unreliable, physically. If she can't stand being fucked fifty times she certainly will not be able to stand eight weeks of winter weather and no shelter, committing acts of violence with, most people admit, no prospect of ever doing anything else, and every likelihood of not doing that for long before you are caught. So what's it to be? Us? On your own? Or what?'

'I don't understand your cause,' replied Ophelia quietly. 'And I don't see how you can expect me to convert so instantly to it. You have hurt me a lot, and my friend more. Yes, we were beastly to that woman last night. But it's not until now that I've ever thought of the possibility that anyone other than the Ones should have any rights. We were brought up to believe that we had achieved civilisation, that we were the elite because we worked, and that everyone else was a parasite. I never had cause to think that the parasites might not like it.'

'I thought you said you didn't understand our cause,' said the top man, a young, tough looking type with scruffy blond hair. 'You seem to understand it perfectly. Now all I need is a sign of your commitment. Take this knife. It is now time to move on. We have some proper clothes you can wear, and we're not long before we must head back to base, so you'll have a short dose of the life to start with. We'll leave you the clothes and we'll go outside. I will return alone in ten minutes. I think you know what you have to do.'

The men went outside. Ophelia carried the unconscious Roxy to the stove where there was still some hot water, and bathed her limbs as best she could. The poor girl was in a bad way, but at least she looked a little better cleaned up. Ophelia laid her friend on her back, arms by her sides. She covered her body with some hay, and looked at the knife. She had no experience of this, but she knew the basics of human biology. With care she placed the point of the knife against the jugular vein of her friend Roxy, and sliced sharply in. The blood ran immediately, large amounts of it, into the hay. Roxy died without knowing a thing. And when Brough came back into the barn, he found Ophelia dead beside her, the knife thrust up from her breastbone into her heart.

[10]

It had taken the prospect of his violent end to make Angela realise that she had strong personal feelings for Lance Brough. Something similar was happening to Ann Richmond. Salkeld, clearly under strain, called to see her at Pleasurehouse 13 and told her that Brough had disappeared in City HX, along with the young female Two he'd been with. It was probable that they'd been killed. The bodies had not been found, but bloodstained clothing had. All the signs pointed to a well-known psychopath as the murderer (Salkeld didn't tell Ann that it was the same psychopath who had burnt his arse with cigarettes all those years ago.)

The story didn't end there. It was possible that there had then been an outbreak of despondency or good citizenship, because the body of the psychopath in question had been found swinging from a lamp-post. Either it was suicide by a depressed killer, or some socially minded self-appointed justice had decided it was time the murders stopped. Things still weren't right in HX though, no question about that. There wasn't very much you could pin down, describe and measure, but things were not right.

Ann had been thinking, and now she had decided. 'Salkeld,' she said. 'I want to go to HX.'

'Don't be ridiculous, Ann. You haven't finished your job here yet. You might have stopped all the moaning and groaning from the Ones, but that's down to your own efforts in entertaining them. If you were to leave, we'd be back where we were – only worse, because now they've come to expect you. No, I want to know what's wrong here. Somebody else can risk their neck in HX.'

'Darling Salkeld, my own very favourite little Twozec. You let your nice friend Ann go for her holidays on the palm-fringed shores of lovely City HX, and Ann will show you her exceptional gratitude. Hm?'

'Ann, look, please, it isn't possible.'

Ann undid a couple of buttons at her neck and fiddled with the waistband of Salkeld's robot-made suit trousers. 'What, not even for your best friend Ann? Who you got into all this in the first place?' The tip of Ann's tongue curled up and touched the outside of her top lip.

'I've told you, it's just not possible,' said a less decisive Salkeld. 'Officially you're still a Onewife. On secondment. How on earth could I explain that you've decided to go for a swim in pigswill instead of producing top-flight theatre and other types of circus?'

Ann walked away, sat down, did up her buttons and crossed her legs, making sure Salkeld got a good glimpse of thigh as she did so. 'Salkeld. I want to go home. I want to go back to my husband.'

'What? You can't do that.'

'Just watch me. Just you watch me.'

And he did. He watched her stroll across to him and put her arm round his neck. She kissed him, and the kiss promised him much. He watched her walk away slightly, turn her back, and slip off her clothes. He watched her turn, come to him, look glintingly and twinklingly in his eyes, and put her hand on his cock which had already stirred itself. She massaged it. She put her hand inside his suit trousers and got it out. She rubbed the end of it against her furry pussy, then knel down and licked and kissed it. She lay on the carpet. Salkeld quickly threw his clothes off and got down beside her. Once more she kissed him, and put all the promises of delights ever made by woman to man in that kiss. She brought her knees up, took hold of Salkeld's great, hard, curved scimitar and guided him in. Slowly at first, then more uptempo, Salkeld plunged and back, plunged and back. Ann was making encouraging breathy noises down her nose. Her legs wrapped around him, her heels pulled him in harder. She was whimpering now, asking him for more. He responded, faster, deeper, and felt her vagina in spasm as she came. Five or six more thrusts and he was there too, gasping and panting.

They lay together for a while on the floor. Then she said 'So what is it, Salkeld? Domestic bliss with little Arthur, or high excitement in HX? Give the wrong answer and you'll never again do what you've just done.' Salkeld gave the right answer which, it was to turn out, also meant never again.

'If you really want to go to HX, I suppose I'd better let you. But you can't go as a Two. You'll have to go as a destabilised Two and live as a Three. That way you'll be more accepted. And provided your destabilisation story sounds solid, you might find a way into whatever's causing the rumblings up there.'

The next night Ann was the only passenger on the ATV which arrived at the Destabilisation Gate outside HX. As was customary, the force field was switched off around the gate and a derisory fanfare was blared out, a recording made by six comic trombone players. Of course, none of the Threes ever bothered to watch. Originally it had been a disgrace to be destabilised and, like the public hangings of old, the vile mob sometimes turned up to watch the victim wriggle even though they knew nothing of his crime and his relative innocence or guilt.

Here in City HX, and the other cities, the concept of disgrace had disappeared beneath a plethora of disgracefulness, and so nowadays the unfortunate destabilised person was thrust without a word or a heckle into the City, with an address to go to and a future of plenty of everything assured. For most, though, it meant that their lives no longer had the slightest meaning. If the Threes thought nothing of a Destab, the Destab thought nothing of the Threes and felt his new plummet in status very keenly. Suicide was common among those destabilised. Some, who had been Threes before they became Twos, managed to readjust to the old life, but very few of those who had always before been outside the City could ever get used to the complete lack of direction, of responsibility, of anything except continuous consumption.

Salkeld didn't know much about this. Ann didn't either. Why should they? Destabilised people were non-people as far as anyone outside the Cities was concerned. Nobody ever kept track of Destabs at all. Not that the people in the cities were that bothered either. The domestic robots were programmed to get rid of bodies in the waste disposal system and then notify the accommodation programme at the computer centre when the apartment was ready for re-occupation. So no city dweller had any cause to get involved in Destab suicides, which almost invariably happened soon after they'd arrived and before they'd got to know the neighbours in any case.

Ann had decided to lay low for a few days, and then to start frequenting places well away from her apartment. Her sudden appearance in these haunts could be explained by saying she was fed up with the spots near

224

where she lived. She could let it drop that she had been a destabilised Two, ages ago, if she was asked by some perceptive slob who noticed that she was different looking from the average Three. And then, having got to know that area well, she had some background to talk about when she started going out nearer her home.

Things went well at first. Nobody in her street thought anything of a stranger occasionally being seen there. She hardly saw her neighbours, and she took care not to let them see her if it could be avoided. All her supplies were ordered via the network and delivered by the pig system, the torpedo-shaped programmed containers which whizzed constantly around inside hidden pipes, dropping off food and whatever else anybody requested. There was no need for her to go out in the neighbourhood – but the more time she spent sitting in her apartment, the less was getting done about finding Brough.

If he was alive and well, she reasoned, he would surely be known wherever young women congregated. Her first resolve, therefore, was to drag the discos. It was not altogether a pleasurable experience. She remembered disco dancing from her own youth, in the glittering clubs frequented temporarily by the temporarily famous. It had always seemed a mindless pursuit to her, a relentless, solo act of endless repetition to music which formed an infinitely long series of identical pieces. But, she was good at it, naturally, and she liked men and the bright lights, so she went discoing.

She wasn't quite so keen on that kind of bright light any more, but she still liked beautiful young men and, she was glad to find, she wasn't the only lady of a certain age lurking around the young folks' top spots in City HX. It was easy for her to sit in the background with a drink and watch the dancefloor, occasionally having a

225

flutter in her nervous system as a chunky blond Brough lookalike passed briefly in front of her.

Nothing very much had changed. Girls danced together. Men watched. There was a difference, however. When a pick-up had been accomplished and the requisite length of time had been spent staring into space while gently swivelling a few joints to the mind-screaming, boringly micro-exact rhythm of computer-composed 'music', the pair didn't do what they'd done in Ann's day. Your place or mine. Like to come back for coffee. Etchings, ha ha. Really interesting collection of Indian erotica I'd like to show you. No, these young people of City HX just went to a couch in the shadows and fucked right there. So Ann was never short of something to look at. She scanned the dance floor and bar for Brough's hair, face, eyes, walk, stance. And she scanned the shadowy couches for a hint of his well-remembered naked body.

Some of the more gorgeous and sensible young men there liked to take the occasional spin among the older ladies. For a start they were less likely to be totally spaced out than the young girls, and they were more experienced, and they wanted it more so they put more into it. Ann was not short of would-be gigolos. There were several different approaches, varying from a kind of nephew-to-maiden-aunt politeness to an ill-mannered, want-it-or-not-you-bitch arrogance whose most abrupt exponent had come up to Ann's table, flopped his dick out, dipped it in her gin and tonic, and flipped the drops at her saying 'If you treat this thing right it'll spray come all over your fucking ugly face'. Ann's response had been to get up as if willing and gently grasp the boy's prick in her left hand while delivering a swinging right uppercut to his testicles. He had gone outside to throw up.

She would stay in a particular club for all the peak hours – say, eleven until three – rather than move around. These places were open almost all the time, closing only for a flush-out and clean by the robots, and people were constantly arriving and leaving, so Ann thought it best to stay put rather than disco-crawl. She might see three or four hundred different young men on any night, and a handful might look a bit like Brough, and occasionally a back view or a long-distance glimpse would set her racing, but always to be let down.

She would try to strike up conversations with some of the girls, thinking they might know Brough, but it was hopeless. They were all morons, the so-called music was too loud, and they obviously thought that a woman like Ann, old enough to be their mother, in their night club was either a fucking cheek you old tart, or the most hilarious thing since Tamsin was so pissed that, when she felt sick while she was being screwed on the dining room table by her mother's boyfriend, she could only think to vomit backwards over her shoulder. Her mother had been furious, making a mess like that on the carpet. Tasmin should know better at sixteen years old.

So usually Ann just looked, and turned away her young admirers, nicely or peremptorily depending on their behaviour. Then one night a young lad came up to her and said 'Hello. You're looking for someone, aren't you?' He seemed pleasant, so Ann looked around her and said she thought that probably all the women sitting, looking, waiting, were just like her. No, the boy didn't mean that. He'd seen her in here and other discos, and she had looked sad and searching, rather than eager and slightly embarrassed and searching. Like the other women. They just wanted a young body

227

to go to work on them. But he felt Ann wasn't after that, was she?

'No, I'm not. I am looking for someone. A particular someone. I don't want to tell you why, but it's important to both him and me that I find him. He's about your height, a bit older, about two years older than you I should say, and he's got blond hair, generally short and untidy, and a snub nose, a few freckles, blue eyes, and he's well built, a bit broader than you.'

'Sounds like Steve McQueen,' said the young man.

'How come you've heard of him?' asked Ann, astounded. 'He was history before I was born, which was, I might say, at least a day or several before you were.'

'I'm into the old films,' he explained. 'They're all there, on the network. Most of the people in HX just want the standard stuff, you know, a minute of scene-setting than it's get your knickers down and stuff this wherever you feel like it. I think that's just boring. So I watch the movies from before the Change. And I came across this one called *The Cincinatti Kid*. So I asked for more of this, and got *Butch Cassidy and the Sundance Kid*. And so on. All terrific. Trouble is, I can't get anybody to watch with me. If five minutes go by and there's no great steaming cock on the screen being sucked by six different women, everybody's bored and wants to go down the pub.'

'I'll watch with you,' said Ann, attracted by this tasteful (and tasty!) boy with the lonely passion for the olden days. 'I'll watch Steve McQueen. Or something different. Do you like musicals?'

'Well, I like music,' he replied.

'Ever heard of a man called Gene Kelly?' asked Ann. 'No? So you've got a great treat in store. Take me home, young man, and together we'll watch *Singing in the Rain*.'

And so they did. When it finished, it was very late. The lad said Ann could stay if she liked. 'I mean, you know, no obligation sort of. Just stay. In the spare room. And then tomorrow we could watch *Bullitt*.'

Ann smiled, went into the spare room, closed the door, and walked up to the communication screen. She asked the network for an instant response. She wanted a negligée, colour black, size etc. By the time she had removed and folded all her clothes and showered, the pig had arrived and unloaded her small parcel. She put on the low-necked nightgown of flimsy black silk and over it a loose-fitting item of the same diaphanous material, tied with a ribbon under her bust. In the mirror she thought she looked like the Empress Josephine waiting for Napoleon. Mind, she was a dirty bitch. She was supposed to have liked him unwashed and smelling of a soldier's campaign. She hoped her young man smelled only of some sharp, keen body lotion – at least, until they got going.

She opened the door quietly. He wasn't there in the living room. Must have gone to bed. His door also revealed nobody, but the sound of water told her where he was. She put the light out in the bedroom and lounged in the open doorway, the lights from the living room behind her. She leaned an arm on the doorjamb, and waited.

The door to the bathroom opened and the boy's hand automatically put out the light behind him. Nothing else automatic happened after that. He stopped, bomb-shelled, by the glamorous silhouette in front of him. A luxurious, generous body was clearly outlined, surrounded by a wisp of something less substantial. Ann allowed him a lingering glimpse before switching on the bedroom light. Now he saw an even more glamorous sight, a woman in the prime of her life dressed in the very finest and most seductive garments possible. She slinked from the door towards him. He dropped his towel, his fingers unable to do anything so common-place as hold on to it. She came up to him, pressed her utterly fantastic body gently against his, took his face in both hands, bent his head down to hers and kissed him. He felt her tongue in his mouth. She felt his prick rising against her stomach.

She led him to the bed and pushed him gently onto his back. Keeping her eyes fixed on his, her fingers went to the ribbon bow underneath her glorious tits. A tiny pull and it was undone. A small shrug and the black silk of the first garment swished to the floor. She walked towards the boy, lying on the bed, arms by his sides, cock standing in a stiff arch bridged from scrotum root almost to belly button. The voluminous silk of the nightgown moved easily over her swaying hips. A double convex expanse of bosom peeped anxiously above the swooping neckline as if trying to get out. She threw a leg across him. She felt for his prick and guided it in, made sure her knees were pinioning his arms, then lifted up the nightdress and spread it over his head.

He was inside a translucent black tent. It was full of the sweet, perfumed aroma of a newly washed body, and the scent of new silk, and in the background the ancient, primitive smells whose names the human race has forgotten but whose meaning every lovemaker knows. He could see, above him, the southern hemis-pheres of a giant pair of breasts with nipples jutting out, a pendulous, swinging, night-time cliff overhang which he was anxious to reach for. Looking down with his chin on his chest he could see a rounded tummy, shaped in shadow and moving up and down and around and around as Ann bumped and ground her way home. There was a darker shadow indicating a patch of hair, and an indistinctly outlined shaft of hardened flesh being alternately revealed and hidden as this miraculous woman raised and lowered herself onto it.

He was desperate to get a hand on those deeply impressive globes with their erect pinnacles looking so tantalising, but he couldn't shift his arms. He wanted to put his hands around the bottom he couldn't see, and feel the secret crevices of her crucial juncture. She kept him prisoner for long enough, until she could tell by his whimpering and her own tidal surge that the big moment was almost here. In a single, magnificent movement she swept the nightgown over her head and away. She shifted her knees and bent down towards him, her hands behind the back of his head, her elbows on the bed. As she explored every nook and cranny of his mouth with her tongue, his hands grasped her bosom, then grappled her arse cheeks sticking up towards the ceiling, then went back to the mighty melons.

He pushed upwards, further into her as she wriggled and jumped, and as she suddenly leaned her head back, eyes closed, lips apart with gasps and little shouts, he felt his own irresistible flush sweep up his stem and out into her twitching, gripping, love-juice-flowing quim. Ann fell flat out on top of him. He cuddled her, content to rest surrounded by this warm, curved, pneumatic personification of sexual bounty.

When they woke it was dawn. He took a bottle of champagne and some orange juice from the cooler while she requested *42nd Street* on the network. They sat on the couch, he in a green and black striped towelling dressing gown, she in her black silk. They sipped the fizz and, in the quiet moments of the film, Ann sounded a few small notes about her past life. The young man came to the conclusion that here was someone who yearned for the old ways, before the Change, someone who might play a useful part in the cause he was so fond of. But he had to be cautious. Nobody in the movement was allowed to make any kind of new contact without first consulting his colleagues and having the potential member checked out by at least two others. He would definitely mention her at the next meeting of his cell. Not only would she be the oldest recruit to the group, he thought, she would have the biggest tits, too. Good thing for the revolution, big tits. Nothing is too big for the uprising classes.

He was uprising too, just at that moment, because at the end of the film, Ann's hand had slid inside his dressing gown and was cradling his balls. Her green eyes were looking with amused intent straight into his. She slipped off the couch onto the floor and knelt in front of him. She parted his gown and searched for his hardening cock with her lips. He sat up, and put a hand down each side of her open neckline and grasped the luscious fruits. As he played with these mammary miracles, squeezing them, teasing out the nipples, feeling their wondrous weight, she took his prick in her hand and slowly, methodically, licked every part of its surface until the entire machine was glistening with her saliva.

She admired her work for a moment, then gobbled it up. He sat there, tits in hand, a mass of deep red hair between his thighs as her head bobbed up and down. It felt as if she was taking the complete length into her mouth, and the movements of her tongue and cheeks and the sucking and the swallowing were the most sensational thing he had ever felt. Very soon he was digging his heels into the carpet as he felt the spunk rise. As the first gush swept into her throat she just kept on sucking and swallowing, and the next spurt and the next were even more brilliant. Eventually he stopped spurting and she stopped sucking. It had been, quite simply, the best orgasm he had ever had. He looked at her in admiring gratitude.

'A lost art,' she said. 'I had to learn how to do it well, or I didn't get any work.'

'What do you mean?' asked the boy.

'In the old days, when I was a young hoofer trying to make my way, along with dozens of other good-looking girls with big knockers and wavy bottoms, the men who ran theatres and agencies expected you to help them make their minds up on such matters as casting. You could do that by impressing them with a mazy tap routine, or with the height and precision of your kicks, or you could get on your knees, whip their cocks out of their trousers and suck for your life. She who sucketh the best, lo, so shall work also be given unto her.'

'Well, thank you to the corrupt old system,' toasted the lad in orange juice and champagne. 'And I'd been told it was all bad.'

'Oh no,' said Ann, getting up and nestling in beside him on the couch. 'It had its good points. Not the least of which was a saying. You scratch my back, and I'll scratch yours. So come on, my cocky young friend. Get busy!'

He understood what was required. He slid onto his knees as they reversed the positions of their previous encounter. She pulled her nightdress up to her waist and wriggled herself forward until her bottom was right on the edge of the couch. His head went in, and she felt his tongue, delicately at first and then strongly and more confidently, scouring her sweet and sour sauce and licking her lips. She shuddered as he found her

233

little sapling, and she grabbed the back of his head in both hands and pulled him in hard. Her legs went over his shoulders as she collapsed back onto the couch. Still he kept in contact, licking eagerly and energetically as she began moaning. She felt herself approaching the climax and she banged her feet in the middle of his back as she gathered speed and he desperately kept up the lunging of his tongue. Bang, bang, bang went her heels. 'Oh, oh, oh,' she cried, and he was buried in a surging, slippery, writhing, leaping pocket of joy with his hair held more firmly than any horse's mane ever was. With a final shout she came, and his tongue was stilled, and she held him there until all the waves of sensation had receded.

Later, as she walked along the street to her apartment, she realised she didn't even know his name.

Ann's life had settled quite quickly into a routine. Go round the discos, go round the pubs, occasionally have a frolic with a man she would pick up. She wasn't getting any nearer finding Brough, but what else could she do? She could go on like this for months, and probably would have done, month after month in this debauched and indolent city. But there were some people here who didn't maintain a constant stupor from drink, drugs and sexual overindulgence. These people noticed things, and Ann had been noticed. Even before her encounter with the young Steve McQueen fan she had been spotted, and when he reported her as a potential member of the underground, it wasn't long before Ann made unwitting contact with the very organisation which knew all about Brough's current whereabouts.

They didn't tell Ann that he'd proved himself in a very short time to be every bit as good a guerrilla as he

234

had been a Twostudent. They didn't tell her that he was already famous throughout the movement.

In fact, they didn't tell Ann anything. Two men and a girl were deputed to get to know Ann and find out what she was doing in HX. They followed her from her apartment into a restaurant, where robots served her with a plain grilled Dover sole fresh from the robot-run fish farm, and a half bottle of Chablis made from grapes grown in the computer-managed ecosystem established where part of Kent used to be, where the soil and climate of any part of the world could be simulated.

Her meal finished, Ann began her usual round of the pubs. She was always willing to talk, and it was easy for the trio of rebel investigators to get her into conversation. The wine flowed and Ann got quite chatty. She told them she'd once been a dancer, that she had worked abroad before the Change, that she'd been a Two for a while but had got into trouble. 'Too much pop,' she said. 'Couldn't stand all the servility, you see. Had to do everything those bastards wanted. No freedom. The whole world arranged to suit the Ones. Don't give a fuck for anyone but themselves. I couldn't stand it, as I say, so I went on the pop. And the next thing I knew, I was a Destab. Still, it isn't so bad. Nothing to do, but no bastard Ones telling you what to do, either.'

While she was in the ladies' lavatory, the trio agreed they didn't believe her. Not entirely. She might be telling the truth, and she sounded as if she was, but the whole thing was too unlikely. On the other hand . . . so they decided they had to keep going. They had to know more. The blond-haired man, who was about twenty-two, handsome in a raffish sort of way but with a look behind his eye that told you there was something else, somewhere else, that was more important than this particular moment – he invited the others back to his apartment. The four of them set off, having picked up a couple of bottles from the robo-vend.

It was a large, third-floor flat with a balcony and a ten-metre sitting room. The blond man and his companions cleared the floor of furniture, programmed the network for music from the old dance bands, and demanded dancing lessons. They foxtrotted, they waltzed, they quickstepped, they cha-cha'd. Then a new sound came out of the system, a sultry, subtle sound redolent with dark passion and hot nights but also funny. Sex with laughs. 'You just sorta stand there, and just sorta do it,' sang the voice. 'And you know how one step can lead to another.' Ann explained that this dance was called a tango, that the singer was a complete original from the mid-twentieth century called Lena Horne, and requested it again from the network.

Her blond partner soon picked up the raunchy sway and the rhythms like mating calls. Ann didn't object when he leaned down and kissed her on the neck. She responded by pushing her pelvic bone up against his awakening monster. He undid a couple of buttons and a catch, and freed her bountiful bosoms into the dimmed light of the room. He kissed there also, and fondled them in wonderment, and sighed as she reached inside his clothes and found something hot and hard. As Miss Horne sang her new-fangled tango, an old-fashioned notion made Blondy push Ann backwards towards the couch. She reclined, cheekbone in palm, elbow on couch arm, as he buried his head in the most luxurious pair he had ever seen. She raised her hips to allow him to remove the rest of her clothes, and took a vigorous cock with a terrific curve in it in her hand as he then knelt before her. She sat up and placed the nut of it between her lips. She swept her tongue around its rim, she tickled the secret little crevice, she licked at the focal point of his nervous system.

She felt his fingers inside her, searching and finding, massaging her into a warm, damp readiness. He slid out of her mouth, bent briefly to kiss her tits and then her quim, then mounted. Not only was his prick very curved; it was exceptionally long too, and she felt an unusual sensation as this great sickle cut a swathe in her private Elysian fields. Then she felt another pair of hands on her nipples. She opened her eyes to see the girl, naked now, a trim, willowy little thing with huge brown eyes and a tiny, uptilted nose. This Miss was massaging the breasts of Madame while the other young sir, a bulky individual with hair all over his chest, was giving her everything he had from behind.

Intentionally or no, the men hit a sympathetic rhythm as the music changed to a big-band sound. 'This,' Ann whispered, 'is called "In the Mood", would you believe?' As the Glen Miller Orchestra swung into it, the blond and the hairy chest swung too. Madame and Mam'selle were umphing and whimpering, and moving to meet their men, Ann shunting forwards and the girl pushing backwards. The girl's gropes on Ann's tits got into time as well, and now all four of them were dancing in the most fundamental way. As his power rose in him the blond could no longer keep to the regular step. He began to speed up, and Ann felt herself slipping into a wine-assisted oblivion of sensation. The girl was shouting 'now, yes, now, yes, yes, yes,' and gripping Ann's tits tighter and tighter. The hairy chest's thighs were slapping against the girl's arse cheeks as he went for goal, and the men shot as the girl shouted and cheered and halloo'd, and Ann went into unconsciousness.

They'd made coffee when Ann came round. Still

237

undressed, they passed cups and cream and chatted about dancing and the stage and what the world was like before the Change. Ann became loquacious. The wine (undoctored) and the coffee (doctored) loosened her tongue, and she got a little mixed up between shows she had been in as a chorus hoofer and a show with which she had been more recently associated. It wasn't apparent to her, but the others easily picked up that she had been a Two until recently and quite a well-connected Two at that. She let nothing else slip, and started feeling randy again at the sight of this pair of well-made young men. They reminded her of another young man, whom perhaps she might not see again.

Her companions were concerned to see her eyes fill with tears. Assuming she was having regrets for her life as a Two they said she needn't worry about what's gone before. This was her new life now. And she forgot to correct them, forgot to tell them that she'd been a Destab for years, and so they knew for certain. She was feeling maudlin, no mistake, and she needed comforting. She sighed with gratitude as the little dark girl leaned over her ample body and breathly kissed her in a line from throat to mons veneris. Ann shifted her position on the couch so the girl could get full access to the crux of the matter, and allow herself to be wafted away on the end of the girl's tongue.

At a signal from Hairy Chest the girl lifted off and he presented his cock to the entrance. The tall blond man had had a long curved one. This new member was thick and short and so hard he could have knocked fence posts in with it. It stretched Ann wide to force its fat way in and his quick, bounding thrusts were tight on her little joystick. He went to work as if he were doing a hundred press-ups in the gym. Ann felt him sweating too, and noticed the tiny droplets forming among the mass of hairs on his body. She wrapped her arms round his bulky mattedness, and linked her feet behind him. The girl meanwhile, standing beside them, had taken his balls in her hand and was fondling them gently as he screwed into Ann. The blond man wanted to join in but couldn't quite think how, until he stood on the couch and put his banana in the girl's mouth.

As Hairy Chest and Ann neared their locked-in climax, the girl let go and concentrated on the cock in hand. Ann and her gorilla were bouncing now, juddering and groaning, and the girl wanted the long curved cock, so she let go with hand and lips and went over to an armchair. She knelt in it, facing the back, with her head on an arm looking back at Blondy and her arse in the air looking like home. The blond man stepped down from the couch, took a few strides and his prick in his hand, and stuck it straight in at the small, puckered option. If the girl had been loud before when Hairy Chest had been rogering her quim, she went totally berserk now the long, curved tool was sliding in and up her bumhole. 'Oh, oh, oh, oh, yes, yes, yes, yes, more, more, harder, harder!' She began making whooping noises, and burbling noises. She lifted her head and with both hands firmly grasped the back of the chair. This meant her rear was a bit lower, and the man had more difficulty, but his semi-circular thrusts went deeper. The girl grappled with the chair back like a lover, and whooped and whee'd and shouted 'oh yes, oh yes, oh yes', and the man thrust harder and faster until he spilled with a final, deepest-of-all thrust which had the girl almost levitating off the chair as she cried out for joy. As the pair of them subsided, and Ann and Hairy Chest unravelled themselves, Ann began to wonder what on earth she was doing here, having a wild party with people far younger than her, and whom she'd only met that night. As the talking drug in the coffee wore off she became quite sniffy and puritanical just like her mother had been. She put on her clothes, said a polite goodnight, and left.

They were waiting for her at her apartment. Four men, young, well mannered, with hard eyes, who asked her if she would mind if they came in for a while. Ann did mind, but they came in anyway. They asked her name, sat down around her, and told her they thought she was a spy.

'Please don't take this personally,' said the main man. 'But I have to tell you that our security here is very important to us. If there is a threat, we have to snuff it out. That's what we are. We are the organisation's snuffers.'

'Organisation? What organisation?' asked Ann, trying desperately to keep the tremble out of her voice.

'You know that already. The revolution. All we want to know is why you are here in HX. If you tell us, we won't kill you. If you do not tell us, we won't torture you or make you suffer a long slow death. We shall simply hang you from the lamp post like we did Pam the Pram, and break your neck. Quick, simple, no mess. We won't know why you came, but that will matter rather less if you're not alive to complete your mission. You have precisely five minutes to tell us.'

They looked at her for about three of those minutes, then the most innocent, nice-looking member of the gang went to a holdall he'd been carrying and took out some thin rope. He began tying it into a slip knot. Ann rapidly concluded that Salkeld and his games were not worth all of this, and told the men everything. She trusted them. She believed they wouldn't now kill her, and she was right. They listened without betraying any motion, foreknowledge or acquaintance with any of what she said. When she'd finished, they told her they were satisfied. She was to wait here, in her apartment, until she was called for. Someone would come when it was time, and she would be taken out of the city and on to another place. She was not to be afraid. Everything would be all right. The person would come tomorrow, or possibly the next day, and she was to have a few things ready to be packed for a journey.

Two nights later a young boy came round, a lad of about thirteen or fourteen. He had a rucksack with him and some clothes. 'You're to put these on,' he said, laying out some thermal underwear, trousers, cotton shirt, three thin sweaters, thick socks, and waterproof top clothes.

'Am I going hiking?' Ann asked. 'You could say that,' replied the boy. 'Anyway, you've got to hurry up.'

OK, my young friend, I'll show you, thought Ann. There and then, in front of him, she stripped to the skin and picked up the underwear. 'What are you goggling at?' she asked him.

'I'm sorry,' said the boy. 'It's just that I've never . . . er . . .'

'Never seen such a big pair of tits before?' said Ann, unkindly, and then felt sorry for the boy. He was obviously a brave lad, and well behaved. She should be nicer to him. 'Here,' she said in a softer voice. She took his hands and put them on her breasts. 'Now, what do you think of those?'

'They're very nice,' the boy managed to say.

'Did you say we had to be quick?' asked Ann, archly. The boy nodded.

So she delved into his pants, took out his frantically vibrating cock, sat on the nearest chair and put it between her lips. She felt it from stem to tip with the end of her tongue. She moved her hand up and down the shaft a few times. The boy, wide eyed, was moaning, so she took as much as she could right into her mouth and sucked hard. He came instantly and copiously, and gratefully. He murmured his thanks as Ann wiped her lips and got dressed. She was to put the rain gear in the sack, along with the boots she saw in there, and go out in her ordinary shoes and a normal winter coat. The boy would carry the sack.

They met someone else on a corner. He took Ann on to another corner, where someone else assumed responsibility for her. They went down some stairs into a cellar. A small party was assembled here, six or seven men and a couple of young women. They were all dressed for an outdoor trek. Ann completed her own dressing and took her place in the middle of the line. They walked down dark and damp corridors then came to some black, oily-looking water. It came up to their knees as they splashed along, through ancient brick archways and tunnels then into passageways cut from rock. The roof got lower. At its narrowest the cave forced them to bend double, their faces touching the water, as they struggled on and up. Suddenly they felt air, fresh air, and they were out. They could look back at HX, some way below them now, and they could look forward at nothing but darkness.

The first part of the journey was the most dangerous. They were in lowish country in the Vale of Craven where a lot of Ones had their country homes. There was much creeping along river banks and through woods, and tip-toeing silently past old farmhouses which were now luxurious dachas, and crawling noiselessly through villages like Lothersdale and Malham which were so much more picturesque now that their wentieth-century buildings, the bungalows and the ouncil homes, had all been demolished.

If the first part was dangerous, the second, much onger part of the journey was a nightmare. They would walk by day if the conditions were right for fugitives – which meant the cloud was down and it was slashing with rain and snow and screaming with wind. At this ime of year the conditions were 'right' nearly every day.

They walked by night, too, if there was no moon. It eemed to Ann that they trudged endlessly through the ame ground over and over. They slogged up and up, hen down and down, and through a bog, and through nother bog, and up and up, and across the snow line, nd through another bog. She hadn't realised there were any places in England as cold and miserable and wild as this.

All she could do was keep going, trying to stick close o somebody, trying not to stumble and fall too many imes. Would there ever be baths full of hot water gain? Would there ever be hot food served on plates in room with table and chairs? Would there ever be a bed? Looking back on it much later, all Ann could emember eating was chocolate bars, and soup made rom powder and bog water, warmed up on a solar stove which didn't work properly.

They slept in short spells, shivering, soaked, inside hick plastic bivouac bags laid down wherever they happened to be. Each time they set off it took less and ess time for the wet to penetrate to the skin, for the cold o penetrate to the bones. They'd given her a pair of boots to walk in, but they weren't a good fit and they hadn't been used much, so she may as well have done he journey in ordinary shoes. All the protection the boots gave her feet against rough ground was soon cancelled out by the blisters they caused – and the were no proof against the mire and the sodden peat and the icy running water.

She developed sore patches on the insides of he thighs where her wet trousers rubbed. She had red weals on her shoulders where her pack straps rubbed She had raw flesh exposed on various toes and parts of feet where her boots rubbed. Christ. Everything rubbed. Everything stuck and unstuck, painfully. The sloshing rhythm of walking was mind-numbing at least and eventually, say half an hour after each restart, he body would come to a compromise over the cold out side, the warmth inside and the wet everywhere, and sort of anaesthetic, semi-comatose status would take over. The only bit of her that stayed active was he mind.

She began to replay scenes from her life. She'd hear that when you died your whole life flashed before you Well, if she wasn't actually dying at the moment sh was fucking near it, and may well be going through al this agony just to get to it. So she thought of the ol days, of Paris, Vienna, Hamburg. Dancing. The lights the music, the fantastic costumes. And now look at her And the parties. Those glamorous nights. Those enor mous beds with silk sheets and hard-muscled youn men with eager cocks that could keep going all night Beds. Huh.

That episode with the agent, in his office. He'd filmed it, the bastard. He always took great delight in showing that film when he had friends round to dinner It was the first time she'd ever sold herself like that, bu she'd never regretted it. What was a fuck, anyway? A cock-suck a day keeps the bank manager away. Ban manager. No such thing now. And there was that tim she'd had no money to pay her troupe and she'd had to go and see the bank manager. Poor little man. Probably hadn't had any kind of fuck for a year, much less the kind I gave him. Christ. There was spunk everywhere. It was even in my hair, I noticed, when I got home.

Wonder what happened to lover boy Brough. Poor lamb. I did like him. Maybe even loved him a little. I certainly loved his red hot prick in my belly. And up my arse. Did I smile then? Better be careful. They might think I'm enjoying myself. And then there was Salkeld. Putting his hand up my thighs when I was dusting the spiders. Didn't I catch him, though, with my foot when I spun round? I must try that again. Maybe I could be a kung fu expert or something. I wonder if they want kung fu experts in the revolution? And Rafferty. He was OK. Not quite my scene. And that boy in the city who liked the old movies. I liked him, too. His hands felt nice. My tits liked his hands. Oh fucking hell, what's happening now?

It was a soup stop. They sat, in the rain, hands quiveringly cupped around a plastic mug of nameless fluid, thick with lumps, but kind of hot and sort of palatable. Better than nothing. This was hard, hard work. They kept to the highest points, to the most remote parts where no warm-blooded creature would willingly go at this season. North they went, over Great Shunner Fell and High Seat, then west over the Howgill Fells, more northerly again to make Hart Crag and Seat Sandal, then west to their destination, a small, hidden valley somewhere in the isolated wilderness bounded by four of the tallest peaks of the Lake District – Glaramara, Great Gable, Bow Fell and Scafell. Up there nobody, not even the Romans, had ever bothered to try and build a road.

In the summer, of course, there had been Ones who came here for the great outdoors, who walked and climbed. But there had been a series of accidents and disappearances. Wild-eyed ramblers returned with stories of how the rest of their party had been dragged off by mountain men and how the sole survivor had made a miraculous escape to tell the tale. By the end of the season that part of the Lake District had been closed 'for ecological restoration' while the Amenities Committee chewed its nails wondering how to wage war on a group of dedicated bandits who officially didn't exist.

But this wasn't summer. No larks were singing now. No eagles floated in spirals above, no grouse exploded with a crackle from beneath your feet. This was winter, wet and cold, and all that exploded beneath Ann's feet was a mess of blood and broken skin. Her shoulders were agony from the straps of the backpack. Her ankle, which she'd turned coming down Mallerstang Edge about three million years ago, had overcome the lead and opium treatment her captors had given it and was now back to full elephant size. But she had made it. They hadn't had to leave her like they said they might. She had kept with them, bog for bog, peak for peak, and she'd lost five or six kilos of weight doing it. She hadn't been this slim since her dancing days. Quite nice really. Makes the old tits stand out. Almost worthwhile doing that walk.

They went through half a dozen checkpoints between crossing the infant Derwent and arriving at the collection of turf-roofed single-storey shacks which made up the headquarters of the revolution. Although the sentries were armed with old-fashioned weapons which fired gunpowder-powered bullets, Ann was sure that no small party of enemy could ever get up here alive, and a big party would be spotted miles away, giving everyone time to disappear.

She was shown into a shack which had ten beds in it.

There was a huge metal dish in the room (Ann had never seen a tin bath before) which a man filled with hot water. He gave her some soap and told her to get in. He was polite enough not to stay to watch. As she climbed in she wondered briefly if it was possible for feet to catch fire under water, but the restorative powers of bathing worked well enough to make her feel halfway human again. She had no clean clothes, so she put on what she'd just taken off, having dried everything on the iron stove which stood in the centre of the room. She didn't know what to do next, so she lay down on a bed.

She slept for fourteen hours. A man woke her up with a hot drink. He was accompanied by a young woman who was obviously his superior, who eyed Ann with more interest, she thought, than an average prisoner might have deserved.

'My name is Angela,' said the girl. 'I am the staff officer in charge of prisoners and the camp itself. However, I don't make the decisions about what should happen to prisoners. Whichever of the field commanders happens to be here at the time – they do that. There's a field commander in now. I'll take you to him. Do not be surprised by his youth, or mine for that matter. This is a young person's game, but then guerrilla warfare always was.'

Ann followed Angela. That name rang a bell. Angela. She'd seen the face before, but it had been on a screen, not in the flesh. By the time they'd walked across a few metres of grassed passageway, roofed with camouflage netting, heather and bracken, she'd remembered. The young female Two who had disappeared in HX. So she wasn't quite as astounded as she might have been when she walked in to a hut to meet the field commander and saw that it was her ex-lover boy, Lancelot Brough.

EPILOGUE

Everyone else might be fucking themselves silly as per normal on a Tuesday, but there was a nasty flashing spot of trouble on Twozec Salkeld's screen.

'What the bloody hell's the matter now?' he shouted.

'During a recent raid on North West Region Distribution Centre,' answered the screen, evenly, 'large amounts of food were taken. The raiders also broke into the emergency armaments store and looted it. Much damage was done to electronic systems and equipment. Recorded pictures of the raiders were analysed as usual. With two exceptions, all participants in the raid were Threes therefore no information exists on them. The exceptions have been identified as Lancelot Brough, recruited from the Ones to the Twos by you, and Ann Richmond, lately a Onewife but seconded as an acting Two to Pleasurehouse 13, also by you. Please explain, Executive Salkeld.'